For Dave and Alison

Six Days

NICK PAGE

MINSTREL
Eastbourne

First published 1992

Cover illustration by Josh Kirby

British Library Cataloguing in Publication Data

Page, Nick
Six days.
I. Title
823.914 [F]

ISBN 0-85476-291-4

Printed in Great Britain for
Minstrel, an imprint of Kingsway Publications Ltd
1 St Anne's Road, Eastbourne, E Sussex BN21 3UN by
BPCC Hazells Ltd, Member of BPCC Ltd.
Typeset by Watermark, Crostwight, Norfolk.

THE FIRST DAY

1

In a magnificent display of sheer, rippling muscle power, Jave forced his eyelids open. It was 6.30 am on the first day and his wrist alarm was bleeping.

'Stupid bleeping alarm,' he muttered. He lifted his arm free of the bedclothes. The wrist unit was slim and rectangular, and not much bigger than an old-fashioned wrist watch. Jave pressed a small button on the side of the unit and the alarm was immediately replaced by the silky-smooth voice of a newsreader.

'And now the headlines again,' it said. 'The Prime Minister talked to the cabinet this morning. Then she spoke to the sofa and had a good chat with the chest of drawers.'

It was 6.31 and Jave was getting seriously concerned about the Prime Minister. Maybe it was true that she was losing her grip. After all, being in your sixteenth term of office must slow you down, even if you didn't have a body to worry about any more....

The morning light slowly insinuated its way into Jave's bedroom, revealing a scene of almost clinical purity. Clothes were folded and piled neatly on a shiny chromium-steel chair; the plush acrylo-carpet was spotlessly clean; all surfaces were smooth, white and shining. The room had automatically cleaned itself again.

Not for the first time, Jave felt that modern technological advantages were not all they were cracked up to be. Everything looked so sterile. There was a lot, he thought, to be said for a good old mess.

Slowly and painfully, he climbed out of bed.

At 6.40 Jave visited his 'de-smell you in one' fully automated Shower-o-Matic, guaranteed to 'make you feel fresh, clean and ready for the day' and which promised to handle all the routine hygiene tasks with delicacy and efficiency. This morning the machine that claimed to be 'more sensitive than your own mother' was as faulty as usual and Jave spent the time between 6.44 and 6.47 cleaning toothpaste out of his nose.

He dressed and wandered through to the kitchen.

There was a gerbil on the breakfast table.

Jave took a plastic canister and poured out a handful of seeds in front of the gerbil.

'Breakfast,' he said.

'About time, baby,' said the gerbil.

'You could have helped yourself,' replied Jave.

'Hey man,' said the gerbil, busily stuffing himself. 'How is I s'posed to open the canister? You' forgetting I is only four inches high?'

He chewed for a minute. 'Man, that sure hits the spot!' he said. 'I'm tellin' you – them caraway seeds is baaaaad!'

It was 7.00 am and the gerbil's name was Frid. Frid was a Robomammal.

The early robots were expensive. It was not the computerised brain, it was the rest – arms, legs, the moving parts. To avoid this expense, some clever marketing manager invented Robomammals.

Using a mixture of neuro-surgery, robotics and sheer guesswork, a chip was grafted onto a mammal's frontal lobe, overriding the animal's brain, but using its central nervous system. It was a marvellous idea (unless, of course, you were the mammal in question), allowing the computerised brain to use the body and abilities of the mammal. This, it was said, would make robots more accessible, more natural. They would get hungry and thirsty. They would even be fitted with personality circuits.

The idea came unstuck when they added voice synthesiser units, allowing the Robomammal to talk to you. Suddenly, your cat, which had always purred or miaowed, told you the weather forecast. Suddenly your goldfish was not only babysitting, but singing lullabyes as well.

Customers couldn't cope. Somehow, they just couldn't get used to arriving home at night to find the rottweiler hoovering the carpet and singing arias from Puccinni. In a society that was already incredibly unnatural, this was felt to be taking things too far.

Sales plummeted and in the end, much to the relief of animal rights protesters, not to mention various domestic pets, Robomammals were discontinued.

Jave, however, did not get rid of Frid. He had won the gerbil in a competition and had become quite attached to him.

Frid did the accounts. He kept the diary. Jave would never have admitted it, but Frid was his only friend. The only problem in their relationship was that someone, and no one at the robotics corporation ever admitted responsibility, had programmed Frid to speak entirely in twentieth-century 'Jive' talk.

'We is in serious need of bread,' said the gerbil, still busy with the caraway seeds.

'Well, use the food tube.'

'Not bread, *bread*. Moolah. Greenbacks.' The gerbil looked impatiently at Jave's uncomprehending face. 'ECUs,' he said.

Jave sighed and took his mug of coffee through to the lounge. The kitchen was an open plan affair, containing nothing much more than a waste disposal unit, microwave and food tube. Anything you wanted could be ordered through the tube. It was never normally necessary for things to be kept in stock, meaning that kitchens were, in the twenty-first century, not much bigger than a large cupboard.

The curtains of the large lounge window swished aside automatically as Jave approached, allowing the grey, cloudy light to slither into the room. Jave stood, nursing his coffee and gazed out through the steadily falling rain at the London skyline. His flat was on the twelfth floor. Although the skyline was clustered with skyscrapers, he still had a fairly good view of the city. Not as good, of course, as the rich people who lived thirty floors above him, but pretty good nevertheless.

Jave liked his flat. The only problem was whether he could afford to keep it.

'How much have we got, then?' he asked.

The rodent, who had entered the room behind him, hummed slightly.

'Nil, my man,' he answered. 'The big zero.'

'Oh bazzin' heck!' said Jave. 'Are you sure?'

The rodent whirred again. 'Certain,' he said. 'We is as broke as broke can be.'

Jave finished his coffee and threw the plastic mug onto the floor. A flap in the wall whirred open and the mug suddenly whipped across the carpet and disappeared into the hole.

'Well,' said Jave, 'maybe something will turn up at work today.'

He grabbed his old trenchcoat and put it on.

Then he climbed out of the window.

2

London in 2050 was not a nice place. Not that it had been particularly pleasant at any other time during the previous 2000 years. But it was worse now.

Over the course of the past fifty years, London had changed. Despite the fact that the capital of Great Britain had been moved elsewhere, London was still dangerously overcrowded. More and more people had crammed themselves into the city, but not the type of people you would really want. Cars clogged the roads and poured out fumes. House prices spiralled ever upwards. Transport systems collapsed, broken by sheer weight of demand and inadequate infrastructure. There was simply no room.

Then came a breakthrough. In 2036, while reading a book of architectural history, a planner named Arfer Pod rediscovered a particularly underrated idea from the mid-1960s. The idea was called 'tower blocks'.

Reintroducing the idea of 'tower blocks' would, Pod reasoned, have three great advantages. First, it would allow you to house more people in less space. Secondly, it would move people away from the streets which, in London, were rapidly turning into violent, dangerous rubbish tips. Thirdly, it would make him extremely rich.

Thus it was that tower blocks for living accommodation started to shoot up again in London. The time was right for them to flourish, because living above the streets was so much easier these days. Shopping was done by vidphone. Telecommuting meant that nearly half the workforce in the country worked from home. Wrist units kept you in touch with what was going on. Community life had broken down anyway, so a little more fragmentation would hardly make any difference.

And the big advantage lay in security. The streets, reasoned the planners, were so dangerous that nobody in their right mind wanted to go near them. This was a way for people to move as far away from ground level as possible. For those individuals who did want to walk anywhere, walkways were built from tower block to tower block to avoid the need even to touch the ground.

But what really changed things was the Sinclair C27 Air Car. Based on a long forgotten Sinclair design, with wings attached, the C27 worked on the principle of negative geo-centricity.

It was, basically, allergic to the earth. This meant not only could it fly, but it could be parked outside your fifteenth floor flat all night. Come the morning, you'd simply climb out of the window and zoom off. And no one could steal it, unless they were prepared to try and jump into it from above.

The natural corollary of all this was that nowadays no one went near the ground. The ground was a dim, ill-lit place where the debris of society collected. The ground was dangerous. The ground was where the poor people went. Anyone who was anyone lived on, or above, level ten which was considered the lowest acceptable height. In most tower blocks, all the floors below the tenth were filled with heating, plumbing, electricity generators and all the machinery needed to make life within the tower blocks acceptable.

The greater your earnings, the further you lived away

from such machinery and the nearer you lived to the top of your chosen block (giving a totally new meaning to the phrase 'living the high life'). The lower your earnings and status, the nearer you lived to the tenth floor. Jave lived on level twelve.

'What are we going to do, then?' asked Jave as they flew over the city.

''Bout what?'

'Well – business,' said Jave. He pushed a lock of brown hair from his face. 'You remember? That place we go to, to be alone every day. That shy little, secluded spot that is called the office.'

The gerbil whirred and bleeped. 'We's tried every business plan,' he said. 'We's tried advertising. It's the sign o' the times, man.'

'Meaning?'

'Oh come on, man,' said the gerbil. 'All this private eye stuff! It ended years ago, baby. You is out of time.'

'Nonsense.' He turned the steering wheel slightly and banked around a slow-moving air tanker.

'It's the truth. I mean, callin' yourself Private Investigator don't help. All the other guys, they's called Security Consultants.'

'They're just the same as me.'

Jave pressed his foot on the accelerator and flicked a switch which opened a vent in the plexi-glass dome of the C27. Fresh, chill air blasted into his face.

'You think so?' said Frid. 'They is cats of a different colour. They have the latest gadgets. They handle high-class stuff.'

'They're spies,' said Jave vehemently. 'Industrial espionage. Licensed burglars. Sneaking around, bugging people's offices, rooting through shredder bins, piecing together little bits of information. I mean, where's the romance? Where's the adventure? They're nothing but shabby, cheap little spies.'

There was a pause.
'Rich, though,' said Frid.

Jave could date to the minute, the moment when he had first wanted to become a detective. It was 21st May 2040. Jave's birthday. He was fourteen. As a treat, his parents took him to the Institute of Visual History where he had been allowed to select and watch any of the six million vids they had stored there. He only picked *The Maltese Falcon* because he thought it was a natural history programme and he was quite into bird spotting at the time.

His parents had tried to make him change his mind. 'You don't want to watch that,' they said. 'It's not about birds. It's very old. It's not even in colour, let alone 3-D.' But, with the obstinacy unique to children when they reject the sensible choice, Jave insisted on watching his selection.

His parents were surprised when they returned ten minutes later to find him sitting enraptured. They were amazed when forty minutes had gone by and Jave was still sitting in the booth, lost in the grainy black and white world that was flickering on the screen. When the film had finished and he had emerged from the booth demanding to watch another one, they were convinced there was something wrong with him.

But to Jave there was nothing wrong. It was merely that his world had changed completely.

In the following days, he spent many an hour wandering around pretending to be Humphrey Bogart, and speaking with a lisp. He bought up every old pulp detective novel he could lay his hands on. If it had not been declared illegal in 2017, he would have taken up smoking.

His parents, deeply worried, booked him time at the Community Mind Unit, but the Psycho-Adjuster who examined him assured them that it was just a phase and that it would eventually wear off.

When he was seventeen, in a deeply emotional moment, Jave bought his first trenchcoat in an antiques shop off the Portobello Heights. The Psycho-Adjuster declared that Jave's 'obsessional behaviour would soon start to diminish'.

When he was eighteen Jave quit school and went to work in the Department of Social Security, the Government agency which monitored internal security and which had replaced the old style police forces in 2014. The Psycho-Adjuster resigned.

His parents, who had always planned that he should be an advertising accounts executive, were distraught. But Jave's subsequent career proved how right he was.

He gained promotion quickly and easily. He came top in his exams for three consecutive years, eventually becoming the youngest Stamper in the entire department and earning a reputation for intelligence, flair, unorthodox petty cash returns and a large degree of eccentricity.

Although successful, his five years at the Department of Social Security were not very happy. He never quite fitted in. The fact was that he was years behind his time. He had been impregnated with an image that was a hundred years old – the image of a loner, a free spirit, a rebel, an old-fashioned, hard-boiled private eye. Although working in the present, he was living in the past.

In the end, the rifts between him and his colleagues, between the loner and the institution, became too great. The day after he had been hauled before his superiors, congratulated on finding the madman who had blown up a total of seven underwear factories for no very apparent reason and then fined a week's wages for wearing 'deeply unfashionable clothing', he won Frid in the national lottery. The Robomammal introduced himself and informed Jave that, among his many accomplishments, he could handle accounts, calculate tax codes and write sales catalogues. Jave decided that the time was right and left a vid-note of resignation.

He quit the Department of Social Security and set up in business for himself.

At 8.47 am on the first day, Jave landed on the roof park, put Frid in his pocket and took the lift down to his office.

The sign on the office door said 'Jave Fleming – Private vest'. It was supposed to say 'Private Investigator' but the other letters had fallen off.

The office was small and shabby, which actually suited Jave fine, because that was the way he always felt Private Investigators' offices should be. There were a couple of old wooden chairs in one corner, a tatty piece of carpet on the floor and a filing cabinet which Jave didn't need (all the files being held securely in Frid's databanks) but which he thought added a certain something to the place. In the filing cabinet, he kept some letters, a packet of paper clips, a dog-eared copy of *Farewell My Lovely* a couple of plastic mugs and a bottle of whisky.

In front of the window there was a desk and on the desk was a vid unit – combining video phone, fax, online database and television. Of course, these days you could speak to anyone simply by using your wrist unit, but Jave liked the look of the unit, which was a model crafted out of old-fashioned black bakelite.

Also on the desk, in the opposite corner to the vid unit was a food tube – a food delivery unit shaped like a small American fire hydrant and made out of shiny chrome.

Jave walked over to the window and lifted the blind a fraction, while behind him, Frid started running through the accounts and singing a Michael Jackson medley.

A few storeys below him began the criss-crossing network of walkways between this tower block and the adjoining ones. It was difficult to see beyond that, to the darkness ten storeys below the walkways, but Jave knew that somewhere below him was the area known as Elephant and Castle. He had been down there a few times. It was not a nice area. He wondered how long his business would continue this way before he too was forced down to live on the street levels, where no one wanted to go.

Jave sighed. Surely others had a better life. Surely others didn't have to sit in a crumbling office block, eternally broke and with only the company of a hip gerbil. He looked down again at the ground level in the blackness below. On the other hand....

It was 8.51 on the first day.

3

During the day, nothing happened. Not only that, but it happened very slowly.

Jave and Frid had several games of chess, which Frid always won, not only because he was a computer, but because Jave invariably got bored halfway through. Anyone who played chess against Jave had only to wait a little while before he would rush in and do something stupid. He always tried to open carefully, to build up his attack, to blend the virtues of patience and strategic thinking, but after about six moves he always went on the all-out attack with all the caution usually associated with lemmings.

Lunchtime came and went. Jave dialled up a cheese and tomato sandwich which arrived in the small food transporter tube situated on his desk, its corners frayed through the heat generated on its journey. The cheese and tomato sandwich tasted good. Not like cheese and tomato, of course. More like, well, steak and tomato, but once you worked out how the transporter affected food molecules, you could nearly always get what you wanted.

He spent the afternoon watching TV. There was nothing much to watch. Fifteen of the seventeen channels were broadcasting game shows of one sort or another. Channel 16 had an Open University programme from 1976. Channel 4 had a religious meeting on, hosted by the Bishop of Swindonopolis, Lou Blynell. Jave watched for ten minutes, waiting for the Bishop actually to say something. He didn't. Jave switched off the TV.

Eventually, Jave cracked. 'This is ridiculous!' he exclaimed. 'Not one single caller. All day I've been sitting here! Why haven't we got any work?'

'Hey, stay cool, baby!' said Frid, who was now singing his way through the Luther Vandross back catalogue. 'Things is bound to get hotter.'

'Oh rubbish,' said Jave. 'No one wants us. No one needs us. I always wanted to be a Private Investigator, and now look at me: washed up at twenty-four.'

'Just stay mellow.'

'I am mellow. I am incredibly mellow. If I get any more mellow I'll rot. I just want some work, that's all. I want someone to knock at the door and come in and throw money at me.'

There was a knock at the door. Jave shot bolt upright.

'How did you do that?' said Frid.

'Customers!' exclaimed Jave. 'Scan.'

Frid's whiskers revolved slowly, and his nose beeped. 'There's two,' he said. 'A chick and a dude.'

Jave pressed a button and the door slid open.

The first of the two figures standing there was a seventeen-year-old boy, with blond hair, bright blue eyes and gleaming white teeth. He would have been handsome were it not for the fact that he had two noses.

It was Kevving, Jave's brother.

The other was a slim, young girl with jet-black hair. She was dressed in a plain, dark green dress jeans, with a gold sash tied across one shoulder. Apart from Ingrid Bergman, in *Casablanca*, Jave thought she was the most beautiful thing he had ever seen.

'Hi bruvv,' said Kevving.

'Hi,' said Jave, trying to look busy. 'How are you doing?'

'Not bad.' Kevving slouched into the office, collapsed into the chair opposite Jave and scratched his left nose. 'You all right?'

'Fine,' lied Jave, trying not to stare at the woman accompanying his brother. He stood up. 'Who's your friend?'

'Oh – this is Chanis,' said Kevving.

The girl walked forward. 'Hello,' she said.

Jave was taken aback. She may have been beautiful, but she had a voice which sounded like someone attacking a pig with a cheesegrater. *Ah well*, he thought, *you can't have everything.*

'Chanis Chones,' continued Kevving. 'You busy at the moment?'

Jave turned. 'No,' he said. 'Not really.'

'Good.' Kevving lay back in the chair and spun it round once, looking at the office. 'Nice place you got here,' he said. 'Real, y'know, atmosphere.'

'Atmosphere' was a word that meant a lot to Kevving. Whatever he did in life, it had to have 'atmosphere'. What exactly he meant by that it was difficult to say, but Kevving was the original party animal. Ever since he had hit his fifteenth birthday he had been up and running – chasing after the good times with that furious desperation that only the really unhappy can achieve. Jave liked his brother a lot. Quite why he liked him he could never exactly say.

Maybe it was his charm. Kevving had charm like other people have freckles. Not only could Kevving charm the birds down from the trees, he could charm them straight into the oven and get them to turn the gas on first.

Kevving grinned and wrinkled both his noses.

Jave sighed. When Kevving wrinkled his noses like that it meant problems.

In the 2030s, it was discovered that people not only wanted children, they wanted well-adjusted, good-looking children. This fact led to the development of the Do-It-Yourself Genetic Engineering Pack.

Jave's parents, appalled at their first attempt (him), had purchased the 'MFI Classic Surfer' kit. This ensured, through a series of manoeuvres too revolting to contemplate, that your child had 'blue eyes, blond hair, rippling muscles and the ability to sing Beach-Boys' songs'.

The limitations of this pack became apparent nine months after its use. True, their baby had blond hair, blue eyes and sang a mean version of 'Help Me Rhonda'. The problem was he also had two noses.

It was the same with all the packs. Babies turned up with additional limbs, bizarre pigmentation, or strange physical abnormalities. In the many lawsuits that followed, the MFI Genetics Division blamed a batch of 'dodgy Taiwanese chromosomes'. The product was hurriedly withdrawn, the lawsuits settled, and pretty soon all that was left was a generation of bizarre children and some very rich parents.

Jave switched his attention away from his brother to the girl who was standing nervously by the doorway.

'I'm sorry, Miss Chones,' he said. 'Sit down, please.' He glared at his brother who was happily spinning himself around in the chair. 'Kevving – get up and let the lady sit down.'

'What?' said Kevving.

'You heard.'

'I told you,' sighed Kevving, reluctantly prising himself out of the chair. 'He's soooo old fashioned it is untrue.'

The girl smiled and sat in the chair. Jave thought she was almost perfect.

'Thank you,' she said.

Apart from the voice.

'So what do you want?' said Jave. 'I mean this is not a social call, is it?'

'Nah,' said Kevving. 'Got a job for you.'

Jave felt his heart leap. Here it was! A strange and mysteriously beautiful woman had come into his office. She would ask him to find the bird. It was the Maltese Falcon all over again.

'Chanis wants you to find something...' said Kevving.

The girl looked at Jave, nervously. She had a small, black nylon wallet with her which she fingered anxiously.

'Kevving said I could trust you,' she said.

'He did?' said Jave, surprised. 'Since when have you ever trusted me?' he asked his brother.

Kevving laughed. 'Personally I don't, but this is business.'

'I want you to find something out for me,' said the girl.

'I see.'

The girl reached into the bag and pulled out an envelope. 'I've got some money,' she said.

She put the envelope on the desk. Frid was on it like a flash, his whiskers revolving as he scanned the envelope's contents.

'Three grand!' he exclaimed. 'Not bad, man.'

The girl looked shocked. Which was understandable, since it is not everyday that a talking gerbil starts counting your life savings.

'Did he...?' she asked.

'Speak? Yes,' said Jave. 'He's a Robomammal.' He pushed the gerbil to one side. 'I'm sorry about the way he leapt on your money,' he added. 'He's got a one track mind.'

'Yeah,' said Frid. 'Living. I'm addicted to it.'

'Now,' said Jave, sitting back down, 'what do you want me to find out?'

The girl looked at him. 'I want you to find the person who murdered my father,' she said.

There was a momentary pause. 'I see,' said Jave. He opened his mouth to say something more, but he couldn't think of anything. 'I see,' he said again.

Chanis, sensing that something more was expected of her, reached into her bag again and pulled out another envelope.

'Here.'

She pushed the second envelope across the desk to Jave, who opened it and took out a hologram.

The gram showed a man, perhaps forty years old, with more hair than Jave had ever seen outside a mattress. Grey hair sprung from his head in great spiky tufts. A huge, bushy beard, the colour and consistency of steel wool, hung from his chin with a vast moustache disguising his mouth. He looked like a lavatory brush with eyes. And it was the eyes that held you. They leapt out from within the thicket of hair like those of a predator. They were black and deep and unreadable.

The man was wearing a big, camel coloured coat, belted at the waist. In his hands he clutched a small black book.

Jave turned the hologram slightly to see a little more of the image. At the back of his head, the man's hair ended in a huge bushy pony-tail. Slung over his shoulder was a black leather bag.

'Is this your father?'

'Yes.'

'He's certainly...unmistakable,' said Jave.

'It's the most recent gram I have of him,' explained Chanis. 'It was taken about a year ago.'

'What happened to him, then?'

'He...he's dead,' said the girl, and Jave thought for one awful moment that she was about to start crying. 'They told me a few days ago.'

Jave slapped a button on his food tube and three coffees appeared.

'All right,' he said, handing one to the girl. 'Let's just start at the beginning, shall we?'

'His name was Abram. Abram Chones. Up until about six months ago, he was working with our church. He was the pastor.'

'What does that mean?'

'Well, he was in charge of the place. He would do everything – organise the services, deal with people's problems, talk to people, encourage newcomers. He ran the fellowship.'

'Where was this?'

'It's a small fellowship, really,' croaked Chanis, her bass voice grating around the room and causing the filing cabinet to rattle. 'We meet in the Camden area, in my flat. It's only on the eleventh floor, but it's quite big. We can't meet openly, you know. That's why it's been so difficult to get people to look for him.'

'Let me get this straight. It's not a registered church?'

'That's right.'

'I see.'

'Anyway – he said he wanted to move on. I guess he felt he had done what he could for us. He wanted to go and start a new fellowship.'

'What did you say to that?'

'Well, I agreed with him. Our church had been growing quite a lot. We thought the best thing to do would be to set up again somewhere else.'

'Does this happen a lot?'

'More than you think, Mr Fleming. I know the government and the media would have you believe that only the official church is thriving, but that's not the case. The real church is going on underground. That's the one that's growing. Not the one you see on your vid screens. That's just a device for selling things.'

Jave smiled. For a moment there had almost been a flash of anger there. He was not surprised. The religion that filled the vid screens was, he thought, a load of trivial pap. He could understand why it made real believers angry.

'I see,' he said. 'So where did he go to set this new church up?'

'He moved to a house on the M25. He'd been out there a few times, checking on something. I don't know what. But he said he wanted to try and do something for the people out there. It's a pretty rotten area.'

'When did this move take place?'

'About six months ago. I saw him on my birthday which was 24th April. That was the last time I saw him alive.'

'Where did he go?'

Chanis reached down into her bag and pulled out a piece of paper.

'His address was 344, Fifth Lane, Junction 25,' she said.

Jave looked at the piece of paper with the address scribbled on it. 'Was that a big place?' he said.

'I don't know. I never went there. Not until...until last week.'

'What did he do when he got there?'

'Again, I'm not sure. He would have started to make contact with a few people, I suppose. He told me he might try and start working with the official church, if there was one. But generally, when you're starting from scratch, it's just a question of getting to know people – finding out how you can help.'

'All right.' Jave paused and looked into the girl's eyes. They looked a little calmer now. Less alarmed. 'So what happened to him?'

Chanis swallowed a sip of her coffee.

'I got a call from Social Security on Friday last week,' she said. 'It was six in the morning. They told me that the place where my father had been living had been firebombed.'

'Firebombed?'

'That's what they said. Apparently someone had planted an incendiary device under the floor. It had blown up sometime in the night – they reckoned around midnight. I can't remember exactly what the bomb was called. A 'P' something or other. Apparently it was very powerful.'

'A P-42?' suggested Jave.

'That's it.'

'They weren't kidding. The P-42 is one of the fiercest incendiaries around. Developed by terrorist groups in Germany some time back. It uses a small but very concentrated charge of heavy napalm with a normal detonator. The napalm is put under intense pressure and when the trigger goes off, it explodes outwards and upwards. Generally, what you get is incredibly intense heat. I mean really intense. But only over a limited area. That's the strength of the P-42. It's a very precise bomb. And it's very, very hot.'

'Yes,' whispered Chanis.

Jave looked up. 'Bazzin' heck, I'm sorry,' he said. 'I didn't mean to go on about it....'

'No, that's OK.' The girl smiled. 'That's more or less what the Social Security said. They hardly found any trace of his body even. Just some fragments of clothing and some hair.'

'Is that all?'

'That's all. They checked the hair and the clothing. It was definitely him. They said the intense heat would have destroyed everything else.'

'Yeah. So what theory are they working on?'

'Well, that's just it. They say that it was probably an accident; that the bomb was intended for someone else. Apparently the area is prone to gang warfare. The police reckon that either he was mistaken for someone else, or....' She paused.

'Or that he was involved in it,' continued Jave.

'That's right. But that's impossible! I know what kind of man he was. He was a good man. He would never have got involved in anything like that. Not unless he was trying to do something about it.

'So, are they pursuing investigations?'

'They say they are. But I don't think they believe it's worth it. He's not the type of person they tend to bother about.'

Jave nodded. That was true enough. There were so many murders reported each week, that the Department could only possibly deal with the really important ones. On the whole, they were pretty accurate in deciding which ones could be solved and which ones couldn't. It sounded like they had already made up their mind that this one was definitely one of the insoluble ones.

And, Jave thought, they were probably right.

Kevving, who had been sitting quietly in a corner, listening to all this, suddenly jumped up.

'So where do we start, bruvv?' said Kevving.

'We?'

'Oh, didn't I tell you?' said Kevving. 'I thought I'd tag

along. Grab a bit of the atmosphere. Doing something different.'

'Don't be stupid,' said Jave. 'This is hard work.'

'Exactly,' said Kevving. 'Something different. Where do we start?'

Jave looked at Kevving. He looked at Chanis. He looked at the money.

He sighed. 'We'll start first thing in the morning,' he said.

THE SECOND DAY

4

Jave woke up the following morning feeling good.

He had a job. He had some money. Then he thought about it. The job was likely to be a blind alley. And his brother was insisting on accompanying him. Suddenly, he didn't feel so good.

He climbed out of bed, annoyed more than ever at the way the room had cleaned and repainted itself.

'I wish,' he said to no one in particular, 'that once, just once, I could wake up to a mess.'

The room didn't answer. But somehow, the paintwork looked aggrieved.

After removing the worst excesses of the Shower-o-Matic's attempt to shave him, Jave wandered through into the lounge.

'You want some breakfast?' he asked the lump of bedclothes on the settee.

'Mmmmphhfflgggh,' said the lump.

'With or without sugar?'

'Mmmph.'

Jave went into the kitchen. Frid was sitting on the kitchen table chewing some seeds. Beside him lay the remains of a plastic canister.

'Couldn't wait,' he said. 'Had to blast my way in.'

'Fair enough,' said Jave.

He punched a series of numbers into the metal console of the food tube. There was a small delay, then a hum, then his breakfast began to appear.

When the food transporter was first invented it was hailed as a masterpiece. No longer would people have to go shopping, they simply dialled up the code and – hey presto – the food would arrive in their house. The only problem was that in the early models something seemed to happen to the food in its journey through the sub-ether. It changed its taste.

Cheese, for some reason, always tasted of steak. Conversely, steak always tasted of mature cheddar. Not that everything was so easily worked out. Tomatoes always tasted of onion, but onion always tasted of anchovies. Fish fingers tasted of pizza, potatoes tasted of chicken vindaloo and satsumas tasted of banana. Big Macs tasted of rotting vegetables wrapped around a dead cat. So no change there.

At first, nothing was done about this. Everything tasted of something, after all, and for many people it made meal times much more exciting. The authorities were content to let the matter rest, until it was discovered that baked beans ended up tasting of ten-year-old, oak-matured whisky. Consequently, whisky sales plummeted and many people took the opportunity to get completely blasted out of their skulls on half a can of Cross and Blackwells.

Action was demanded, particularly by the proprietors of Old Jock's Sporran-Warmer, who were enraged to find that they had sent out 3000 bottles of oak-matured baked beans in tomato sauce.

Scientists worked day and night, and eventually the wrinkles in the system were ironed out and everything ended up tasting more or less as it should. They could never get rid of the cheese problem, however, as it always tasted like steak.

Pancakes with maple syrup, hot coffee, a warm roll and butter, orange juice; the ingredients of Jave's breakfast were all fine. It was just the cheese....

It was 9.30 am on the second day, and Jave was flying across London. He had a passenger.

'Chanis is very worried, you see,' said Kevving, scratching his left nose.

'Tell me again, about her father.'

Kevving sighed.

'His name was Abram. He was a Christian.'

'And since when have you been involved in Christianity?' asked Jave.

'Not long.' Kevving looked out from the Sinclair C27 at the London landscape. 'I just happened to find myself outside their building. But this lot are different, y'know. Not like the official church.'

'Do they sing spirituals?' enquired Frid, Jave's gerbil, sitting on Jave's shoulder. He began to sing. 'Swing low, sweet chario-o-t...'

'Do you mind? I'm trying to drive,' said Jave. 'I don't need a black pentecostal gerbil deafening me.'

'Chanis is, well, different,' continued Kevving. 'She leads this group. They care for people.'

'Why don't they look for Abram's killer, then?'

'Don't be stupid, bruvv,' said Kevving. 'It might be dangerous.'

'Yes,' said Jave. 'I had a feeling anything you're involved in would be dangerous. I don't know why, but in my mind there's a very strong association between the words "Kevving" and "dangerous". And also, "stupid", "irritating" and "extremely painful" come to that.'

'I don't know why you're so skagging touchy,' said Kevving. 'You'd think you'd be pleased to get a job.'

'What makes you think that?' said Jave, irritated.

'Oh come on,' said Kevving. 'Anyone can tell you haven't been doing too well. Your office looks like a pit.'

'It's supposed to look like that. It's atmospheric. Humphrey Bogart never had a clean office.'

'Humphrey who?'

'Bogart. He used to be in films. Hundred years ago.'

'Oh,' said Kevving with the tone of voice of the terminally bored.

'Target area approaching,' said Frid. 'M25 dead ahead.'

The previous night, Jave had spent a further couple of hours finding out all he could about Chanis' father. It did not boil down to much. They had lived in London, where Abram had brought up Chanis on his own. Then, during the boom, he had moved north to work as a tunneller on the North Sea tunnel. When that had finished, they moved back to London and joined the church there.

Not long afterwards, Abram became the pastor. He had been good at his job, a sensitive and deeply religious man who cared for the poor and lonely. Maybe because he was poor and lonely himself, Jave thought, although he did not suggest this to the man's daughter.

The unofficial church had grown under his leadership to the point when, six months ago, he had decided to move out, by which time, Abram had been in charge of the church for six years.

And there it was: a girl with the voice like a water buffalo. A man with too much hair and a strong faith. And a bomb capable of melting the strongest steel to a puddle.

It was 10.00 am on the second day. Jave delicately manoeuvred his C27 into the street below him. Turning the negative geo-centricity counter to 'toleration', he let the car land with a slight bump. The motors hummed quietly and then faded.

Ahead of them there was a sign: 'Social Security – Authorised Personnel Only'.

Beyond it was a tangled ruin of metal and rubber and blackened, charred concrete.

Jave climbed out of the car, joined by Kevving.

'Nice area,' he said, sarcastically. He looked up the street. At the end there was a massive lorry bearing another, much larger sign.

'Church of the Blessed Commuter' it read. 'Established 2036'.

The M25 had always been plagued by congestion, but when the great jam came in 2030, no one knew it was the beginning of the end.

It started normally enough, motorists slowing from their standard 0.85 miles per hour to a dead halt. Across all twenty lanes, motorists waited in their cars and lorries for the jam to clear. After three or four hours, they began to get impatient. Nothing happened. Night fell.

It was during the second day of the great jam, that people began to realise something was wrong. Absolutely nothing was moving. People abandoned cars and walked to their destinations, sick of the whole mess. For those who stayed with their vehicles, supplies had to be flown in. Days stretched into a week, weeks into a month and still nothing moved. People were now commuting to work from their cars, returning after a hard day's labour to spend the night on the motorway.

After a while, services and amenities sprang up, frequently much better than the people had at their own homes. So they stayed. Some bought up cars next to them and knocked through, creating much larger vehicles with bedrooms, bathrooms and jacuzzis. Of course, that meant that these cars could never move again, but there didn't seem much chance of that anyway.

The problem was, no one knew what was actually causing the great jam. Ordinary theories didn't make sense, and, desperate to find a solution, traffic chiefs called in philosophers and mathematicians.

The philosophers looked at the problem, ate several free lunches and explained that the M25 jam was a problem with no end and no beginning. They illustrated this unhelpful statement with Möbius strips, ideas from Zen and episodes from an old TV programme called *Neighbours*. Then they went home.

In the end, an enterprising minister in the Deptartment of Transport solved the problem by declaring the M25 a residential estate and handing it over to the Deptartment of Housing. No one made a fuss, because the PM, during a period of disorientation while her nutritional jelly was renewed, had appointed a hairbrush to the post of Minister of Housing. Unsurprisingly, the hairbrush did nothing.

Now, twenty years later, the M25 had become a huge, circular city around London. Lorries had been knocked together to provide maisonettes and shops. Streets and communities sprang up. The M25 had, at last, found something it was good at.

Jave looked at the church for a moment. Then he turned back to the sign forbidding entry. He walked straight past it and over to the remains of Abram Chones' house.

5

The area told Jave very little. It had once been a medium-sized lorry, in a particularly shabby area of the M25.

Now it was nothing more than a pile of rubble, black and twisted by the heat of the blast.

'Wow,' said Kevving, picking his way among the twisted sheets of metal. 'I wouldn't have liked to have been in here when this went up.'

'You wouldn't have known much about it,' said Jave. 'When those P-42s blow, they shoot a flame straight up. I saw one once in a Security display. I'm not surprised they found hardly anything left of the guy. They say the heat can just vaporise people. Everything – flesh, bone, muscle – just turns into steam.'

'Not hair, though.'

Jave thought back to the gram of Abram Chones that Chanis had shown him. He was not surprised. There was so much hair it would have taken the equivalent of a forest fire to get rid of it all.

'So what kind of zeke normally uses these bombs?'

'Zeke?'

'Hip slang, bruvv. You wouldn't understand.'

Jave shrugged. 'Normally, they're an amateur's weapon. I mean, they're very powerful, but they're also very unreliable. They may go off, they may not. You can't time them. Half the time, they blow up in the face of the guy who's making them.'

'Maybe Abram Chones was making one, then?'

'Not unless he was making it underneath his lorry. According to Chanis, Security said the bomb was placed under the lorry. Look...' Jave gestured at the wreckage. 'That must be the floor over there.'

He pointed towards a large sheet of twisted metal that had been thrown some yards away from the area. It had a jagged round hole in it, the sides curled upwards in a lip as if someone had pushed a red hot poker through a piece of plastic.

'But when they do work,' said Jave, 'they really work well.'

They clambered back out from the wreckage and past the sign.

'So what do we do now?' said Kevving.

'Well, you can do what you want,' replied Jave thoughtfully. 'But I'm going to church.' He pointed at the huge lorry at the end of the road, its neon church sign glowing in the dismal morning air.

'Shall I come in with you?' said Kevving.

'No,' said Jave. 'Just stay out of trouble.'

Chanis had told him that Abram was going to try and make contact with the local church. Well, thought Jave as he walked up the road towards the darkened entrance of the massive lorry, you can't get much more local than this.

Inside the church was dark and cool. It had once been several large container lorries, but, at some point in the past, it had been knocked together to form one huge square lorry, with smaller lorries attached to form little side chapels.

As the figure came towards him, Jave reflected how little the uniform of the clergy had changed over past centuries. Still the long black cassock, still the white dog-collar (now called a non-human-collar after protestations from the Canine Defence League that the old name was 'dogist'). If the uniform hadn't changed, however, its filling certainly had.

'Hello,' said the vicar. She was a rather stately, forbidding woman with grey hair, grey eyes and, unfortunately, grey teeth.

'Hello,' said Jave. 'I wonder if you can help me. I'm looking for some information. About the lorry down the road.'

'Which lorry's that?'

'The one that isn't there any more. The one that blew up.'

The vicar looked, Jave thought, momentarily startled. It was only a flicker before she regained her composure.

'Are you from Security?' she asked.

'No, I'm working on behalf of someone. The daughter of the man who was in the lorry at the time.'

'Ah yes,' said the vicar, shaking her head. 'Such a tragic accident.'

'Accident?'

'Well, according to the police. They think he was mistaken for someone else.'

'Did you know him?'

The vicar shook her head and said, 'I don't think so.'

'Maybe you saw him around?'

'I really don't remember.'

Jave pulled the hologram out of his pocket and showed it to the vicar. She looked at the picture, but, Jave thought, not for long enough to take any of it in.

'No,' she said, 'I can't remember him.'

'Are you sure?' persisted Jave. 'His name was Abram Chones. His daughter said he moved to these parts about six weeks ago. She seemed sure he would have made contact.'

'No,' said the vicar. 'I would remember someone like that.'

'Well, maybe you heard about him in the neighbourhood?'

The vicar looked distastefully at him.

'I've already told you,' she said, 'I've neither heard of, nor seen this man.'

'So you did.' Jave smiled. 'Well, sorry to bother you. Nice church you got here.'

The vicar looked round proudly.

'We think so. We do our bit in the community.'

'I'm sure you do. I'm sure you help a lot of the poor people out there. It's a pretty rough neighbourhood.'

'Yes,' sighed the vicar, 'it is a little insalubrious. But it all depends on what you mean by help. Ultimately you need to encourage people to help themselves. It's no good just doling out food or money. You've got to go deeper than that. We realised this many years ago. The poor are part of society, there's not a lot we can do. After all, didn't Jesus himself say, "The poor will always be with you"?'

'I don't know. Did he?'

'Yes. He did.' The vicar looked slightly annoyed at Jave's interruption of her rhetoric. 'The church should echo society. The poor are wanted, one might almost say demanded, by society. It's the church's role to reaffirm our society, to change it from within. It is our place to uphold society, not to undermine it.'

She looked at Jave and smiled patronisingly.

'This is nothing new. The churches decided many years ago that they should not confront society. Our role should be one of discussion, of support, of affirmation.'

'Abram Chones was very concerned about the poor.'

'As are we all. Now if you'll excuse me....'

'So you can't tell me any more about this man?'

There was a pause. The vicar looked like she had trodden in something nasty. 'I didn't catch your name.'

'I didn't drop it,' said Jave. 'The name's Fleming, Jave Fleming. I'm a Private Detective.'

'I didn't think we had any of those any more,' said the vicar.

'We haven't. I'm a dinosaur. A living antique.'

A steely quality came into the vicar's eyes. 'I thought I'd made it clear, Mr Fleming,' she said. 'I've never seen him before.'

Jave put the hologram back into his pocket.

'Well, then, I won't take up any more of your time. I wouldn't want to keep you from affirming society and all that.'

He turned and wandered back out of the massive lorry, and down the steps onto the crumbling tarmac. Once outside he dropped something from his pocket. There was a scuttling sound.

Jave crossed what had once been the fast lane of the M25 to a large, glass-fronted plasti-build structure called 'The Central Reservation Diner-A-Go-Go'. He ordered a coffee.

It was not long before the vicar came out. From where he sat drinking, Jave watched her stand in front of the church lorry for a moment before striding off between the parked houses with their gaudy window boxes. If he had been closer he might have seen the small gerbil following her, his whiskers revolving and making a barely audible whirring sound.

After she had gone, Jave took his coffee and sat at the counter. He took out the hologram of the man he was hunting. The figure was hairy – his grey bushy beard and uncombed hair making him look like his head was losing its stuffing. There was something almost unreal about him. He looked back at Jave with eyes that gleamed, two beads of blackness in a sea of hair.

6

'Any luck?' said Kevving, sitting down at the next chair.

'Yes and no,' said Jave. 'The vicar was lying. She's gone off somewhere.'

'Shouldn't we be following her?'

'I told Frid to do it.'

'So what do we do now?'

'We wait,' said Jave. 'Where have you been?'

Kevving smiled. 'Detecting, of course,' he said. 'I have got *some* brains you know.'

'I know,' replied Jave. 'It's just a shame they're nowhere near your head. What have you found out?'

'This,' said Kevving, 'is Hemma.'

He gestured towards the counter. There was no one there.

'Who is?' said Jave.

'I am,' said a voice. Jave leaned forward and looked over the counter. The woman standing there had pale, straw-coloured hair that seemed almost translucent. Her eyes were as blue as the Caribbean and flecked with green. She wore a bright red waitress' uniform which bulged in what Jave considered all the right places. The only problem was that she was only three feet tall – yet another casualty of the defective gene kits. Still, Jave thought, as her eyes twinkled at him, it was better than having two noses.

'Sorry,' said Jave. 'Didn't see you there.'

'I've been talking to your brother,' said Hemma. 'Isn't he sweet!'

Kevving flashed a smile at her and wrinkled his noses.

'Yes he is, isn't he?' said Jave. 'He's so sweet, he's been banned by several dentist associations. He rots people's teeth.'

Hemma giggled. 'You're moderately funny too,' she observed.

'Thanks very much.'

'Anyway, I showed Hemma a hologram of Abram Chones,' explained Kevving. 'She's certain she's seen him around here.'

'I recognised his bottom,' explained Hemma. Jave looked surprised. 'Well,' she went on, 'when you're my size it's all you see of people. He used to come in here for a doughnut sometimes. He was ever such a nice man.'

'Did he say what he was doing?' asked Jave.

'No, not really. He used to talk about getting his hands dirty.' The diminutive figure thought for a moment. 'He used to get quite upset over the people here. Over the living conditions.'

'I see. Did he have anything to do with the church over there?' asked Jave.

'Dunno,' said Hemma. 'None of us have much to do with it really. Oh, there are quite a lot of people from the bigger cars, the ones with pools and all that, who go often enough. But the church keeps itself to itself really.'

Jave swallowed his coffee thoughtfully.

'Where did he live?' he said.

'I'm not sure,' said Hemma. 'Like I said, he didn't come in here that much. I just recognised him from your brother's description and from the gram. He was the guy who lived up the road, wasn't he? The guy who got blown up?'

'That's right. Were you around at the time?'

'No. It happened at night. We're only allowed to open until half-eleven, you know. It's the local licensing laws. I heard the explosion though. I guess most of us did who live locally. It was amazing. The whole sky went bright red for a moment.' Hemma's face looked like an excited child describing a firework. 'Then there was just a lot of smoke and flames and stuff. The fire department flew in pretty fast.' She laughed. 'There are quite a lot of fires around here one way or another,' she said. 'Normally when people want the insurance.'

'So you didn't know Abram Chones well?'

'Not really. He hadn't been around here long.'

'Is there anyone else who might know him? Neighbours or anyone?'

She shook her head. 'Not his neighbours. All those lorries around him are warehousing, as far as I know. He was the only guy who lived in that area. And the only guy who would want to,' she added. She thought for a moment. 'I guess MacWhirter might know something about him. I saw him chatting to the guy sometimes.'

'Who's MacWhirter?' asked Kevving.

'MacWhirter the Lender. He runs the credit agency up at the next junction.' Her voice was ice-cold.

'Sounds like you don't think much of MacWhirter,' said Jave.

'Not many people do,' she said. 'But you know how it is. We all need credit.'

'So where do I find this guy?' enquired Jave.

After another coffee and Kevving spending some time chatting up other members of the restaurant staff, Jave and Kevving made their way up through the cars and lorries following Hemma's directions.

Their destination lay at what was once junction 5, slightly up the slip road. It was a tall lorry, its cab now boarded over and the tyres long since deflated. The sign over the door said: 'MacWhirter's Credit Mart – Goods Bought and Sold. Credit Arranged.'

Into the side of the lorry there had been cut a door with some steps leading up to it. The door was heavily reinforced and bolted from the inside. A large sign said: 'Go Away, We're Closed.' The two windows either side of the door which held the window display were covered with wire mesh. There was another sign, hand-painted which read: 'Beware of the Grizzly.' Whoever owned this lorry didn't want anyone getting in.

Jave tried the door.

'Locked,' he said. He glanced at his wrist unit. 'Closed early, or gone out or something.'

'Do we wait?' asked Kevving.

Jave didn't answer him. He looked in the windows.

The display made a sort of catalogue of modern spending. All human trade was there. Well, almost all, represented by a vast array of goods awaiting their owners. Goods used to secure desperately needed loans. Goods that waited, like orphans, for owners who would never come to redeem them.

There were musical instruments – old-fashioned guitars and brass instruments along with bright glittery synthesisers. There were hologram takers, along with the holograms that they had taken, cased in silver frames. There were bangles and bracelets, their once golden gleam now tarnished and dirty, strings of cream-coloured pearls, rings with holes where once jewels had been set; lockets, open and empty. There were old-fashioned watches and their modern cousins the electronic wrist-units. There were radios, TVs, and hi-fi of all descriptions. There were coats of black, brown, cream, beige; and shoes and hats and baggage. There were 'puters and vid screens; paintings and mirrors; chairs, tables and even an ancient commode. There were goods of every kind.

But they were not whole objects. They were strangely vacant, bereft of what once gave them life – their owners. They were gifts without receivers. The flotsam left on the shores of happiness once the tide had gone out.

Jave looked in the window for a minute. He looked at the items left by other people. Something in there looked familiar, but he couldn't put his finger on it. It was probably just that everything looked familiar. Depressingly familiar. He turned back to Kevving.

'Let's have a look round the back.'

Behind the lorry it was dingy and dark, an alleyway between MacWhirter's lorry on one side and a large articulated on the other. There were a couple of wastebins, an old plastic canister and an empty bottle of Old Jock's Sporran-Warmer.

The back door into MacWhirter's lorry looked pretty

rotten, in order to fit in with the rest of the alleyway, but it was just a disguise. In fact the back of the lorry was as secure as the front.

Next to the door, however, was a small window. Jave took off his scarf and wrapped it round his fist. He smashed his fist into the window. There was a slight pause and then a stab of pain shot up Jave's arm like a missile.

'What are you doing?' said Kevving.

'Breaking and entering,' gasped Jave. 'Although the only thing I'm breaking is my hand.'

He looked at the window. It was perfectly unscarred. It seemed to glow slightly, almost with self-satisfaction.

'Bazzin' intelligent glass!' said Jave. 'This guy is serious about security.'

'Let me try,' suggested Kevving. He walked up to the window and looked at it. It shattered into a thousand fragments.

Intelligent glass was developed in response to vandalism, break-ins and the ever present problem of window cleaning.

It was basically toughened glass, but with a small microcomputer linked to its atomic structure. This meant that the glass could actually look at what was happening around it and react accordingly. If it saw someone about to spray something on it, it would alter the atomic structure to reduce the surface friction to an infinitesimal level. Paint would then just slide off it. If the glass saw someone trying to break it with a brick it would strengthen itself to whatever level it felt necessary.

This magnificent breakthrough, which totally revolutionised home security, succeeded because the computer was programmed with a database containing hundreds of millions of examples of 'reality' which it matched against what it saw outside. Thus, when it saw something happening outside, it would check it against the examples in its memory and work out what was going on. Then it would react accordingly, as Jave had just found out.

This vast memory bank also gave it data which it could use as a check on its own status. As long as what it saw outside could be matched against its databanks it was obviously in good condition. If what it saw seemed to have specks on it, the glass would realise that it was dirty and automatically clean itself. If what it saw was blurred it would alert its owner and arrange for its own replacement.

In extreme cases, where for instance what it could see and what it knew reality to be like differed fundamentally, it would realise that something very basic was wrong with itself. Accordingly it would commit suicide by shattering itself. Of course, such occurrences were extremely rare and would take an extraordinary breach in reality, such as the existence of a man with two noses. It never seemed to occur to the glass that reality could be at fault.

Inside, the lorry was very dark. As soon as they opened the door they were assailed by a horrible smell – a smell of sweat and stale, rotting food.

'Wow!' exclaimed Kevving. 'There are times when it's no fun having an extra nose.' He found a light and switched it on.

The room they were in was a small kitchen, with transporter tube, waste disposal unit and sink. The place was filthy, the sink stained and dirty. There were piles of old clothes everywhere and old plastic containers that had once held transported food.

Kevving looked around disdainfully, holding his noses. 'Not keen on housework, is he?'

'Come on.'

They passed through the room and opened a door into the dim and dingy shop area of the Credit Mart.

The main room of the vehicle was large, but appeared smaller through the sheer amount of goods crammed into it.

On the right hand side of the room was a counter with an old-fashioned electronic till. Behind the counter were glass shelves filled to overflowing with jewellery, watches, wrist units, hologram units, old coins, scraps of material, electronic devices and even leather-bound books. Next to the till was a big jeweller's felt cloth. Jave could just imagine the figure of MacWhirter laying out the goods to be pawned on the black cloth, spreading the pathetic hoard out in front of him, turning it over and peering through an eyeglass, while the unfortunate pawner waited nervously to see how little he would be lent.

To the left of the counter, against the front wall of the vehicle, there was a rack of coats. Jave wondered what desperation a man must be in if he was prepared to come in and pawn his coat.

He looked away from the coats and back to the counter. He stiffened.

To one side of the counter there was a foot sticking out.

Slowly, Jave walked to the counter and looked over to the floor behind.

On the floor between the counter and the shelves on the back wall, there lay a small, wiry man with ginger hair and a ragged ginger beard. He lay, one knee drawn up almost to his chest, his body cramped into a space too small for it. Around him there were old cameras and radios and wrist units and laser pens which he had knocked from the shelves as he fell.

MacWhirter's face was blue, his eyes bulging like a fish's and his tongue lolling grotesquely from one side of his mouth. Drawn tight around his neck was a cloth belt

– probably one from the many greatcoats that hung from a rack to one side of the shop. He had been strangled. He was lying facing the back of the counter, his open eyes staring at the drawers with a kind of fascination.

Kevving came up behind Jave.

'Weird place this,' he said. 'It's like a...oh, bazzin' heck!' Jave could hear his brother take a deep breath. 'Is he dead?'

'Well, if he's not,' replied Jave, 'he's very uncomfortable.'

The corpse looked shrivelled, almost like a mummy. Jave went round to the back of the counter and felt the pawnbroker's hands. They were as cold as his trade.

'MacWhirter?' whispered Kevving.

'Looks like it,' said Jave.

'Who was it?' said Kevving, breathing in deeply through his noses.

'How the bazz do I know?' said Jave. 'I only just got here.'

He looked round the lorry. 'Doesn't look like anything's missing,' he said, 'although with this lot it's difficult to tell. Thieves would surely have taken more of the expensive stuff. Made more of a job of it.'

He stood up and checked the till. The key was still in the lock and the drawer opened easily. It was full of coins and notes.

'So whoever it was, he didn't want money,' suggested Kevving.

'No.'

'Oh, wow.'

Jave looked at his brother. He realised that even for someone as basically weird as Kevving, coming across your first corpse was not likely to be a run-of-the-mill experience.

'Look,' he said, 'why don't you go and wait outside? There's nothing more you can do in here.'

'No, I'm all right,' said Kevving. 'It's just a bit of a shock, that's all. I mean, you think the zeke's alive and waiting to answer questions. And there he is. A complete deadoid.'

'Yeah.'

'So, if it wasn't money and it wasn't thieves, what else could it be?'

'Oh come on, Kevving!' Jave was exasperated. He felt somehow uncomfortable. Not with the fact that there was a dead man at his feet, but with the fact that his brother was there asking questions. It didn't seem right somehow. 'There could be hundreds of explanations,' he said.

'Such as?'

'Well, I don't know! Revenge maybe. After all, MacWhirter's not a popular man. Could have been the last straw for someone. Or to hide something.'

'Hide something?'

'Look, men like MacWhirter, they buy and sell. They lend money. They're dealers. And not only in goods like all this. Often we're talking about information.'

'So he could have been killed because he knew something?'

'Yes. Or even because he didn't know something.'

Jave looked round the shop. 'It wouldn't be hard. All you'd have to do is come in as a customer, look at the coats, bring one across to the counter and wait till MacWhirter's back is turned.'

Kevving grimaced.

'After that,' continued Jave, 'all you'd have to do would be to lock the front door and walk out through the back. The door's self-locking back there.'

'So, what do we do?' Kevving's voice sounded hushed and strained.

'We report it of course. Only not just yet. I want to have a look round first, before the Social Security get here. Keep a look out round the back. Tell me if anyone's coming.'

Kevving disappeared into the back room, relieved to get away from the grotesque figure that lay, distorted, behind the counter.

Jave pulled a pair of gloves from the pockets of his trenchcoat and slipped them on. Quickly, but carefully, he worked his way through MacWhirter's pockets. There was nothing much. A few hard ecus, some receipts, a scribbled shopping list. Finally, from the pocket of MacWhirter's waistcoat, Jave pulled a scrap of paper, torn from a notebook somewhere.

One side of the scrap was blank, but the other was written on in pencil. The writing was large, but very neat and almost scored into the paper with the weight of pressure. It was a single name 'Charlie Harris' and a number, '2025'.

Jave folded the paper and put it back in the waistcoat pocket. Then he rose from the body and started, methodically, to search the shop.

Ten minutes later, Jave took off the gloves and stuffed them back into his pocket and pressed a button on the old black vid unit that stood on a shelf behind the counter. The unit bleeped once.

'Number,' said a dry, automatic voice.

'Social Security, please,' said Jave. 'I'd like to report a murder.'

A few minutes earlier, Kevving had slipped out of the shop and into the street behind. They checked the street thoroughly. Jave locked the back door behind him, crossed the kitchen area back into the shop and unlocked the front door of the shop. Then he turned the sign round to read 'open'.

Just like the alleyway behind the shop, the street in front was completely deserted except for a mangy cat scavenging under one of the vans.

Jave couldn't have said why exactly he thought it was better to keep Kevving out of it. He just knew, from long experience in the Social Security Department, that it never helped to complicate things. Best leave sleeping brothers lie, with no one aware that Kevving had ever been there.

And anyway, thought Jave, standing by the vid unit, close to the cramped body of the dead man, no one would even care.

But if no one cared about Kevving, someone had certainly cared about MacWhirter; cared enough to kill the man by strangling him with the belt from a coat.

And, search as he might, Jave had been unable to find the coat to which the belt belonged.

7

'So you thought you'd just do your good citizen bit, huh?'

The man who was speaking was tall and thin and dressed entirely in black syntho-leather. The black hair that topped his round head was frizzy and cut in what had once been known as an 'afro'. It surmounted a face of such deathly whiteness that it was almost transparent. From a distance Social Security Stamper Hook looked like the letter 'i'.

From close up, he didn't look any better. His pale, watery-blue eyes with their pink rims were permanently hidden by a pair of sunglasses. His thin, wiry hands ended in dirty and broken fingernails. He had never been known to smile. Except when he didn't mean it.

What other people could never see, of course, was the incredibly hard life that had brought him thus far. His parents had died in a bizarre bowling accident when he was only three. He had been brought up by a maternal aunt, a woman so strict that she only allowed laughing on alternate Saturday evenings after six o'clock.

And if that wasn't bad enough, all his life Stamper Hook had suffered from a cold. For as long as he could remember, he had been plagued by a nose that, while not blocked, invariably dripped like a leaky tap, giving him a permanent sniff.

With such a terrible and deprived background, one would expect even the best balanced person to turn out badly. But even so, those few people who did know his history felt that Stamper Hook had over-reacted.

Part of his over-reaction was to become the nastiest official in the Department of Social Security. It was not a nice job being a Stamper. It brought a person into contact with the very dregs of society. It was a job which constantly brought the employee face to face with brutality and violence; a job which meant hours of interrogation, strong-arm tactics and, ultimately, locking up people for years and laughing unpleasantly.

Stamper Hook loved his job.

His black leather coat flapped irritably about him as he wandered around the shop.

'You know how it is,' said Jave. 'Just trying to be a responsible member of society.'

'You've had a complete change of character then, Fleming?' asked Hook. He laughed, but it didn't sound like a laugh. It was short and brittle, like a cough. 'I don't remember you ever having such high morals when you worked for Security.'

Jave smiled. 'I've matured, Hook,' he said.

'Stamper Hook, to you.'

Few could have seen the way that the police force in Great Britain was to change in the twenty-first century.

It all started through fears about civil liberties. By the end of the twentieth and the beginning of the twenty-first century, people in Britain were becoming seriously concerned about the amount of information the police had about them. Huge police databases had been compiled containing all manner of information about individuals. People felt it was intrusive, it was unconstitutional, it was an unjustifiable invasion of privacy.

Eventually the public outcry was so great that in a moment of relative lucidity, the Prime Minister decreed that police records would be drastically reduced.

The public rejoiced, but what they didn't realise was that police records were relatively incomplete compared to those held by another Government department. All the information on police files, and much more, was held in the archives of the Department of Social Security.

As mechanisation and computerisation forced more and more people out of work, as the average living age skyrocketed and the retirement age was reduced to forty-three and a bit, the Department of Social Security had to amass more and more information about the population.

From where they lived and what they did for a living, to how much they weighed and what car they flew, the Social Security, through its multiplicity of claim forms, knew it all.

So, reasoned the Government, why not simply switch information bases? Since Social Security already knew so much, people would never notice them finding out a little bit more.

And so it proved. People were so relieved at the reduction of the police database that they failed to observe the increasing detail of Social Security forms. No one seemed to notice that Form D38 (claim for child benefit) included the question: 'Are you now, or have you ever been, a member of the Communist Party?' No one spotted that Form UB29 (claim for unemployment benefit) included the question: 'What is your opinion of King William?' No one seemed to mind that Form 76E/2 (one-off claim for injury or mutilation suffered through contact with a yak) asked for such information as 'blood group', 'favourite colour' and 'maternal grandfather's inside leg measurement'.

This usurpation of the police's role took another step during the great depression. When the economic crash came in the twenty-twenties, over eighty per cent of the population awoke to find themselves without a job. There were so many people out of work that the Department of Social Security had to set up its own police force to man the Security offices and ensure the safe transportation of benefit money. They were also responsible for vetting claimants.

Thus, by 2025, the Department of Social Security had a massive store of information on virtually the whole country, as well as its own private security force which carried out its procedures and protected its offices. It was only natural that, when in the following year the Government disbanded the police force, it merged them into the Department of Social Security.

Police Constables were now known as 'Clerks' and Sergeants as 'Assistants'. The highest grade of Social Security officer was known as a 'Stamper' after the old Social Security staff who dealt with National Insurance stamps.

'This man....' Stamper Hook gestured at the counter, where the forensic droids were busy whirring and humming around the body.

'MacWhirter.'

'MacWhirter. Tell me again how you came to be involved.'

Inwardly Jave sighed. He had known it was going to be like this as soon as Stamper Hook walked through the door. Stamper Jonn Hook was renowned throughout Social Security as an officer with all the charm, tact and intelligence of a mentally retarded pit bull terrier. He smelled about the same as well. In his years at

Social Security, Jave had learned to keep out of Hook's way – especially if you wanted an intelligent conversation.

Jave repeated the details of what he had been doing there, leaving out only a few minor details – Kevving's trick with the intelligent glass and the fact that he had searched MacWhirter's body. He omitted mentioning these because through some hunch, some detective's intuition, a Holmesian 'sixth sense', he suspected they would lead him to the murderer. Also, he knew it would really irritate Stamper Hook.

And yet there was more to it than that. Jave had the feeling of having wandered into a bigger puzzle than he had foreseen. It was too much of a coincidence. No sooner had they come looking for MacWhirter than they had found him murdered. Of course, Jave had no proof that this murder had anything to do with the murder of Abram Chones. Any number of people had motives for murdering men like MacWhirter. Nevertheless, Jave felt that the less he told Social Security, the better.

'So,' Jave concluded, 'I came to have a talk with MacWhirter and found him like this.'

'And the window smashed and the back door open?' asked Hook, suspiciously. 'Or did our little Private Eye indulge himself in a bit of breaking and entering?'

Jave didn't answer that question.

'The front door's open,' he pointed out, careful to use the right tense.

'Maybe you wanted to help yourself to a few things first, eh?' said Hook, his long, thin nose twitching. 'Maybe you had reasons of your own to get rid of MacWhirter.'

'If I'd wanted to steal things I'd hardly have called in and reported this, would I?' said Jave. 'And especially not if I'd strangled the guy.'

'Double-bluff!' said Hook. 'That's what you want me to think.'

'Look, Hook,' said Jave, suppressing his irritation, 'I came here looking for someone. I had information that MacWhirter might know where he is. All right, I admit I had a bit of a look round before I found the body, but that's it. I don't want to get mixed up in a murder enquiry.'

'So you say.'

Stamper Hook sniffed. 'What's the job you're on?'

Jave paused. Should he tell him? He decided he didn't really have an option.

'Chones,' he said. 'Abram Chones. Killed last week. P-42 bomb vaporised the guy. The daughter wants me to find out who did it.'

'Sounds like a nobody,' said Hook. 'Still, that fits. A nobody looking for a nobody.' He snapped out a laugh at this enormous witticism. 'So why would this nobody be involved with MacWhirter?'

'Dunno,' replied Jave. 'I'm not even sure that he was. It was just that he was the only person that anyone round here could remember Abram Chones talking to.'

'What did he do, this Chones?'

'He was the leader of a church.'

'A church,' Stamper sneered. 'So that's what you do with yourself these days, is it Fleming? Thought yourself so high and mighty, didn't you, leaving us poor foot-sloggers to set up on your own? The great Jave Fleming, Private Detective. And what do you end up doing? Acting as nursemaid for a bunch of religious nuts who aren't man enough to do their own dirty work. So much for the great detective!' He sniffed triumphantly.

'Still got your cold I see,' said Jave.

Stamper Hook's eyes flared angrily, an effect which was entirely lost on everyone in the room, because he always wore dark glasses.

'Listen, sonny,' he said to Jave. 'You'd better be telling me the truth, because if I find out you've been lying to me, I'll rip your intestines out through your nose.'

'Thanks,' said Jave, 'I'll bear that in mind, if ever I decide to lie to you.'

There was a bleep from one of the forensic droids.

'Drrroid Thirrrty-One, reporting, sirrrr,' it buzzed. It was a small, plump droid, which resembled an ancient vacuum cleaner with a lot of flashing lights. It had a loose panel which buzzed and vibrated every time it spoke. 'Body checked. No fingerrprrints. Surrrrounding arrrea, checked. Minorrr objects retrrrieved forr further examination.'

'OK,' growled Hook.

'Furrtherrr scans of the immediate locale being undertaken by myself and Drrroid Thirrrty-Eight.'

Behind him, a small, squat droid bleeped excitedly.

'That's me!' it said.

'Fine,' said Hook. 'Carry on. Now....' He turned to continue his investigation, but was interrupted again by the droid.

'May I say what a pleasure it is for Drrrroid Thirrty-Eight and I to be worrking alongside you, Stamperr. Needless to say, we will do all within our powerrr to bring this case to a successful conclusion.'

'Fine. Just get on with....'

'No, rrreally,' insisted the droid. 'It's the peak of my carrreerrr. It's the proudest moment of my shorrrt existence.'

'Look, will you just....'

'And mine too!' said Droid Thirty-Eight. 'I mean, woweee! Hot Diggety-dog! I mean, when we heard that we were going to work with Stamper Hook, we were just thrilled, really we were. I've been a fan of yours from way back....'

'That'll do!' shouted Hook.

'Of course, some droids were saying that you're about as intelligent as a small soapdish, but I put them right, I can tell you.'

'That's rrrright!' said Droid Thirty-One. 'And anyway, what you lack in intelligence, you make up for in per-rrseverrrence....'

'Shut up!' yelled Hook.

There was a silence. Some colour had actually come into Hook's face – two red patches on his gaunt, taut cheeks. They looked like large spots.

The droids bleeped, nervously.

'Look, you pair of mechanical morons,' said Hook, menacingly. 'I don't want to listen to this load of rubbish. Just get on and do your work.'

He turned round and made to continue interrogating Jave.

Behind him, there was a low electronic burbling.

'There, there,' Droid Thirty-Eight was saying. 'He's not worth it.'

'I thought I told you to be quiet,' said Hook, coldly.

'I'm sorry,' sniffed Droid Thirty-One. 'I'll be all rrright in a minute.'

'He set his heart on this assignment,' said Droid Thirty-Eight, accusingly, to Stamper Hook, 'and you had to treat him this way. He didn't deserve this.'

'I've had about enough of this,' muttered Hook.

'You...you ought to be ashamed of yourself!' said Droid Thirty-Eight to Hook. 'Treating him this way – a droid what's given his life to the service of Social Security staff like you. You're not fit to plug in his diodes!'

'Listen,' said Jave, 'I think I ought to be going.'

'I haven't finished with you yet,' said Hook.

Behind him Droid Thirty-One started a sort of long, protracted, electronic wailing.

'He hates me!' he was saying. 'He despises me!'

'Forget him!' said Droid Thirty-Eight. 'He's not good enough for you!'

'But I love him!' wailed Droid Thirty-One.

Droid Thirty-Eight swivelled slightly and turned two

red flashing lights on Stamper Hook. 'Look at what you've done to him!' he said grimly. 'Well I hope you're satisfied. You...you swine!'

'Look, I didn't mean to upset you,' said Hook, trying to make amends.

Jave felt this was a good moment to make his exit.

'I'll see you around,' he said to no one in particular.

By the time Hook had succeeded in calming down the droids, Jave was sitting in the Central Reservation Diner, drinking a cup of coffee and wondering what to do next.

8

When Jave arrived back at the office, he thought that someone had added a gargoyle to the decor. Then he realised that he'd told Kevving to meet him here.

'So what happened then?' asked Kevving, thoughtfully chewing an opple. 'Did you report it?' said Kevving.

'Of course I reported it. What option did I have? You go into a place and find a murdered man, you've got to report it. They're bound to find out sooner or later. And then it just looks bad for you.'

'Who's on the case?'

'Hook.'

'Hook?'

'Hook.'

Kevving thought for a moment. 'He doesn't like you, does he?' he said.

'You could say that. He thinks I'm something you tread in.'

Jave went to the food tube and punched in a number. 'You want anything?'

'No, I'm eating an opple.'

The opple was developed as a mixture of an orange and an apple.

It was a revolutionary fruit, not in itself (it had no real advantages, apart from allowing people to eat an apple in segments) but for what it represented. For the opple was the first tangible product of the new science of crypto-biology.

Crypto-biology was a development of the old art of grafting that gardeners and horticulturists had used for centuries. While standard grafting could only work between two basically similar kinds of plant life, crypto-biologists discovered that it was possible to graft entirely different characteristics onto fruit and vegetables. Not only did they mix greatly differing fruits together, producing results such as the opple, but during the mixing process, they managed to graft on neuropeptides – the chemicals in the brain that exert strong influences on moods, emotions and general behaviour.

The opple was a mixture of orange, apple and happiness, producing a very nice feeling in the mind of the eater. The summerberry was basically a strawberry with added lethargy, giving the eater the feeling that, wherever and whenever he was eating it, he was actually in the middle of a lazy, warm, August afternoon.

It was generally agreed, however, that the triumph of crypto-biology came when scientists matched a banana with the neuropeptide that encouraged psychoanalysis, thus creating a banana that actually peeled itself.

There was a buzz from the food tube and a plastic cup of Old Jock's Sporran-Warmer appeared. He gulped it down. It wasn't even that he liked whisky that much. It just felt like the thing to do at the time.

'This is all your fault!' he accused Kevving.

'My fault? How is it my fault?'

'I knew it was a mistake letting you come along. I knew it!'

'Wait a minute, bruvv – you're the one who wanted to break into the place.'

'So what? If you hadn't been there I wouldn't have been able to, would I? And then I wouldn't have found the body and I wouldn't have had Stamper Hook on my back as he undoubtedly will be once his droids have calmed down.'

'Oh, sit down,' said Kevving, 'and have another drink. You're getting everything out of proportion.'

Jave did as he was told. Surprisingly, Kevving was right.

'I mean,' said Kevving, 'look at it this way. Things are happening, right?'

He leaned back as if he'd made his point.

'So?'

'So what?'

'So things are happening.'

'Yeah,' said Kevving, tapping the side of his noses conspiringly. 'I mean *really* happening.'

Jave looked at his brother. 'Look,' he said, 'this may come as something of a surprise to you, but the man we found back there was dead. He was not "happening". He had happened. This is turning out far more complicated than I thought.'

Kevving laughed. 'But you're not going to give it up, are you?'

Jave smiled. 'Give it up? Why should I? Things are really happening.'

He punched another number into the tube and two more cups of Old Jock's appeared.

'Here,' he said.

Jave drank his whisky more slowly this time and looked at his brother who was gulping it down like opple juice.

'There's something I don't understand,' he said. 'What are you doing mixed up in all this?'

Kevving shrugged his shoulders. 'Just lending a helping hand,' he said.

'That's just it,' said Jave. 'I've never known you show any interest in helping anybody before. You used to help yourself, of course, but mostly to my money. So what's changed?'

Kevving leaned forward, his eyes twinkled excitedly.

'It's this church, bruvv. These people,' he grinned. 'They're nice. I mean, OK some of them are right bazzers – fifty years behind the time and with porridge between the ears, but they're still OK, you know? They care about me.'

He looked down and twirled the empty plastic cup in his hand.

'Before I met Chanis, I was in a bad way, y'know? I was on some heavy stuff. I was suffering from the whole bit – shaking, hallucinating, the works. Some of them hallucinations were real heavy.'

'I can guess. Last time you met me you told me a giant rabbit was trying to nibble you to death.'

'Yeah, that was a bad one,' agreed Kevving.

'Then there was that time when you dialled me up and told me that all your hair had turned yellow and fallen out.'

Kevving looked up. 'That wasn't an hallucination, bruvv. It had.'

'So what happened?'

'Well, I fell into this church one day. I mean really fell in. I was living in the level above and I leaned a little too far out. Went straight through the glass roof.'

Jave laughed.

'No laughing matter, bruvv,' said Kevving. 'I fell straight onto the dried flower arrangement. I'm still trying to remove some of the pampas grass to this day. Some of the dudes thought I was an angel.'

'They must have been blind.'

'Well, anyway, they picked me up and pulled some of the flowers off me and generally looked after me.'

'Why?'

'I dunno. Just because they thought it was the right thing to do, I guess. So I sort of stayed there. I mean it's not a church. It's not an official meeting or anything like that.'

'You know they're not allowed. Any meeting like that is supposed to be registered. It has to take place in an official place of worship.'

'Yeah, but you can't blame them. I mean they've got all this life and there's the registered church....'

Jave leaned back and shook his head. 'I don't know what to make of you, really I don't. I know you're supposed to be the insane one of the family, but this is taking things a bit far.'

There was a scampering outside in the hallway and a hiss as Jave's door opened.

'Hey dudes!' said Frid, jumping up onto the desk. 'What's going down?'

He reached a furry paw into a small plastic canister on Jave's desk and took out a pawful of caraway seeds. 'Man, I is hungry,' he said.

'Oh,' said Jave, 'you didn't miss much. Just a murder.'

'A murder!' exclaimed the gerbil, spluttering seeds. 'Oh man! How come I always miss the action?'

'It's for the best,' replied Jave. 'You know you only get over-excited. I'll tell you about it later. First, I want to hear what happened with the vicar.'

The gerbil settled down to tell his story. 'Well, I followed the lady,' he said. 'Right after she left you, she went rushin' through them streets like she was in a race.'

'Did she fly somewhere?'

'Not at first. First she went down them backstreets to some small lorry on the side. I reckon she was making some kind of visit.'

'Where was this lorry?'

There was a slight whirr from somewhere within the gerbil as he activated his memory banks.

'Clockwise lane six. Lorry VKY 330JJ,' he said. 'Just north of the church, and towards the next junction.'

'Who lives there?'

'According to my address banks, the lorry's owned by a dude by the name of Marc Shoeban.'

'Shoeban? Funny name,' commented Kevving. 'Could have been a sick old dude that she was visiting.'

'Yeah, and I could be the Prime Minister,' said Jave. 'Anyway, we can check that place out tomorrow.' He turned back to the gerbil, who was just taking another mouthful of seeds. 'Where did she go after that?'

'Well, I nearly lost her,' said Frid with his mouth full. 'I'm telling you, that chick may be big and ugly, but she's fast. She went north and then across a couple of lanes, right to one of the junctions. Went into some kind of shop. I tried to follow her, but this place had some mean security systems and they closed the front door. I couldn't sneak in nohow.'

'Did you scan the place?' asked Jave.

The gerbil looked hurt.

'Of course I did, man. I got heat readings – there were two of them in there. Anyway, she didn't stay more than a minute. She came running out of that place like it was on fire. I'm tellin' you, baby,' the gerbil puffed out his cheeks and looked about him for effect, 'she sure looked scared.'

He grabbed another caraway seed in his tiny paws and popped it into his mouth.

'So I followed her. She went straight back to the church. Next thing I know there's a flyer taking off from the roof and she's on it.'

'That's all?'

'That's all.'

'You didn't get a trace on where she was going?'

Frid looked aggrieved. 'Hey!' he said. 'I'm only a gerbil. I'm not air control. You dig?'

'Why didn't you run up there and leap onto the back?' asked Kevving.

'Because I is not completely insane,' said Frid. 'If you want a stunt gerbil, go somewhere else.'

'So anyway,' said Jave, 'we know she went to this lorry to see this Shoeban guy, or to make a call or something. And after that she went to this shop and in the shop she saw something that scared her.'

There was silence in the room. 'This case is getting complicated,' Jave said.

He walked over to the window in his best Humphrey Bogart walk – the walk of a man solving a crime.

'Why are you walking like that?' asked Kevving.

'Like what?'

'Like a constipated heron.'

Jave sighed and relaxed his pose. No one ever called Humphrey a constipated heron, he thought. At least, no one who lived to talk about it.

Out of the window, London was settling down to a hot night.

Lights dotted the plate-glass cliff faces of the enormous tower blocks that reared up into the sky. Just a few floors below him, the walkways were gradually emptying as people made their way into the safe harbours of their homes. Homes where everything was secure and safe. Tight, sealed; hermetically sealed little boxes where life was controlled, arriving only through the carefully planned spontaneity of the TV chat shows.

These were the homes of the well-off people where no one ever got murdered and no one ever went missing.

'Somewhere,' Jave said, 'there is someone who knows everything we're trying to find out. Somewhere there is someone who is the key. Or maybe not.'

'What do you mean?' asked Kevving, joining his brother at the window.

'Well, that's what I'd like to think. That there's someone out there who has all the answers. But the truth is it's never as easy as that. People only ever know a fragment of the truth. There never is that mythical being who sees the whole picture.'

He took a sip from the plastic glass in his hand. 'I spend all my days scrabbling around trying to piece together a jigsaw puzzle with too few pieces. All I really want in life is someone who can see the whole picture. But he doesn't exist.'

'Oh, I don't know,' said Kevving.

Jave looked at his brother, who was standing by his side, staring into the twilight and picking one of his noses. Was that what Kevving had found? When he fell through the skylight into that church, had he found the one person who saw the whole picture?

Suddenly a thought struck him. He turned back to the gerbil who was still busily stuffing his face.

'This shop,' he asked. 'What was it called?'

The gerbil looked up, his whiskers full of caraway seeds.

'Oh, didn't I say?' he said. 'It was a weird place. Buying and selling and all that. It was called MacWhirter's.'

THE THIRD DAY

S.D. - 4

9

It was 7.30 on the third day and Jave was trying not to wake up.

His wrist unit was bleeping again. He thumped his wrist against the wall and the bleeping stopped. There was an angry buzz and then the voice of the radio announcer slithered into action.

'The Prime Minister will meet with the cabinet tomorrow, according to informed sources in Swindonopolis. Uninformed sources said they didn't know anything about it.'

Jave switched the radio off and opened his eyes. The room was so clean, it hurt.

When the brochure spoke about a room that automatically cleaned itself each night; where you could set the wall colour, temperature and light to whatever you wanted, Jave thought it was too good to be true. It was.

Jave's bedroom, like every room in his flat, was a model of efficiency. Every night the sensors hidden in the wall scanned the apartment for anything out of place, identified it and cleaned it up. If it was rubbish it was sucked into the waste disposal chute to wind up eventually on the ground many storeys below. Clothes were retrieved by wiry steel arms with filament-thin fingers which shot out of the walls, grabbed the clothes and took them to the laundry automatically. Objects such as books were replaced in pre-programmed places.

But that wasn't all. Every night, as if to demonstrate the cleanliness of the surroundings, the flat reset the colour of the walls to a brilliant white. Each morning, therefore, Jave woke to a room with all the homeliness and individuality of an intensive care ward. He had tried to persuade the room not to do this, but it always did. This morning was no different.

'Room,' Jave said, through thick, sleep-heavy lips.

'Yes?' said the room cheerfully.

'Not white,' said Jave.

'I'm sorry?' The synthesised voice seemed to come from all around Jave. Only if you knew the room intimately would you know that small octophonic speakers were concealed behind strategically placed furniture.

'I keep telling you.' Jave was too tired to be irritated. 'Not white. The walls. Change the colour.'

'White is chosen to show the occupant that the room is spotless,' explained the room with a touch of annoyance. 'I am programmed to institute a white reset every night after cleaning.'

'Well don't. I want another colour.'

'Certainly,' replied the room. 'What would you like? There's white with a hint of peach; white with a hint of rose; white with a hint of beige, or how about white with a hint of white?'

'White with a hint of white?'

'It's like white, only brighter.'

'No white!' shouted Jave.

'You've got to have white,' said the room. 'It's got to be white with a hint of something.'

'All right,' said Jave, 'I'll have white with a hint of complete black.'

The computerised voice sounded upset.

'Black?' it enquired. 'Are you sure?'

'Of course I'm sure.'

'I don't know about that....'

'Look,' said Jave, 'either you do what I say, or you will be room with a hint of axe, understand?'

There was a tiny, but discernible, 'Hmph!' The room went black and Jave got up.

After breakfast, Jave gave Kevving his detailed instructions for the day.

'Stay here?' complained Kevving. 'What do you mean "stay here"?'

'Look,' said Jave, finishing his syntho-coffee, 'you'll have to stay here today. This could be time for a bit of undercover work.'

'I'll be OK,' said Kevving. 'I blend into the background.'

'Blend into the background? How can a man with all the subtlety of a bull hippo blend into the background? When you come with me, I might as well run around wearing a large sign saying, "Detective at work."'

'I won't say anything.'

'Kevving,' Jave explained, 'you've got two noses. I mean, people notice these things. Even the most unobservant people tend to notice a man with a hundred per cent bonus in the nose department. You'll just have to stay at home.'

'But it's boring,' complained Kevving.

'So be bored. It'll do you good. You get too much excitement anyway.'

'I'll tell you what,' said Kevving. 'I'll call Chanis and let her know what's happening.'

Jave felt a lurch in the pit of his stomach and his knees suddenly started to waltz with each other. He remembered the stunningly beautiful girl who, the day before yesterday, had walked into his office.

'Well, look,' he said, 'don't frighten the girl. I mean try and keep the subject away from the murder. Don't be tactless.'

Kevving looked hurt at the mere thought of Jave accusing him of tactlessness. 'I'm not a complete moron, you know,' he said.

'Oh,' replied Jave, 'is there a bit missing then?'

'Don't worry, I'll be sensitive.'

'Sensitive,' muttered Jave as he climbed out of the window a few moments later to the waiting Sinclair. 'He's about as sensitive as a sumo wrestler.'

In the pale, cold light of the early morning the M25 seemed eerily empty. There was hardly anyone on the spaces and Jave's footsteps gave metallic echoes as he walked down the thin spaces between the cars and the trucks. Beside him, Frid scampered from shadow to shadow.

The lorry they were looking for was small and shabby and looked uncared for.

'I don't know who this Shoeban bloke is, but he doesn't earn very much,' said Jave. He pressed his hand to the flat metal plate at the side of the door. There was a buzz inside.

Jave waited for a while, but no one came to answer the door.

'Scan,' he ordered.

'No body heat anywhere, so no one home,' said Frid, his whiskers whirring. 'Or if there is, they're dead.'

'Don't say that,' said Jave. 'It'll happen.'

He examined the outside of the lorry. It was a cheap aluminium-sided, twelve wheel job that had previously been a frozen food container. You could still see the faded paintwork on the side where there once had been the legend: 'Bird's Eye Octopus Portions – A Leg for the Whole Family.'

In the past someone had knocked a door in the side – a cheap wooden affair that now hung somewhat unsurely on old and rusty hinges. None of the homes on the M25 was exactly luxurious, none in this junction anyway, but this one gave shabbiness a bad name.

Jave pushed at the door. It swung open. He looked down at Frid, who was standing by his feet.

'Did you do that?' he asked.

'Nope,' said Frid. 'Must've been unlocked.'

'Do we go in?'

The gerbil looked at his owner.

'Do ducks float?' said Frid.

They went in.

The room was cold and damp. The metal floor of the lorry was uncarpeted and the room was sparsely furnished. In one corner there was a camp bed with an old ragged sleeping bag on it. On the floor by the bed was a small halogen reading lamp, but without a bulb. At the end of the bed there was a wardrobe with only one door. It looked empty. Opposite the camp bed was a desk, a set of drawers and a chair. The desk was piled with scraps of paper, old envelopes, a paperback without a cover and other such refuse. Likewise, the floor was littered with scraps of newspaper and old plastic bags. By the bed there were two old paperbacks, both without their covers and with torn pages. It was as if someone had dumped their week's garbage in the lorry. The pile on the desk was surmounted by a dirty plate and a mug that seemed to have incubated an entirely new life form.

There was a doorway with a ragged curtain across it in one corner of the lorry. It led into what had once been the cab and what was now a tiny, cramped kitchen with a rudimentary microwave, a broken food tube and a sink full of dirty cups and dishes.

'You going to search in there?' enquired Frid.

'I don't think so,' replied Jave, closing the curtain. 'I've not been innoculated recently.'

They turned their attention back to what could only be called the living room because someone had actually been living in it.

'Do you reckon he slept here last night?' asked Jave, looking at the bedclothes.

'Don't know,' answered Frid. 'Ain't no latent heat. But he could have got up early this morning.'

'Well, let's have a look around.'

Frid went to have a look around the floor and in the wardrobe, while Jave went through the papers on the desk.

They were mostly just circulars, adverts, catalogues and free newspapers. There was little there of personal value, and the only envelope Jave found with Marc Shoeban's name on it was a *Reader's Digest* prize raffle. As he sorted through the pile, Jave began to suspect that Marc Shoeban never threw anything away that he received through the post, but that no one ever sent him anything worth keeping.

At the bottom of the pile, however, Jave struck gold. Or gilt, perhaps.

Underneath the pile of junk mail on the desk, there was a plastic-coated ticket with the name Marc Shoeban on the front. It was a residential permit, the kind that people had to have to prove rights to their property.

The front of the card gave the man's name, the agency that had sold him the van and the amount he had paid. Marc Shoeban had purchased the van only seven days before. He had paid the agents – Everyglade ('Our Houses are your Homes') – a tiny amount for the property. On the rear of the ticket was what Jave was looking for: a photo of the man.

Marc Shoeban was wearing sunglasses in the photo – small, round lensed glasses with silver frames. He was clean shaven with short, cropped black hair. His skin was very pale. He looked to be in his mid- to late-forties, although it was difficult to tell because the photo was not very good.

Jave studied the face. It told him nothing. There was nothing in the photo to indicate a profession or any real distinguishing features. The only thing that struck Jave was the paleness of the skin. Maybe Shoeban had a profession that kept him indoors. But there was nothing else of any importance. The photo was basically just head and shoulders. Below that, Marc Shoeban was wearing a black garment of some kind, but the picture was not detailed enough to tell Jave exactly what it was.

Frid scampered up beside him. He was carrying something.

'Found something,' he said.

'So have I,' said Jave. He showed the library card to Frid. 'Recognise him?'

'Something within Frid whirred.

'No.' he said. 'Not seen him in the past few days.'

'Oh well,' said Jave. He put the library card back on the desk. 'What have you found?'

'This,' said Frid. He handed Jave what he had been carrying.

Jave turned the flat, white square over in his fingers. It was a hologram. And staring out from the hologram were the features of Abram Chones.

10

'Well, proves one thing,' commented Jave as he sat in the Central Reservation Diner-A-Go-Go.

'What?' asked Frid.

'It proves a link between the vicar and Abram Chones. Either she knew him directly, or she knew of him.'

'Through the Shoeban dude.'

'Exactly.'

'But if she knew the guy, why would they want him out of the way?'

'That is a good question.' Jave took a sip of coffee. 'I wish I knew the answer.'

'Well, do we go and see the vicar chick again?'

Jave swallowed the last of his coffee and stared for a moment at the dregs in the bottom of his cup.

'We go and see the vicar again,' he said.

It was raining as they left the Central Reservation Diner-A-Go-Go and crossed towards the big, black hulk of the Church of the Blessed Commuter. Jave turned his collar up and looked up into the iron coloured sky. There was nothing but cloud, however far he looked. Nothing but grey, impenetrable cloud.

As Jave began to climb the steps up to the church, Frid slipped away into a darkened doorway to the right. Jave continued into the huge lorry.

It was dim and cool. The church was largely deserted. Jave paused just inside the door and shook the rain from his shoulders. Then he began to wander slowly down the nave, looking around him while his eyes adjusted themselves to the darkness of the church interior.

It was an amazing building. From the inside, one would never have guessed that it was formed entirely of massive, old container lorries, welded together and knocked through, stacked on top of each other, put together like building blocks. On the outside you could see where one container had been welded to another – the building looked like a huge patchworked cube. From the inside, however, it was a church, dim and cool and quiet.

At the end of the nave was the altar, flanked by two enormous neon candles and an automatic incense burner. The altar had been designed in keeping with its surroundings – a thick slab of metal, polished to a brilliance and mounted on two oil drums. These rudimentary elements gave to the altar a strange, modern kind of grandeur, a reflection of the beauty latent in even the most uninspiring objects.

The wall behind the altar, however, had a modernity of an entirely different kind. From the other end of the nave, Jave had thought at first that the wall was covered by a silvery kind of tapestry. Only when he was close to it did he realise that, from floor to ceiling, the wall was filled with an enormous video screen.

There was a small brown cleaner droid sweeping the floor.

'Excuse me,' said Jave.

'Sir?' said the droid, wheeling over to him in one slick movement.

'That screen – what's it for?'

'It's a video screen, sir.'

'Yes, I realise that, but what do they show on it?'

There was a slight pause. 'Videos, sir.'

Jave stared at the droid.

'And TV broadcasts,' suggested the droid hopefully.

'What kind of videos?' asked Jave through gritted teeth.

'Oh, I see, sir,' said the droid. 'Those'll be the videos by the Bishop.'

'The Bishop?'

'Bishop Lou of Swindonopolis,' said the droid. 'Surely you know of him?'

'Yes,' said Jave, 'I know of him. But is this his church? Surely it's in a different area or whatever.'

'Diocese,' said the droid helpfully. 'Yes it is. But the Bishop's so wonderful and popular, sir, that many churches up and down the country take his video show each week. It saves on the expense of having their own staff, you see, sir. So all the poor people, who haven't got their own vid screens can come here and watch the Bishop every Sunday morning, large as life as it were.'

'I didn't realise he was that big,' said Jave looking up at the massive screen.

'No, sir, he's not,' replied the droid. 'They enlarge the picture, you see.'

'No, I meant...oh never mind.'

'Anyway, sir,' continued the droid, 'the Bishop's a real star. His TV and radio shows are syndicated throughout the world. And to think our vicar here knows him!'

'She does?'

'Oh yes, sir!' The droid bleeped with reflected pride. 'He sometimes visits her here. She's helping with his campaign.'

'What campaign?'

'Why, to become Archbishop of Canterbury.' The droid glowed with either pride or overheating.

'I didn't think they had campaigns. I thought they chose them some other way.'

'What way?'

'Well, I dunno. Prayer or something.'

'Don't be silly, sir,' chuckled the droid, turning in a little circle at this human idiocy. 'An Archbishop has to be chosen carefully. Delicate negotiations, consensus, votes, calling in favours and all that. You have to promote your candidate. The church is very much in favour of choice and the free market.'

'Even in Archbishops?'

'Even there, sir!' The droid emitted a little whirr of glee. 'And to think that our vicar is a part of all this!'

Jave remembered why he had come.

'Speaking of which, where is your vicar?'

'She's in the parish office, I believe, sir.'

'Where do I find that?'

The droid gave a click. 'Come this way.'

The droid clicked again, a small red bulb in its top flashed twice, and a door in the right hand wall of the church slid open to reveal a brightly lit corridor. Jave followed the droid down to a large glass walled suite of rooms labelled 'Parish Office'.

'If you ask in there, sir, one of the scriveners will help you.'

Jave pressed the metal panel set in the side of the office wall and a glass door swung open.

The office into which he walked had the air of a small business. There were personal vid screens and two scriveners busy printing off labels and sending electronic mail messages. Unlike the church, the parish office was bright and well-lit.

'Can I help you, sir?' enquired a tall scrivener. She had a large mouth and too many teeth for Jave's liking.

'I'd like to see the vicar please,' said Jave.

'Reverend Shamworth's a bit busy at the moment,' said the scrivener, tapping away at her keyboard. 'I think that's right, isn't it, Sharong?'

Sharong was standing at the other side of the office, doing something strange with a 3-D copier.

'Mmmm,' said Sharong. 'Parish business.'

'Parish business, I'm afraid,' said the first scrivener. 'Only available for those in desperate need of pastoral help.'

'That's right,' said Sharong from the far corner. 'Desperates only, love.'

Jave tried to look like a man in desperate need of pastoral help.

'It's quite urgent,' he pleaded.

The scrivener smiled sympathetically. 'Well, I'll try,' she said.

'Oh, could you?' said Jave pathetically. 'You don't know how grateful that would make me.'

'What name shall I give?'

Jave thought for a moment. 'Marc Shoeban.'

The scrivener pressed a button down by her side. Somewhere, something buzzed.

'Yes?' said an irritated voice that came from a small speaker somewhere behind the scrivener's head.

'Sorry to disturb you, Reverend Shamworth,' said the scrivener, 'but there's a man here to see you.'

'Can't it wait?' asked the vicar. 'I'm having my lun...er, a time of private prayer.'

'He says it's urgent.'

'They all say that.' There was the sound of chewing. 'Who is it, anyway?' asked the vicar through a mouthful of food.

'A Mr Marc Shoeban,' replied the scrivener.

There was a slight pause and then, gratifyingly for Jave, the sound of someone having a very bad coughing fit. Jave hadn't a clue who Marc Shoeban was, but whoever he was it was someone the Reverend Shamworth wasn't expecting.

'Send him in!' spluttered the vicar in between coughs.

The scrivener pressed another button by her side and a door clicked open.

'In to your left, Mr Shoeban,' directed the scrivener.

'Thank you,' said Jave. 'You've made a desperate man very happy.'

'We do our best,' said the scrivener.

'Oh, we do,' echoed Sharong.

Jave walked in.

The vicar's room was sparsely but tastefully decorated. There was a plain white desk with pens, pencils and a number of plain brown files carefully arranged. There was the obligatory food tube, a shelf of books and a couple of clean white chairs. The white carpet under his feet was thick and spongy. On a hook to his left hung the vicar's black cassock, looking like someone had thrown a bottle of ink against the white wall. On the wall by the hook there was a framed gram of Bishop Lou in mid-platitude. Jave noticed some writing in the bottom left hand corner.

The vicar was dressed in a striking scarlet cassock that stood out against the whiteness of her office. As Jave entered, she had her back to the door and was putting some old food packaging in the waste tube.

'You've got a nerve coming here,' she said. 'Haven't you already had more than enough? Don't you know there's been someone asking after...'

She turned and stopped abruptly, her face turning the same colour as her cassock.

'What...who...what are you doing here?' she finally exploded. Jave sat down in one of the beautifully upholstered chairs.

'Don't mind me,' he said. 'You just carry on with what you were saying.'

'How dare you!' exclaimed the vicar, gradually regaining her composure.

'You were saying there's been someone asking after Abram Chones,' said Jave. 'Only you didn't quite finish the sentence. Was that what you were going to say?'

The vicar sat down behind her desk with a regal composure.

'I don't have to answer questions from you,' she said. 'A jumped-up, half-price Social Security Stamper who has wheedled his way into my office under false pretences!'

Jave paused.

'I've never quite understood that phrase "false pretences",' he said. 'I mean, can you have "true pretences"?' He thought for a moment. 'Well, anyway, let's get down to business.'

'If you don't get out of my office at once,' said the vicar, 'I shall call the Social Security.'

'No, I don't think you will.'

'Oh, won't I?' She put out a long bony finger and started to punch in a number on her vid screen. The light on the screen came on, bathing her face in an eerie green glow.

'No, you won't,' said Jave, 'because when they come you'll have to tell them what you were doing in the shop of a man who was murdered.'

Her finger stopped in mid-number punch.

'What do you mean?' she demanded.

'Does the name MacWhirter mean anything to you?' asked Jave.

Very slowly, the vicar pressed the clear button on the vid screen. The light went out.

'What are you saying?' she said, licking her thin lips.

'You were followed, you know,' said Jave, 'when you left here after our conversation yesterday. You went first to a lorry owned by a man called Marc Shoeban, then you went to see MacWhirter. Then you came back here and flew off somewhere.' He paused and looked at the vicar. Her eyes were fixed on his and her thin, grey face looked trapped and surprised.

'In between your exit from the shop and your return to this little place,' Jave continued, picking his words carefully and looking closely at her face, 'MacWhirter was murdered.'

She relaxed, slightly. Jave noticed her hands grip the white plastic of the desk less tightly. He had made a wrong move. Only slightly, but it was wrong.

'Are you implying that I killed this man?' asked Reverend Shamworth.

'I don't know,' answered Jave. 'All I know is that a little later there were Social Security droids all over the place, a Stamper leaping about like a bull in the Royal Doulton factory and a dead body.'

The vicar looked at Jave for a moment. Then she sat down in her chair. She moved slowly, like a cat settling itself down for a sleep.

'So I'd like to know what you were doing there,' said Jave, 'and what you discussed with MacWhirter.'

'What I was doing there is up to me,' said the vicar. 'And as for discussing anything with Mr MacWhirter, I didn't discuss anything with him.'

'You didn't speak to each other?'

'No.'

'Why not?'

The vicar had an almost triumphant expression on her face. Yes, thought Jave, she was like a cat. A cat with a mouse to play with.

'Because, Mr Fleming,' she continued, 'he was already dead.'

Jave stared at her.

'Already dead?'

'Exactly, Mr Fleming,' said the vicar. She had recovered her composure. The game had turned now that she had startled Jave. She had the initiative. 'So, you see, I couldn't have discussed anything with him.'

'All right,' said Jave, 'if he was already dead, why did you shut the place up?'

'I didn't know he was dead when I did that. You see, Mr Fleming,' she said, turning again and staring out of the window, 'Mr MacWhirter and I did have something to discuss, something...personal. It was our habit to do so in an atmosphere where we knew we would not be disturbed. I went in, called out to tell him I was there and, before going and finding him, I closed the door securely and put the "closed" sign up.'

'He wasn't in the shop?'

'Not that I could see. Once I'd made sure we weren't going to be interrupted, I called out again and went over to the counter. It was only then that I saw....' Her voice trailed off. 'It was only then I saw what I saw,' she concluded.

'So why didn't you call the Social Security?'

'What makes you think I didn't?' she answered. 'The fact was that I didn't have my wrist unit on me and I didn't know if there was one in the shop. I left the place and came back here to call.'

'Looks a bit suspicious, doesn't it?'

'What do you mean?'

'Rushing away from the scene of the crime.'

'Mr Fleming,' the vicar looked condescendingly at her

interrogator, 'I have a certain position here to maintain. I was innocent of any involvement in the crime. I knew that. It seemed more prudent to keep out of it.'

Jave thought hard for a moment.

'It's a nice story,' he said. 'A good bit of quick thinking. For a vicar you lie very convincingly.'

There was a flash of anger in the vicar's eyes. 'What makes you think I'm lying?'

'Because my Robomammal scanned the place while you were in it,' said Jave, who thought it was time to regain the offensive. 'He picked up two live beings in the shop. Two. That means MacWhirter can't have been dead when you were there.'

The vicar's already pale face drained of even more colour, and her face seemed to blur into the white walls of the room.

'What?' she spluttered. 'That...that's not....'

And then she fainted.

11

Jave leapt from his chair and rushed round the desk. Reverend Shamworth lay prone on the plush carpet, having fallen heavily from to her chair, but nothing seemed to be broken.

He rose from kneeling next to her body and walked to the door of the office. It swished open.

'Excuse me,' he said to the busy scrivener. 'I wonder if one of you could bring a glass of water or something? The vicar's fainted.'

'Fainted?' said Sharong, in alarm.

'Yes, I'm afraid so.'

The scriveners began to twitter in little spasms of alarm, before one of them got their act together enough to come into the office bearing a plastic beaker of water. Fluttering madly, Sharong knelt by the body of her employer and lifted the vicar's head while holding the beaker for her to sip.

Jave took the opportunity of this display of employee-employer care to look round the office again.

The gram on the wall was indeed the Bishop of Swindonopolis: Lou Blynell in all his glory. The writing that Jave had spied when he first entered the office read: 'To Alecks, with warm, cuddly blessings, Lou.' Truly, thought Jave looking at the slowly recovering figure on the floor, this woman was a fan.

He went to the window and looked out onto the murky street scene of the M25, while the vicar slowly recovered herself. After a while she got up, sat back on the chair and said to the still fussing scrivener, 'All right, you can leave me now.'

'Are you sure you'll be all right?' asked Sharong. 'You don't want me to ring the medics or something?'

'No, I'm fine. Really I am.'

'But what happened?'

Jave looked at her and shrugged his shoulders. 'It was probably just religious ecstasy,' he suggested.

The scrivener, who by now was viewing this strange man with a large degree of suspicion, emitted a small 'hmph' and stalked out of the room.

Jave walked back round the desk and sat down.

'Feeling better?' he asked.

The vicar looked derisively at him. 'I'll bet that makes you feel wonderful, doesn't it?' she said, feeling at her non-human-collar. 'Seeing me faint like that. Did it make you feel powerful? All macho?'

'No,' said Jave. 'It didn't. I just felt sorry for the carpet.'

The vicar shook her head. 'Well, I feel sorry for people like you,' she said, 'digging around in people's private lives trying to trick them into answering your prying little questions. What's it like to do such a dirty job?'

'Well, it beats working for a living,' said Jave. 'If I didn't hate getting up in the morning even more, I'd chuck it in and get proper employment. But never mind that. What made you collapse like that?'

'Can't you leave me alone?' the vicar pleaded with a hint of desperation in her voice. 'And anyway, why should I tell you anything more?'

'I don't know,' said Jave. 'Maybe because of my boyish charm and engaging nature. Or maybe because I could still shop you to Social Security. I know a Stamper there who could rip you into little pieces. You'd end up begging him to allow you to faint.'

He gave as cruel a smile as he could muster. The vicar took a nervous sip of her water. Jave wondered how anyone in their right mind could take his act seriously.

'It was true,' she said after a while, 'what I was saying. It was true.'

'Then how does that explain the two readings?' asked Jave.

'I don't know...or, rather, I can guess.' She looked at him almost weakly. 'You see, he was dead when I got there. So, if there were two readings in that place....'

'The murderer must have still been there,' completed Jave.

'You see?' said the vicar, shocked. 'I could have been killed!'

'Yes,' said Jave. 'Instead of old MacWhirter who obviously doesn't matter.'

'I didn't mean that.'

'It's certainly a convenient explanation,' said Jave.

'It's true.'

'So why did you go and see MacWhirter?'

'That's none of your business.'
'I can make it my business.'
'You can try.'
There was silence. Jave tried another tack. 'Who's Marc Shoeban?'
'No one,' said the vicar. 'That is, no one you'd know.'
Blank wall again.
'And how do you know Abram Chones?'
Suddenly, and with a certain fury, Alecks Shamworth burst into life. 'I hardly met the man!' she yelled. 'I only saw him in church. He knew...' there was a slight pause, 'a friend of mine,' she continued. Her voice quietened down. 'That's all.'
'Now you're really lying,' said Jave. 'Shame on you. And you a lady of the cloth.'
Shamworth said nothing.
'I think you knew Abram Chones,' continued Jave. 'I think he was here.' He leaned close to the vicar. 'I think you know what happened to him and you're scared witless that the same thing's going to happen to you. So why don't you make it easy on both of us and tell me what you know?'
'I've already told you,' replied the vicar. 'He came here briefly. I don't know where he is now.'
'Perhaps your friend would know?'
'Who?'
'This friend that Abram Chones knew.'
There was a flicker in Reverend Shamworth's eyes.
'No, he wouldn't,' she insisted. 'And anyway, he's moved away now as well.'
'What's his name?'
'That's none of your business, either. If you think I'm going to let you have the names and addresses of my friends you must be out of your mind.'
'OK, have it your own way,' said Jave. 'To tell the truth, I'm surprised to hear you've got any friends.'

The Reverend Shamworth glared at him. 'I've never been so insulted in all my life!' she said.

Jave leaned even closer.

'You ought to get out more,' he said.

Once more, the vicar turned bright red.

'You know,' said Jave, 'you've turned some lovely colours during the course of our chat. It's like talking to a chameleon.'

'Mr Fleming,' said the vicar, 'I think you ought to leave before....'

'I know, before you call the Social Security. We've had this conversation before. I'm going.'

He turned and made for the door.

'But I'll be back,' he promised.

His exit would have been more dramatic if he hadn't walked straight into the door post, but on the whole he felt the talk had gone well. And there was no doubt the woman was seriously rattled. All that bothered him now was whether she was telling the truth.

He crossed through the office, past the watchful stares of the two females.

'Thanks very much for your help,' he said to them, 'but I've decided to become a Muslim.'

At the Central Reservation Diner-A-Go-Go, Hemma was waiting.

'What can I get you?' she asked.

'I'll have a whisky,' said Jave.

Hemma pressed a button and a small plastic bottle of Old Jock's Sporran-Warmer appeared on the table.

'How are you getting on?' she enquired.

'Not bad,' said Jave. He smiled. From the top of the church a day-glo orange Sinclair air car had taken off. He knew who would be driving.

'I heard about MacWhirter,' said Hemma, climbing onto the table.

Jave watched the C27 rise into the air, turn and begin to head off west.

'Yeah,' he said.

'Just out of curiosity,' said Hemma, 'that wasn't you by any chance?'

''Fraid not,' replied Jave. 'He was dead when we got there.'

'Not that it matters to me,' said Hemma. 'And when the Security came round I didn't tell them nothing.'

Jave looked at her and smiled. 'They already knew,' he said. 'I reported it.'

'Oh,' said Hemma. 'Listen, your brother....'

Jave poured the whisky into a plastic beaker and raised it to his lips.

Then the world fell apart.

As the plexiglass window of the diner shattered into a thousand fragments, Jave was thrown from his chair across the room and slammed into the bar. Behind him, bottles smashed and plates fell to the ground. He was hit in the chest by a saltcellar and then three chairs fell on his head. Through the rumblings and the shakings Jave looked up to see the diminutive figure of Hemma flying through the air saying, 'You couldn't give me his address, could you?' She crashed fairly and squarely into Jave's face, smashing his head back against the bar. Just for a moment, Jave's world turned bright red and he felt like his brain was falling out.

After a while the dust settled and Jave picked himself up. At first he thought that he was bleeding, but a quick check revealed that he was covered in whisky. The diner was a complete mess. Apart from the broken window, there were chairs and tables scattered everywhere, broken glass, smashed crockery and the front door blown off its hinges.

He picked Hemma up.

'Are you all right?' he asked.

Hemma dusted herself down.
'Only I thought he was really cute,' she continued.
Jave looked at her, bewildered. Maybe his brain *had* fallen out.
'Who?' he said.
'Your brother,' she replied, beginning to clear up.
'You're taking all this very calmly,' he said, at which point Hemma began to scream hysterically.
Other customers came up and began comforting her. They had been fortunate in sitting further back in the shop. They were just very, very dusty.
'What happened?' asked Jave.
'Looks like an air car explosion.'
'It was amazing,' exclaimed one. 'I was just watching it fly off when all of a sudden "bang"!'
'An air car...' repeated Jave. He turned round desperately. Outside in the street there was a stream of people rushing up the road to where some charred remains and tangled metal lay on the ground.
'No!' he said.
'Is something wrong?' asked a customer.
'That air car,' said Jave slowly. 'My gerbil was on it!'
Jave skidded out of the diner (helped by the fact that the door was no longer attached to the doorway) and raced up the street to where the tangled mass of metal lay, still smouldering on the ground.
The force of the blast had blown out the plexiglass windows in lorries and houses up and down the street (the intelligent glass had, of course, seen it coming and remained in place looking smug), littering the street with broken glass and shop signs. There were pieces of paper fluttering in the breeze, curtains flapping through the empty window frames and clouds of dust slowly settling on the dirty road.
'What happened?' yelled Jave as he arrived at the scene.

A small crowd had already gathered around the ruined vehicle, staring in ghoulish fascination at the wreckage. Others, less ghoulish, were helping injured bystanders with their cuts and bruises.

'The thing just blew up,' said a man who was sitting on the ground near the wreckage holding a piece of rag to a cut over his left eye. 'One minute it was flying through the air, the next minute there was this explosion, and it fell to the ground. Look at my suit – it's ruined!'

Jave reached into the vehicle and picked up a piece of bright red cloth.

'Yeah,' he said. 'Bad luck.'

Of the vicar herself there was hardly anything left except a few shreds of cloth and something black and lumpy which Jave preferred not to think about. The air car had only been about fifty feet up when the bomb had gone off and it had dropped like a stone. But it was obvious that the machine had been melted well before it hit the ground. The frame of the C27 was blackened and warped like a piece of wax put through a flame. Whatever had happened to it, it was hot.

Jave's mind went back immediately to the remains of Abram Chones' lorry just down the road. Another firebomb? Or just a tragic accident?

'I don't know,' the man complained, 'it ought not to be allowed. There ought to be some kind of law against it, letting unairworthy vehicles fly around like that. I mean, look at my suit! I shall sue.'

Jave turned suddenly and grabbed him by the lapels.

'If you don't shut up,' he hissed, 'I will alter the positions of your limbs so that you'll never wear a suit again!'

'Get him off me!' yelled the man in surprise. 'I'm a disaster victim, I am! Get him off me!'

Jave would have started altering the unfortunate individual then and there, but arms from the crowd reached round him, pulling him away from the man and propelling him away from the wreckage.

'Now come on, sonny, no need to get nasty,' said a voice. 'We've all had a bit of a shock, you know.'

'You don't understand!' screamed Jave, shaking off the arms that had held him. He pointed dramatically at the ruined air car. 'My gerbil was in there!'

There was a dramatic pause.

'No I wasn't,' said Frid.

'Yes you were,' insisted Jave wildly, turning and addressing the furry rodent at his feet. 'I sent you to follow her and now you've been completely blown up.'

'Oh, my mistake,' said Frid.

Jave blinked. Then he stared again at the gerbil by his feet. Frid wrinkled his nose and rotated his whiskers happily.

'Oh bazzin' heck!' Jave said with relief.

After another look at the wreckage, Jave wandered away from the crowd and sat down on the pavement, resting his head against the wall of a nearby lorry. The back of his head ached where he had struck it against the bar and it hurt to blink. Frid had fetched him a piece of cloth soaked in ice cold water and Jave clamped it gratefully to his forehead.

'All right,' he said, 'why aren't you in there?'

'Hey man!' said Frid, climbing onto Jave's shoulder and looking at the back of his head, 'that's a mean lump you got there.'

'I know,' replied Jave. 'Answer the question.'

'Oh,' said Frid, 'no need, baby. See, I was on the back of the car, but she got one of these vehicles with the automatic navigation controls. You just punch in the co-ordinates and the car does the rest. So once I seen these co-ordinates I jumped off. Figured I might as well save myself a journey.'

Jave looked down at his hands. The piece of cloth that Frid had soaked in water was the red cloth Jave had plucked from the vehicle.

'I'm...I'm glad,' he said. 'I thought you'd...well, you know.'

'Hey, baby,' said Frid. 'Doesn't you guys know we gerbils have eighteen lives. We is twice as cool as cats!'

Jave smiled.

In the distance, there suddenly rose the eerie wail of sirens, like the crying of distant birds. Like vultures coming to pick at the carcass.

'Come on,' he said. 'Let's go and get cleaned up.'

On the way back to Jave's Sinclair, they checked out the diner.

Jave was worried about Hemma.

'I hope she's all right,' he said to Frid. 'She was pretty weird right after the explosion.'

They picked their way through shattered plexiglass, fragments of bottles and upturned furniture until they found Hemma, sitting on the bar and drinking a large brandy.

'Look at this place!' said Hemma.

'Yeah,' Jave sympathised, 'it's bad.'

'Bad?' repeated Hemma. 'Bad? It's bazzin' brilliant! I mean, think of the insurance! We'll get a complete redecoration!'

'I think she's recovered,' said Jave to Frid. 'Are you sure you're not hurt or anything?'

'No, no, I'm fine,' said Hemma happily. 'I landed on something soft.'

'That,' replied Jave, wincing at the memory, 'was my head.'

'There you go,' said Hemma. 'You can't get much softer than that.'

Jave sighed. 'Let's go.'

'Hey!' shouted Hemma after them. 'Sorry I landed on you and all that. Nothing personal.'

''S OK,' said Jave. 'You had to land somewhere. We'll

be back once you've redecorated.'

'I owe you a drink,' shouted Hemma. 'And don't forget to give me your brother's phone number!'

On the way back to the car, Jave's head began to ring.

'I think I'm concussed,' he complained to Frid. 'I can hear bells.'

'It's your wrist unit, man,' said Frid. 'Someone's ringing you.'

'Oh, yeah.'

Jave pressed a button on his wrist unit and up flicked the small vid screen. The screen flickered, went blank and was then filled with the features of Kevving.

'As if I didn't feel bad enough already,' muttered Jave.

'Hey, bruvv!' said Kevving. 'Are you all right? You look awful.'

'Talk about the pot calling the kettle black,' said Jave. 'Anyway, I'm OK. It's just that I've got someone tap dancing on the back of my eyeballs.'

'Anyhow, Chanis just called,' Kevving went on. 'She just heard on the vid news about some explosion on the M25. Near the church. Thought you ought to know.'

'I know,' said Jave. 'I was near to it.' He looked away from the screen. 'What am I saying?' he muttered to himself. 'Near to it? I was in it.'

'Hey!' said Kevving. 'Stonk out! How come you're always where the action is?'

'Listen,' said Jave. 'It was an explosion, right? Big thing. Makes a loud noise and throws things around. I had a three-foot-high waitress land on my head. It wasn't a pleasurable experience.'

'Sounds like one to me.'

'Not when she's travelling at thirty thousand kilometres an hour.'

Kevving laughed. 'Yeah, but look on the bright side, eh? I bet it had atmosphere, bruvv.'

'Yeah. It certainly had atmosphere. But never mind that,' said Jave. 'I want you to do something for me.'

'Yeah?'

'I want you to call Chanis back and ask her to come to the flat this afternoon. Tell her to bring anything that she's got that was her father's. Anything she can lay her hands on.'

'Why?'

'Because I tell you to, you stupid great....'

'OK, OK,' interrupted Kevving. 'Calm down. You've been in an explosion.'

'I'll meet you at the flat soon.'

'Right. Drive carefully.'

The vid screen blinked off and then folded down and slipped back into Jave's wrist unit.

'Good advice,' commented Jave as he took one last look down the street where an Air Ambulance was hovering over the tangled remains of the ex-vicar of the Church of the Blessed Commuter.

'So what happened to the vicar, then?' said Jave to Frid as they flew back across London. The Sinclair hummed happily on auto pilot, which was just as well, since Jave had spots in front of his eyes.

'Some kind of malfunction on her car, I guess,' replied Frid. 'Pretty bad coincidence, though.'

'Yeah,' Jave agreed, 'pretty bad coincidence. I mean, what is there on a Sinclair that can explode?'

'How about a bomb?' suggested Frid.

'A bomb?'

'Well, look at it this way,' continued Frid, 'Chones is incinerated, MacWhirter is found strangled and now the vicar's car blows up. They've got to be linked.'

'You mean the same person behind all three?'

'That's right. And what happened to the vicar is just the same as what happened to Chones. Only about fifty metres higher up.'

Suddenly Jave became aware of what he was doing.

'Frid,' he said, 'do you realise that we are flying across London.'

'So?'

'So, the last person we talked to was blown up in an identical car. The one before that was strangled. And we're the link between them!' Jave felt a panic rising in his throat. 'We're going to die!'

Frid's whiskers revolved. 'Only if you try to drive, man,' he said. 'There's no bomb on here according to my scan. Calm down. You don't think that I'd get on an air car I hadn't checked for bombs?'

Jave relaxed. 'Just checking,' he said. 'Anyway – these co-ordinates you were talking about. The ones where the vicar was heading. Where are they?'

'Can't tell for sure,' replied Frid. 'Somewhere in Swindonopolis, I reckon. I got some extra data files back at the office which I can download if you want to pinpoint them exactly.'

'We'll call in there on the way back home.'

They landed on the roof of the office block. As they made their way down to Jave's office, Jave felt increasingly that the floor was wobbling up and down. He paused to steady himself against the wall, but that didn't help, because the wall was doing the tango.

'Are we in an earthquake?' he asked.

'Nope,' said Frid. 'But the sooner we get you home to bed, the better.'

As Jave arrived at his office door, he thought something was different. The door looked the same, the letters were still missing, the plastic paint was chipped and the carpet worn. The corridor was still dingily oozing cheapness from every air duct. But something was different. Then Jave realised what it was. There was a huge black insect standing by the door. He couldn't be sure, but it looked like some kind of giant praying mantis.

'I knew something was different,' Jave said to Frid. 'He wasn't here before, was he?'

The insect turned to look at them as they approached. It spoke.

'So, you're back, Fleming,' it said.

'It talks!' said Jave. He began to laugh. 'And it sounds just like Jonn Hook!'

The insect looked puzzled.

'Are you all right?' he said. 'Is he all right?' he repeated to Frid.

'He's had a knock on the back of the head, baby,' explained Frid.

'That's right,' said Jave, nodding. A stabbing pain ran through his head and the walls changed from the tango to the foxtrot.

'Oh dear,' said the insect, obviously not meaning a word of it. 'Well, perhaps he needs a nice bit of peace and quiet.'

'You do sound like Jonn Hook,' said Jave to the insect.

The insect looked annoyed. 'I *am* Jonn Hook,' he said.

'That,' replied Jave, 'would explain it.'

'And you, Fleming,' said Stamper Hook, 'are under arrest.'

He began to chuckle quietly, a sound not unlike a hyena throwing up. 'Do you hear me, Fleming?' he cackled. 'You're under arrest!'

Jave stared wildly at this strange, insect creature for a moment and then, suddenly, the walls were no longer dancing, the floor was no longer waving up and down and the insect was no longer an insect but the well-known figure of Jonn Hook.

This sudden clarity of vision hit Jave with all the sickening effect of someone putting a dislocated limb back into place. A look of horror filled his face as he realised what was about to happen. It was not the arrest that horrified him, it was the fact that he was going to throw up.

So he did.

All over Stamper Hook.

12

'You don't seem to understand, Fleming,' sniffed Stamper Hook. 'We've got all the evidence we need.'

He pulled a grubby handkerchief from the pocket of his black leather trousers, blew his nose into it, and then examined the contents as if expecting to see a long lost friend.

Jave turned away. The room in which Jave was sitting was small, and coloured the same kind of grubby white as Stamper Hook's hankie. It had nasty brown stains on the wall and it smelled atrocious, due mainly to the presence of Stamper Hook around whom the odour of what had once been in Jave's stomach still lingered.

'You were the first person to report the murder of MacWhirter,' said Hook, 'and now you're the last person known to have seen Reverend Shamworth before she died.'

He stopped, snuffled slightly and put his hands together. There was a small crack from his fingers as he pushed his hands together with excitement.

'So what do we conclude?'

Jave looked at him.

'What do we conclude?' repeated Hook.

'We conclude I need a medic,' said Jave.

'We conclude,' continued Hook, ignoring him, 'that you are up to your neck in this business.'

He leaned on the table that stood in front of where Jave was sitting and pushed his face close to Jave's. Through the aching pain in his head, Jave could see the pock-marked, pale skin and the red-rimmed eyes lurking behind the dark glasses, like two rats in a sewer.

'And you're going to tell me all about it,' said Hook, leering.

'I've already told you.'

'You told me nothing!'

Jave didn't see the hand coming. The palm smacked into his cheek, knocking his face to one side and making his head explode. The room went dark for a moment and all the jumbled memories in Jave's head swirled around like rubbish in the wind.

Jave had been brought here in a Social Security air car, driven by a small Clerk called Chenkins. Chenkins had a limp and the IQ of a fence post. Jave had met Chenkins six years ago, when Jave had first joined the Department. Chenkins had been a Driver-Clerk then and he was still a Driver-Clerk now. Indeed, all the evidence suggested that Chenkins would always be a Driver-Clerk. The job had become part of the man. Like the limp.

The small journey from Jave's office door to the air car waiting on the roof was a foreboding of the longer journey to come. The Stamper had done nothing but try, ineffectually, to wipe the contents of Jave's stomach from his leather coat. In between his attempts he spent his time cursing Jave.

'You've stonking ruined it!' he complained. 'That's only what you've gone and done. Ruined it!'

'I didn't mean to,' said Jave. 'You looked like an insect and then you didn't.'

He shut up though, because the Stamper had hit him in the mouth.

'Shut up!' he yelled. 'You bazzin' skag! You've ruined my coat.'

Chenkins who, though small, was very strong, pulled Jave's arms behind his back and threw him into the van.

'Watch it, Chenkins,' said Jave, as the doors locked. 'My stomach can wreak a terrible revenge.'

After a journey which made Jave feel like the little metal ball you always hear inside an aerosol can, the car came to rest. Chenkins opened the door, pulled Jave out, and marched him into the lift and down into the basement of the Department of Social Security where Stamper Hook had his 'offices'.

For a while, they left Jave in near complete darkness. Jave sat in the dark room, feeling almost peaceful. Then his eyes filled with pain as the lights were thrown on, and Stamper Hook entered the room.

Then the interrogation began.

'Now look what you've done,' said Hook with oily sarcasm, as Jave tried to shake the pain out of his head. 'You made me lose my temper again.'

'Stupid me,' said Jave.

He licked the corner of his mouth which had started bleeding again.

'Do you want more, eh?' asked Hook, leaning very close. 'Enjoy it, do you?'

Jave shook his head. 'You smell of sick,' he said.

Hook went rigid. 'You lousy skag!' he shouted. 'I don't! I've washed!' He stormed up and down the room, swearing at Jave. 'I've skagging well washed!'

'Well, what do you want me to say?' asked Jave when the Stamper had stopped shouting.

'I want the truth!'

'I've told you the truth. I was sitting in a bar and the world exploded. And now I'm ill. It's concussion or something.'

'Yes, so you keep telling me,' said Hook. 'But that doesn't explain why you killed the vicar.'

'I didn't kill the vicar.'

Hook's hand swept in an almost lazy arc. It crashed into the side of Jave's head, snapping it back again.

'Why did you do it?'

Jave shook his head.

'I can go on all night, you know,' said Hook, quietly.

'I've explained,' said Jave, through thick, bruised lips. 'I've explained what happened. I went to see the vicar, pursuing some enquiries. She didn't help. Then I left. I was having a drink in a diner when her car exploded nearby. I mean, I didn't know it was going to happen. If I'd known it was going to happen I wouldn't have been thrown backwards off my chair and into the bar, would I?'

'You're lying,' said Hook. 'And I'm going to find out the truth.'

Jave slumped in his chair and tried to stifle the urge to laugh.

Hook was a maniac, well known for his Neanderthal investigation techniques. But, while both the criminal elements and Social Security officers knew that Hook was a 'slapper', as such Stampers were known, both sides viewed him only with contempt and ridicule, because he didn't even use physical threats with any imagination. He just hit you. Not hard, but often. And in the end, he never got what he wanted. Jave knew he would never be charged with murder, because Hook would never get the evidence he needed. He just hoped that Hook would get bored of hitting him soon, so he could go home to bed.

There was a hiss in the corner of the room and a door opened.

'I brrrought some coffee,' said a voice.

Hook spun round angrily at the interruption.

'What are you doing here?' he yelled.

'I thought you could do with a little coffee,' said Droid Thirty-One. He trundled over to the table, lights flashing on and off, and put the coffee down. A small sensor came out and scanned the room inquisitively.

'Is it me,' he enquired, 'or is there a funny smell in here?'

Hook seemed to quiver slightly.

'All right,' he said, 'you've delivered the coffee, now get out.'

Droid Thirty-One seemed not to hear him for a moment. There was a slight, almost imperceptible, bleep.

'I'll just check out this smell,' he said.

His motor whirred and he sped across to the door.

'Drrroid Thirty-Eight!' he called. 'Can you smell something?'

Jave looked around him. His jaw ached where Hook had been using it as a punchbag and his head still felt like someone was drilling somewhere inside. He reached out and took the coffee which was hot and sweet.

'I don't want the smell checked out!' Hook was saying. 'I'm investigating a case, you miserable little....'

There was a whirring sound as Droid Thirty-Eight rushed into the room.

'Poo!' he said. 'What a whiff!' His scanner spun round and round. 'Is it the drains, or what?'

They both advanced on Jave.

'He doesn't look too clean,' commented Droid Thirty-Eight.

Their scanners spun round.

'Don't look at me,' said Jave, through painful lips. 'I'm not a well man.'

'You're not, are you?' agreed Droid Thirty-Eight. A slight humming sound came from deep within the droid.

'My initial scan reveals concussion and bruising around the mouth,' he said. 'But at least you don't smell.'

'Thanks,' said Jave.

'Look...' said Stamper Hook from the other side of the room.

Droid Thirty-One spun round.

'I can still sense this horrible smell,' it said.

'Me too,' said Droid Thirty-Eight.

They started to work their way round the small room. Jave sipped his coffee and watched Hook grow more and more uncomfortable.

Finally they both stopped in front of the Stamper.

'Now look here,' Stamper Hook protested, looking like a trapped animal, 'as your commanding officer...'

'Phwoooooaaarrrr!' said Droid Thirty-Eight. 'It's you!'

'Oh Stamperrr,' said Droid Thirty-One reproachfully, 'you haven't been looking after yourself prrroperly, have you?'

'Look, it wasn't my fault,' said Hook. 'It was him!'

'I mean, think of yourr position,' said Droid Thirty-One. 'You'rrre a starrr, sirrr. You have to think of grrrooming.'

'Yeah,' agreed Droid Thirty-Eight, 'I mean you're a Stamper, aren't you? Stampers don't go round smelling of, well, vomit.'

'It's not my fault!' protested Hook angrily. 'He chucked up all over me when I arrested him.'

'Now, now,' said Droid Thirty-One reproachfully, 'we're not at home to Mr Tell-Tale. I'm sure he couldn't help it. The poorrr man's not at all well.'

Stamper Hook looked suspiciously across at Jave.

'What do you mean "not well"?' he demanded. 'Can't you see the skag's lying through his teeth?'

'You forget, sirrr,' said the droid. 'I have the honourrr of being yourrr forensic drroid – trrrained in all forrrms of medical diagnostics. My scan rrrevealed severrre concussion and shock.'

'But he's lying!' insisted Hook. 'He can't be suffering from shock! He knew it was coming.'

'Droid Thirty-One's accurate, oh great one,' Droid Thirty-Eight confirmed. 'This Fleming man is in shock.'

Hook looked like he was having an attack. Even for a Stamper of his limited mental abilities, he could see that his theory was going out of the window.

'All right,' he said, 'but he still knows more than he's telling.'

'I've told you all I know,' repeated Jave. 'I have no idea who is killing these people. But it wasn't me.'

'You can't prove that.'

'And you can't prove it *was* me. The fact is that I'm in shock. Your droids have told you. Now how could I possibly be in shock if I'd set the whole thing up?'

'You could be acting shocked.'

'How could I act shocked?' said Jave wearily. 'Ask your droids. This is real.'

'Don't bring them into it,' shouted Stamper Hook. 'Miserable pair of reject dustbins....'

The droids swung round and beeped grumpily.

'Well, at least we're not smelly,' said Droid Thirty-Eight.

'I give up!' exclaimed Hook.

'In that case,' said Droid Thirty-One, happily, 'might I suggest that you let Drrroid Thirty-Eight and me clean you up?'

'What?'

'And disinfect you,' added Droid Thirty-Eight.

'And sprrray you with arrromatic scent,' put in Droid Thirty-One, getting excited.

'And anoint you with exotic oils and unguents!' yelled Droid Thirty-Eight.

'Ohhhh!' said Droid Thirty-One. 'What an honourrr, to be servants of the grrreat Stamperrr Hook!'

'But I don't want...' began Stamper Hook, to no avail.

'And smear your hair with hyssop juice!'

'Leave me alone... hyssop juice?' said the irate Stamper.

'Well,' said Droid Thirty-Eight, 'maybe not hyssop juice.'

'But a man of your calibre should be highly grrroomed,' said Droid Thirty-One. 'It's a sign of powerrr.'

The Stamper thought for a moment. He hadn't realised this.

'Is it?' he asked.

'Assuredly,' said Droid Thirty-One.

Hook sniffed himself.

'Well, I suppose it would get rid of this smell...' he said.

He strode over to the chair where Jave was finishing his coffee. The hot sweet drink had cleared Jave's head a bit, although his lip was swollen and painful.

'All right, Fleming,' he said. 'You can go for now. I've got better things to do with my time than waste it on rats like you.'

He turned from the table and crossed to the door of the interrogation chamber. 'But don't think this is over, Fleming,' he said, as he was leaving. 'You're still number one on my hit list.'

Jave looked at him. Whatever his robots said, the man would never be 'highly grrroomed'.

'Thanks,' said Jave. 'It's nice to know you care about me so much.'

'And you're under all day curfew, you hear? I want you to vid in every hour. I want to know where you are at all times.'

Jave nodded solemnly.

The idea of all day curfew was that offenders or suspects had to call in to Social Security Headquarters every hour to let them know where they were and what they were doing. This would have been a reasonable enough system had it not been for the fact that, at present, over 18 million people were known to be under all day curfew. Which meant that every hour 750,000 people were supposed to call in. Or, put it another way, 12,500 every minute. So to cope with this demand, Social Security should have had at least 12,500 vid lines. Instead of which they had one vid line manned by a ninety-year-old man called Albert. Who was deaf. In other words, Jave was free to go.

As the droids led Stamper Hook from the room with promises of turkish baths and strange emollients, Jave's head stopped booming and echoing.

With effort, he pressed a button on the wrist unit and raised his arm to his mouth.

The frightening face of Kevving flickered into view.

'Hey, bruvv!' said Kevving. 'What's going down?'

'Shut up,' said Jave. 'Shut up and come and get me.'

'You're not arrested then?'

'Well, they were going to execute me, but Hook decided to go and have a bath instead.'

'Right. I'm on my way.'

Jave stood up and felt his stomach leap within him.

'And Kevving,' he added. 'Bring a bucket.'

13

It was mid-afternoon when the Social Security released him.

Frid came for him, piloting the C27 automatically, through a small cable which was plugged into the drive console of the air car. Quite where it plugged into the gerbil, Jave didn't like to think.

Back at his flat everything was as clean as ever.

Well, everything except Kevving, who lounged on one of the settee-bags, one arm thrown negligently over his head, looking, as ever, like the hedge through which someone had been pulled backwards.

'Hey, bruvv!' he said as Jave climbed in through the window. 'You look like you've been through some real atmosphere.'

'You could say that.'

Frid scampered into the flat after parking the air car securely.

'The man's been into a scene. You dig, baby?' he said. 'Like the dude needs some TLC.'

A figure rose from the opposite side of the room. It was Chanis. She was dressed in a sparkly suit that seemed to shimmer as she moved. Her dark hair was tied back with a light green ribbon. She looked pretty and petite and vulnerable. Jave felt sick again.

'Hi,' he said, trying to affect a nonchalance that he was nowhere near possessing.

'Hello,' she croaked. Jave winced. He had forgotten, through a mixture of infatuation and sheer absent-mindedness, that she possessed such a ridiculous voice. It was like having your inner ear sandpapered.

'What happened to you?' she asked.

'Oh nothing much,' said Jave. 'Got caught in an explosion, then arrested by Social Security and then interrogated by a man whose idea of recreation is to take a short walk on people's heads. Pretty normal day, really.' He paused and wiped a hand across his forehead. 'Do you mind if I sit down a minute?'

'Of course not,' rasped Chanis. 'You look all done in.'

As he allowed himself the luxury of being helped across the room to sit down, Jave caught a look at himself in the 3-D mirror. 'All done in', he felt, was putting it rather mildly. He looked crumpled and dry, like a leaf in autumn. His face, which never looked particularly healthy at the best of times, appeared to have been bleached, except for the eyes which were red and sore, like a couple of hot coals in some dirty snow. His clothes looked as though they had died of old age. Even his hair looked old.

All of which was extremely annoying, because he was actually feeling a bit better.

'I'm not looking my best, am I?' he said.

'Frid said it was concussion,' said Chanis. 'You just need some sleep, that's all.'

'What about you?' asked Jave. 'Did you bring the stuff I asked for?'

'Never mind that now,' said Chanis. 'Have a drink and some sleep first. You'll feel better after some rest.'

She was proved right. Jave didn't realise how tired he was until, after a stiff drink, he made the long walk into his tiny bedroom, tore off his clothes and fell into a deep sleep.

When he awoke, it was dark outside. He climbed out of bed, noticing that the clothes he had thrown off only six hours ago had been washed, dried, tidied up and arranged tastefully on a chair. Grimacing at the joys of modern life, Jave made his way to the bathroom.

Standing under a shower of hot water, he felt a hundred per cent better. The headache had gone, the water splashed against his face as if it were driving away the pain. Yes he felt good....

He emerged from the shower, and from his room, clean, fresh and ready to face the challenge of a new day. It was a bit annoying, therefore, to find that it was still evening in the old one.

'What's the time then?' he asked.

''Bout nine,' said Kevving. 'You've been spark out for six hours.'

'I feel like it should be morning.'

'Don't worry. It's only Rave-Lag,' said Kevving.

'Rave-Lag?'

'Yeah, like you feel after a really good party. Your body clock goes AWOL. You wake up, you don't know what time it is. Doctors call it Rave-Lag. It's like jet-lag only more fun. Have some breakfast.'

'Shouldn't that be dinner?'

'Nah – it's all relative. Whenever you wake up, that's the time for breakfast. The time of day's got nothing to do with it.'

Jave looked suspiciously at his brother. 'I don't know,' he said.

'Oh, loosen up, bruvv. You know, I was reading this Rom the other day. In the Philippines, years ago, they used to call Westerners "the people with gods on their wrists". That's you all over, that is.'

'I can't help it,' protested Jave. 'I've always been keen on regularity and order. I suppose I'm a reactionary at heart.'

'But what does it matter?' said Kevving. 'I mean, it's not the end of the world if you have breakfast at nine o'clock at night, is it? You need to loosen up, bruvv. You're getting old before your time.'

Jave's mind slipped back to that brief glimpse of himself in the mirror six hours earlier. The old man, creased by time.

Kevving was right.

'Good point,' he said. 'You're right, I should loosen up a bit.'

Full of this new resolution, he punched a breakfast code into the food tube, which delivered a hot cup of coffee, a bowl of something hideously healthy that looked like budgie-droppings, some hot croissants and an orange juice.

He set to with gusto. It was one of the best meals he had ever had. He was not even put off his food by the sound of Chanis when she entered the room.

'Are you feeling better?' she grated.

'Much better, thanks.'

'You looked awful when you came in.' She came over and sat opposite him. 'Did they hurt you much down at Social Security?'

Jave thought about this for a moment.

'No, not really,' he said. 'I reckon it was three things – first I'm one of their own – or used to be. Even Hook takes that kind of thing into account. Secondly, he's not very good at it. Mostly, you could see the slaps coming and roll with them. It's all a matter of timing.'

'And the third thing?'

Jave tried to look like Humphrey Bogart.

'I'm pretty tough,' he said nonchalantly. He affected, a 'pretty tough sort of guy but with a heart of gold' posture, which was ruined as he knocked hot coffee into his lap and leapt up from the table with a yelp.

Chanis laughed, a noise which sounded like someone was having trouble with some plumbing.

'You're not half as tough as you like to think,' she said.

Jave grinned. 'Well, maybe not,' he said. 'But on the other hand I think I'm three times as tough as anyone else. So that still makes me one and a half times as tough, doesn't it?'

14

Jave found Frid sitting in his normal place behind the central heating device. The gerbil had his walkman on and was listening to 'The Very Best of James Brown'.

'Oi!' said Jave, poking the gerbil with his foot.

'Hey, my man,' said Frid. 'I mean get down and owwww!'

He executed a neat little spin, moon-walked for a few steps and then took off his headphones. 'That baby sure could hit it,' he said.

'Let's talk,' said Jave.

Frid climbed up and sat on his shoulder.

'You feelin' back together?' he said.

'Yeah, great.'

They walked to the window and the automated curtains, sensing his presence, slid apart. Jave looked out over the enormous, sprawling mass that was London.

It was still a bright world, even at night. Huge video screens clung to the side of skyscrapers advertising all kinds of products that no one could ever need, but everyone would always want. Yellow lights shimmered and showered onto the walkways, deserted though they were. From every home, yellow-white lights beamed out into the night sky while, above them, the orange headlights of air cars lit up the sky in an endless beam. Everywhere, man shone a light in an attempt to conquer darkness – the last true wilderness.

Everywhere? Not quite. Down below the level of the walkway there was nothing but a deep and dense blackness, giving the walkways themselves the appearance of paths across a lake, or a sea. There, ten storeys down, and thirteen below where Jave was watching, there was the street level, the place where the darkness was still supreme.

There was the place where no one would willingly go, but many ended up. A place of rubbish and refuse and debris. An ocean of people scratching whatever living they could among the tips and the squalor. It was the flipside of society, the thought that everyone avoided, the illness-ridden face in the mirror.

Jave shivered slightly. He was no stranger to the street level – he had been there many times through his work, both privately and, more frequently, with the Social Security. But he had never been there while it was dark. No one in their right mind went there in the dark.

'You all right?' enquired Frid.

'Just thinking,' said Jave. 'Anyway,' he turned away from the window and let the curtain slide to, 'while I was having my chat with Hook, did you check those co-ordinates?' he asked.

'Yeah,' said Frid.

'So where was she heading?'

'Swindonopolis way,' said Frid, coyly.

'Swindonopolis?'

'To be precise and on the case, baby,' said the gerbil, 'she was going to the Head Office of Anson Enterprises.'

Jave frowned. 'Anson?' he said. 'They're vid stuff, aren't they?'

'Vid programmes, radio shows, tapes, music – the whole entertainment business,' said Frid. 'And, unless I'm wrong, she was going to the head man himself.'

'How do you know?'

'Because the co-ordinates are so precise, baby. I mean not just Swindonopolis. Not just that building. But the private car park to the penthouse suite.'

Jave thought. 'Could anyone land there?' he said. 'I mean, was she going to complain or something?'

'Uh-uh,' said Frid, shaking his small, furry head. 'We are talking corporate UK here. The big boys in Europe. And this guy in the penthouse is the Chairman. We are talking Melling Anson, Chairman, President and main man.'

Jave ran his fingers through his hair.

'Well, at least we know where she was going,' he said, stating the obvious with uncanny skill.

They went back to join the others who were sitting watching the vid.

'What did you two do today?' asked Jave.

'Nothing much,' replied Kevving. 'I called Chanis and told her to bring all that stuff you asked for.'

'So you been going through that?'

'Well, we were waiting for you,' said Kevving. 'We got it all here.'

'I brought what I could lay my hands on,' said Chanis. 'But I don't think it will be much help. It's all from quite a long time ago, I'm afraid. From when he was young. He never kept much stuff from when he was older. Or if he did, I don't know where he kept it.'

She pulled out an old, plastic suitcase from behind the lounger and opened it. Inside there was a pile of paper, grams and old-fashioned photos from Abram Chones' youth.

The first picture that Jave pulled out was a young Abram, considerably less hairy than he was to become, standing with a smallish, blonde woman. She was not stunningly attractive, but she had a kind of delicacy about her in the way that she stood, in her almost bashful smile towards the camera. Abram, on the other hand, stared straight ahead at the camera in a good-natured way, as if daring it to take him on. Funnily enough, although he had short hair, it didn't look right. It looked as if he had had long hair, the kind of hairyness which he was later to achieve, but that he had temporarily had it shorn. He looked like an Old Testament prophet who had joined the army.

'Is this your mother?' asked Jave, holding the picture out to Chanis.

'Oh, yes,' said Chanis. 'That's Mother. Not that I ever knew her, really. She died when I was born.'

'I'm sorry.'

Chanis shrugged.

'It was one of those things. Something about a drug shortage. They could have saved her, but they couldn't get hold of the right stuff. But I never knew her. Dad always took care of me. I never missed her, but Dad....'

She let the words hang in the air.

'He never remarried?' said Jave as they began to take out more pictures and papers.

'No. It was soon after that that he joined the church. I guess that took up most of his time.'

'Maybe it was what he was looking for,' said Jave. 'Something to fill the gap.'

Chanis looked at him.

'I don't think the church could fill that gap,' she said. 'I'm not sure that anything ever did. He had his faith of course, but that was a different kind of relationship. It's always a mistake to think that people join the church on some kind of emotional rebound. I mean, that may be why they go there in the first place, but emotionally it's no substitute. It doesn't even pretend to be.'

'But the church helped him?'

'Oh yes. The people were lovely. They always took a hand in looking after me and supporting him.'

They continued to sort through the papers and photos. They were mostly the usual family stuff – old school reports, Christmas cards from long ago, photos of Chanis growing up and of Abram and his daughter in various places at various times. There were holiday snaps galore and then holograms of Chanis replaced photos, at roughly the same time as the woman replaced the girl.

'You only got a gram unit recently, then?' commented Jave.

'Two years ago,' said Chanis. 'The gram you've got of Dad is the last thing I took. Dad was never interested in technology or anything like that. We never even had a vid unit or anything.'

By the time they reached the bottom of the suitcase,

Kevving had drifted off to switch on the vid unit. Chanis was sitting against the wall, her knees drawn up against her chin, lost in thoughts of her own.

At the bottom of the case were some very early photos, maybe twenty or thirty years back, of Abram at school. At first, Jave couldn't make him out. Then they found him, sixteen years old and smiling forcedly in the third row of his class. He still looked like a prophet. Only very young. An apprentice prophet.

There was pencil writing on the bottom of the picture: 'Year Three Students, 2020–2021.'

Jave scanned the photo. There were young faces – hopeful, surly, bland – all the expressions one would usually find in eighteen year olds.

The young Abram stood among his contemporaries, part of the crowd yet somehow separate. He was staring ahead of him, the same challenging stare into the camera that Jave recognised from the picture of Abram and his wife. It was an oddly disconcerting stare, made doubly so by its juxtaposition with the expression of the boy standing next to Abram. The boy was standing in the back row, three from the left. He had sandy blond hair and wore glasses, and he lit up the picture with a smile of almost dazzling whiteness. Somehow, even through a thirty-year-old photo, this boy's expression shone out.

'What's this?' said Jave, brandishing the photo at Chanis.

Chanis unfolded herself from where she had been sitting and crawled across to see what Jave was studying with such interest.

'Oh,' she said, 'Dad's old college photo. He told me about that. Showed it to me once.'

'Where did he go to college?'

'That was abroad. In Italy, I think. His parents, my grandparents that is, were in the Navy. They moved about a bit.'

Jave pointed at the boy in the photo standing beside the young Abram.

'Who's this?' he asked.

'No idea,' said Chanis. 'There's a list of names on the back.'

Jave flipped the picture over and looked along the list of names. Sure enough, most of them were Italian names – Sergios and Giovannis and Maradonnas.

He scanned a finger across the list of names that made up 'Back row (l to r): Mazucelli, Stephano; Pirelli, Giuseppi; Chones, Abram.'

Then his heart skipped a beat at the sight of the next name in the list: 'Harris, Charles L.' He stared at it.

'Are you all right?' said Chanis. 'What is it?'

Jave pointed to the name.

'Harris, Charles L,' he said.

'What about him?' queried Kevving coming over and joining them.

'You know the last time I saw this name?' said Jave.

They shook their heads.

'It was written on a piece of paper, which I found in someone's pocket.'

'Whose?' whispered Chanis.

Jave took another look at the photo, at the smiling, straightforward features of 'Harris, Charles L.'

'MacWhirter's,' he said. 'I found it in MacWhirter's pocket.'

THE FOURTH DAY

15

Jave did not sleep much that night. The facts were whirling through his mind, like leaves being blown by the wind; facts that somehow ought to form a pattern, but that stubbornly resisted such organisation.

There were still too many unknowns. Who was Charlie Harris? Who was Marc Shoeban and why had the vicar visited him two days ago? It was the names and the faces that bothered him. The lurking familiarity of the face in the photo. The blank incomprehensibility of that face on the card in the dim and dingy lorry.

When he eventually drifted off to sleep again, he was racked by dreams of lorries with dark alleys between them, smiling faces that gleamed at you from shadows and, curiously, by the recurring figure of an estate agent who kept saying the word 'boing'. Perhaps it meant something.

He woke around six o'clock. It was earlier than his normal waking time and allowed him to catch his room in the very act of tidying up. Small mechanical arms were removing clothes that he had thrown down when getting into bed, and moving the furniture back to what the room considered ergonomically pleasing positions.

'Stop it at once!' he ordered.

'Sorry?' said the room, sounding startled.

'Stop clearing up!'

'You have woken early,' said the room sounding as though it had been caught stealing from the fridge.

'I know,' said Jave.

'Your routine has been interrupted.'

'Best thing to do with routines,' said Jave.

Reluctantly, the small metal arms began to slide back into recesses in the white walls.

'Try and get some more sleep,' said the room.

'I don't need more sleep. I need you to stop clearing up.'

Soft music began to fill the air, and it suddenly became very warm.

'I am programmed to care for you,' said the room. 'Sleep would be best.'

The atmosphere grew heavy. The music was gentle and soothing. A subtle perfume filtered into the room through the air conditioning ducts. Jave began to drift back to sleep.

He swung out of bed. He was skagged if he was going to be defeated by a room.

The music stopped abruptly.

'What are you doing?' enquired the room.

'Getting up,' said Jave. 'So get rid of the perfume, turn the heating down and put some snorking colour on those walls!'

Immediately the room cooled to a less oppressively soporific temperature and a horrible beige tint invaded the wall space.

'I don't like the way this relationship is deteriorating,' said the room.

Jave pressed a button on his wrist unit to pick up the news.

'The vacancy for the seat of the Archbishop of Canterbury is still provoking much comment among the few people who remain interested in such things,' said the silky-smooth voice of the radio announcer. 'Hot favourite for the post is the media-star Bishop Lou Blynell of Swindonopolis. Bishop Lou is reported to have said that he is "too humble a man to seek such high office", but informed sources say that, as the first Bishop superstar, he is the only man who can keep fading interest in the Church of England alive.'

The voice paused for a moment. 'And some late news just in is that the Prime Minister has solved the problems of London's ageing water mains. She's decided to flood the disused underground system.'

Jave switched it off. There was nothing on there about the explosion that had wrecked the vicar's air car, nor was it likely that there should be.

In modern Britain, violent death was so commonplace that it hardly made the news any more and anyway, present thinking in Social Security circles was that reporting such events only led to more of them.

There had been a spate of 'competition killers' in recent years, spurred on by reports of other people's exploits to grislier and more violent deeds of their own. The 'Cleethorpes Strangler' had been succeeded by the 'Blackpool Stabber'; the 'Maniac Axeman' was followed by the 'Crazy Machete Wielder' and then by the 'Completely Out of His Tree Loony with the Big Pencil Sharpener'.

What it was that suddenly overheated in these people's brains had always been the cause of much debate. But to Jave it was simply fame. The simple, evil old urge for notoriety that had always lain at the heart of such activities from Jack the Ripper through to presidential assassinations and onwards. Some people paid a terrible price for someone else's fifteen minutes of fame.

Was this killer similar? thought Jave, but he dismissed the thought. There was a cold-bloodedness about these killings. They were not the attention-grabbing depravities of some maniac, but the calmly efficient, clinical activities of the professional.

He thought about things for a while. It was the fourth day of the investigation, and the obvious move was to follow up this name – Charles L Harris; the name that he had found in the waistcoat of MacWhirter; the name on the picture in the bottom of the suitcase; the name that linked the murder of MacWhirter with that of Abram Chones.

After enduring his morning humiliation at the hands of his Shower-o-Matic, Jave walked into the kitchen. Frid, for once, was still asleep, curled up in the remains of an old cornflakes packet he had stuffed down beside the heating system.

He opened a bleary gerbil eye as Jave punched some numbers into the food tube.

'Wha's time?' he muttered.

Jave looked at his watch.

'Six-thirty,' he said.

The gerbil uttered a small sigh.

'I hope you don't expect me to do anything yet,' he said. 'I's resting.'

The food tube gave a sort of disgruntled ping to reveal some hot buttered toast, its edges slightly curled due to the matter transference process, and a cup of syntho-coffee.

Jave took the food and, munching a piece of toast, went into the lounge.

The prostrate figure on the lounger was uttering a noise that sounded like a hippo with sinusitis. When a man with two noses snores thought Jave, you know about it.

He crossed the room and stood in front of the curtains, which swept back compliantly.

Over London, the sun was making a valiant attempt to

break through the mass of low, dirty clouds that filled the sky. The result was a sort of blur as if someone was shining a light behind some grey sheets.

London was beginning to come to life. Below the window where Jave was watching, the walkway droids were sweeping the rubbish off the walkways, letting it fall the ten storeys or so to street level.

There was steam rising from the ground level, as the heating systems of the great tower blocks kicked into life. Their vents were placed between the walkways and the ground, an arrangement that generally resulted in a sort of lower level of cloud, a blanket of steam and smog that, to a certain extent, hid the shambles of the ground level from the prying eyes of those on the walkways and above.

As the droids swept the rubbish over the edge of the walkways, this rising steam caused an updraft which made some of the lighter refuse hang for a moment, swaying like ragged kites in the moist air, before fluttering gradually into the darkness and mist of the ground.

Through the mist, down on the ground, Jave could vaguely make out dim figures, scurrying around in the showers of rubbish, hoping against hope that something valuable, or even edible, would be thrown from the walkways and land in their lap.

There was little hope of that actually happening. Such was the efficiency of the walkway droids that anything valuable was usually recognised and returned. Normally, it was not returned to the owner, but to the corporation which financed the cleaning robots; a corporation which made a healthy profit each year by selling back lost goods, pocketing dropped ecus and blackmailing anyone who'd dropped incriminating evidence while strolling on the walkways.

Behind Jave, the noise from the four-fold holes of Kevving's nostrils ceased abruptly.

'Wha's time?' he said.

'Do you know, you're the second person who's said that to me this morning,' said Jave.

Kevving looked at his watch.

'Six-thirty-seven,' he said with disgust. 'Call that a time?'

'Couldn't sleep,' said Jave. 'Too much to think about.'

Kevving struggled from beneath the bedclothes to sit a little more upright and stare at his brother through sleep-caked eyes.

'All that Harris stuff, you mean?'

Jave nodded.

'Harris,' he said. 'Charles L.'

He crossed to the table in the corner of the room, sat down, and took out a large pad of plastisheet and a stylus.

On a fresh page he wrote 'Abram Chones' in one corner and 'MacWhirter' in another. Then, in the centre he wrote 'Harris' and in the bottom corner he wrote 'Shamworth'.

He looked at these names for a moment and drew a line between 'Chones' and 'Harris' and likewise between 'MacWhirter' and 'Harris'.

A shadow fell across the board. Jave looked up to see Kevving, mummified in his bedclothes, standing looking at the piece of paper.

'There are links, you see,' said Jave. He thought for a moment and then drew a long line between 'Shamworth' and 'MacWhirter'.

'What about this Shoeban guy?' Kevving pointed out. 'Doesn't he also link people?'

'That's right,' said Jave, sucking the end of his stylus. 'He should be in the middle here, next to Harris.'

'Maybe he is Harris?' suggested Kevving.

Jave shook his head.

'Not according to the photos.'

'Could be plastic surgery?'

'Well, it could be. But if it is, it's of a very high standard. They look totally different.' He sucked the end of the stylus. 'I don't know,' he said. 'Those photos. There's something odd about both of them. The Harris one – he reminds me of someone. Someone I've seen.'

'And the Shoeban photo?'

'Well, the same kind of thing. Somehow, it's not right.'

'Not right?'

Jave shrugged.

'There's just something about Shoeban that doesn't seem right. I can't put my finger on it.'

He started doodling on the plastisheet.

'Anyway,' said Kevving, 'if we could find out more about both of them, we'd get somewhere.'

'And where, into all this, does Anson Enterprises fit?' mused Jave.

'Who?' said Kevving.

'Anson Enterprises,' said Jave. 'That's where the vicar was heading yesterday before she was killed.'

'Anson?' repeated Kevving to himself. 'Oh, you mean the vid people!'

'You know them?'

'Sure – they make vid programmes. Some good ones too. They used to do horror stuff. You know, things like *3-D Monsters from Space* and *I was a teenage Tax Inspector*, that sort of stuff.'

'What do they do nowadays?'

'Oh, all kinds. They've diversified or something. They do quiz shows and concerts. Even religious stuff.'

'Religious quiz shows?'

'You know – services and all that. Gospel slots. That's probably what the vicar was interested in.'

'Yeah – she had this big screen in the church.' Jave thought for a moment. 'So it was probably just something to do with that why she was going to Anson Enterprises. Probably just paying her monthly rental or something.'

He looked at the piece of plastisheet and underlined the names Harris and Shoeban. In the absence of any actually activity it made him feel as though he was getting somewhere.

'So,' he said to Kevving, 'what we have to do, is find out about our friend Harris. Then we have to figure out why the mysterious Marc Shoeban had a gram of Abram Chones in his lorry.'

'But first,' said Kevving, 'let's have some more kip, eh?'

16

The offices of the Social Security Department looked no more inviting than they had done twenty-four hours ago.

As he circled above the huge, off-white concrete tower that housed the information sections, Jave wondered how he ever came to work in that place for so many years. It worried him. If his youthful idealism, fired by images from old films had made him work as a Clerk and then a Stamper for the Department, what proof had he that anything had changed now? Was he still fired by the same kind of daydreams? And what, this time, were they getting him into?

He thought about the job he was doing. Inevitably it was inextricably mixed up with images of Chanis. Chanis, who made Jave feel all the things he felt he ought not to feel. The detective-client relationship, he knew, was based on mutual respect and professional detachment. His relationship with Chanis was based on her looking at him and his brain going on holiday.

He was never normally like this. He normally

approached jobs carefully. First rule of survival, he always told himself. Check out the job. This game is full of dodgy characters who would not only sell their own grandmothers, but throw in their grandfathers and a free car phone as well.

As he circled down to land on the roof of the building he felt that this time was different. Today he was approaching his task with all the self-preservation instincts of a particularly depressed kamikaze pilot.

As if to back up his thoughts, a voice came from his pocket.

'You sure you want to do this?' said Frid.

'Of course I don't want to do this,' Jave replied, switching off the C27 and climbing out. 'But can you think of any other way?'

There was a pause.

'We could all go home and back to bed,' suggested Frid.

Jave ignored him and descended the stairs.

The bored officer at reception said nothing when Jave asked him for curfew office, other than look Jave up and down with contempt.

'I'm supposed to report there,' said Jave. 'I'm not sure where to go, or how to do it, but I didn't want to get into more trouble.'

After a further disgusted stare, the officer extended a pudgy, fleshy finger.

'Right hand lift,' he growled.

'Thanks,' said Jave, trying hard to look like someone overawed by the place.

He entered the lift and the doors hissed shut.

'Curfew office,' he said.

The lift thought for a moment.

'Stonk me,' it said. 'We don't get many people going there.'

'I thought I was supposed to report in every day?'

There was a low mechanical laugh and the lift wobbled slightly.

'Well, you're supposed to,' it said. 'But if we all did what we were supposed to do, nothing would ever get done, would it?'

'I think I'd better report all the same,' said Jave.

'All right,' said the lift with a sigh, 'but it's a waste of time, believe me.'

The lift descended into the bowels of the Social Security Department for a few seconds before stopping with a slight bump. The doors hissed open.

'Here we are,' said the lift. 'Don't get too excited.'

Then, with a sigh and a hiss of the closing doors, it was gone.

Ahead of Jave was a large door saying 'Curfew Office'. Behind it, Jave could hear voices. Instead of going through this door, however, he turned down a corridor to his left and passed through a door marked 'Service Personnel Only'.

The door, as Jave remembered, led to a flight of metal stairs, rarely used and down which Jave clanked and clattered his way. A couple of flights down he came upon another door marked 'Hard Copy Area'. He opened the door, which creaked complainingly, to reveal a bleak and empty corridor ahead of him. It was, as he had hoped, completely deserted and, indeed, looked as though hardly a soul had been along there for about twenty years.

Jave padded along the corridor past several frosted glass doors labelled 'Hard Files – Do Not Enter'. Behind the frosted glass there were no signs of any movement.

At the end of the corridor was a door which was identical to the other three in design, but which bore a sign saying 'Hard Copy Department – Reception'. He knocked at the door, waited for an answer that didn't come and entered.

Behind the door there was a small and shambolic office. A wooden counter ran across the width of the office at chest height. On the counter was a small button with a sign taped to it saying 'Press for Service', a ledger which looked as though it had not been opened for years, a well-chewed pencil, a plastic mug with a dried brown coffee stain in it and a small placard saying 'URGENCY IS NO EXCUSE FOR RUDENESS'.

Beyond the counter was a chair and, stacked along the rear wall of the office piles and piles of files, folders, papers, journals, magazines, the odd paperback book and sheafs of letters tied up with bits of string. This mountain of paper ran from floor to ceiling like three-dimensional wallpaper.

Beyond the counter, to the left hand side, was a door into one of the other offices.

There was no one about.

Jave pressed the button for service.

Somewhere, deep in the heart of the adjoining offices, a bell rang. It seemed to echo through the deserted rooms, bouncing here and there between piles of paper. As the last notes died away there was a kind of pause and the slight, almost silent, sound of dust settling. Jave leaned against the counter and waited.

After about a minute and a half, a figure appeared behind the frosted glass of the door on the left. It was small and stooping and seemed to pause for a moment.

'Who's there?' enquired a voice that sounded as though it had been filed away for many years.

'My name's Fleming,' said Jave. 'Stamper Fleming.'

The door slid open and a face peered out. It was old and bald and fringed with white hair that looked as if clumps of cotton wool had been stuck at random on the sides of the man's head. A pair of old-fashioned wire-rimmed glasses perched on top of a big, fleshy and red-veined nose. Behind the glasses, tiny grey eyes peered and flickered with the look of an animal coming out of a long hibernation.

Jave held up a card in a plastic case. He hoped the man's eyesight was as bad as it seemed and that he wouldn't have to explain why he was holding up a plastic card which would guarantee the bearer ten per cent off the cost of a bottle of Old Jock's Sporran-Warmer.

'Stamper Fleming,' he repeated. 'I want a word with you.' Jave snapped the card case shut and tried to talk in an authoritative tone. 'I need some information.'

The figure edged out from his lair. He was wearing the blue and grey uniform of a Social Security Administrative Official. Or, at least, the uniform as it had been in 2022.

'Stamper, you say?' said the old man. 'Not often we get visited by a Stamper, sir.'

'No,' said Jave, 'I shouldn't think it is.'

'In fact,' said the old man, 'the last visitor we had at all was eighteen months ago.' He paused and brushed some dust off one of his arms. 'And he was lost,' he added.

Jave looked around him. 'And you are?' he enquired in a boredly official tone.

'Clarke, sir. Clarke Clark.'

'I'm sorry?' said Jave, who for a moment thought the man was clucking.

'Clarke Clark, sir. It's my name.' The old man chuckled. 'Clarke is my first and second name, sir, although each is spelled differently. The first Clarke having the benefit of a posterior "e".'

'I see,' said Jave, struggling to grasp what was happening. 'Well, Assistant Clark....'

'Not Assistant, sir,' said Clark with a smile. 'I'm a Clerk.'

'A Clerk,' uttered Jave, with a sinking feeling.

'That's right, sir,' said the old man with a smile of complete triumph. 'Clerk Clarke Clark at your service.'

'Right,' said Jave, 'Clerk Clarke Clark.'

The old man continued chuckling.

'Quite an amusing coincidence, don't you think, sir? Three names, sounding the same, but actually spelled quite differently.'

'Astonishing,' said Jave, drily. 'One of the seven wonders of the nomenclature world.'

'I'm glad you think so, sir,' said the Clerk excitedly. 'It's not everyone who thinks it so interesting.'

'I can't imagine why.' Jave coughed. 'Anyway, Clerk...er...Clark, I want some information.'

'Information, sir?' asked Clerk Clarke Clark. 'Of what manner and ilk would that be?'

'Regarding a particular name.'

'I see.'

'The man I'm after is called Harris, Charles L Harris.'

The Clerk looked at Jave, without moving.

'Charles L Harris,' he said.

'That's right.'

The Clerk didn't move.

'If you'll excuse me, sir, why do you want the information?'

Jave tried to look official.

'What do you mean?' he asked. 'That's hardly for you to question Clerk Clark. Just give me what I require.'

Still the Clerk didn't move.

'Do you not have a computer, sir?' he enquired.

'What's that got to do with it?'

'If you'll forgive me, sir, I was just thinking that it was a bit odd, with you from upstairs where there are all those computers and stuff, coming all the way down here to ask me to look something up for you. I mean, without offence, sir, you could look it up yourself at the touch of a button.'

Jave looked at the man. There was nothing on his face to indicate suspicion or anxiety, just a bland, genial mask. And two tiny eyes that darted about behind the glasses. Jave realised he had misjudged his man.

'All right,' he laughed, shrugging off his official demeanour. 'Found out. I give in.' He leaned against the counter in what he hoped was a chummy sort of way. 'Between you and me, Clerk,' he said, 'it's not exactly an official enquiry.'

'Ah,' said Clerk Clarke Clark, 'a personal matter, is it?'

There was, noted Jave, still a steely look behind the eyes.

'No, not personal,' said Jave. 'Well, not exactly.'

He leaned closer to the old man. 'The thing is,' he said, 'we were having a bit of an argument. You see, I'm an old-fashioned sort of Stamper – more leg work and talking to people and all that sort of thing. Whereas some of my colleagues...' he waved his hand in the air dismissively, 'they're all computers and desks and all that sort of stuff. Well, you see, they were claiming that all the information they needed was there at the touch of a button. They were making all these claims for technology.

'Well, I said that all this technology was all very well, but that you can't replace people.' He looked at the Clerk and noticed, with satisfaction, a slight thawing in the icy grey eyes. 'It's what's up here that matters,' he continued, tapping his forehead, 'not what you can type into a computer board. So we had this challenge, to find out something about a name – them by typing it in, me by looking out a file.

'And I said I'd be able to find out much much more by reading the file and looking at all the old records than by looking at the bare details on a computer form. So here I am.'

The old man looked at Jave. He didn't move. 'I see, sir,' he said. 'Some kind of bet.'

'No, not a bet,' said Jave. 'A challenge. A contest. But, well, if you can't help me...' he shrugged his shoulders and played what he felt to be his last card, 'I'll have to tell Hook and his boys that I was wrong.'

The eyes behind the glasses lit up like fireworks.

'Hook, sir. Would that be Stamper Jonn Hook?'

'That's the one,' said Jave.

'Ah well, if it's a contest with Stamper Hook then I'm right with you, sir. Between you and me, sir, I've never found the gentleman to be a very congenial character. He was wont, once upon a time, to come down here and shout at me, for no very apparent reason.'

'I shouldn't let it worry you,' said Jave, who had suddenly warmed to this old man. 'He does that to everyone. The bloke's a dork.'

The old man chuckled, and said, 'Couldn't have put it better myself, sir. A dork, indeed.'

'So what's the score?' said Jave. 'Can you find the file?'

'Oh, I can do better than that, sir,' said Clerk Clarke Clark, chuckling and rubbing his hands together as if he were relishing some private joke. 'I think you'll find that they're in for a surprise about "Harris, Charles L".'

'You mean you know the name?'

'I remember the case, sir. Or cases, I should say. And I think you'll find the computer details are somewhat scanty.'

'Why's that?'

'The files were destroyed, sir. About twenty years ago.'

'How come you remember all this?'

'Oh, I've been here in this Department for thirty years now, sir. I remember most of what I see. Of course, now that everything goes on computer and nothing's written down I don't see anything to remember. But that doesn't mean that I forget what I *have* seen. And I remember Charlie Harris.'

He beckoned to Jave.

'Come through, sir, if you've got a moment.'

Jave smiled. 'Of course. I'd only be watching computer screens upstairs.'

He jumped up onto the counter and slid down onto the other side. Clerk Clarke Clark opened the door into the back office and led the way into the dimly-lit interior.

17

Once inside the next room, Clerk Clarke Clark led Jave through a bewildering maze of files. The files were piled each side of the two men. They were hard copies of files that had now been computerised but which had been compiled many years ago as back-up copies in case of a massive computer failure. Modern computer technology made such failure virtually impossible, but old habits die hard, and the powers that be still thought it best to keep the back-ups. Just in case.

The files stretched back many years. They piled up above Jave, from floor to ceiling, forming walls and passages through which the Clerk led the fake Stamper.

'Here we are, sir,' said Clerk Clarke Clark. They had arrived at a small space, amid the piles of records. Into this space, the Clerk had brought a couple of armchairs and a table. He had converted it into a room of his own, with a pile of old books, a vid screen on a small cupboard and an ancient kettle with a cable that snaked away somewhere under the stacks of paper.

'Very nice,' commented Jave.

Clerk Clarke Clark replied, 'Well, it's a comfortable place to work, and, like I said, there's not much to do these days. Tea?'

'That'll be great.' Jave looked around him. 'Where's the food tube hidden?' he asked.

Clark laughed. 'There's no food tube here, sir. I'm afraid I'm a bit old-fashioned for those things. I wouldn't have one if you paid me. They make the food taste metallic, if you ask me.'

The old man gestured to a chair and Jave sank into the comfortable and well-worn cushions. Clerk Clarke Clark opened the cupboard and produced two mugs and a teapot. He boiled a kettle. He found some milk and some sugar. Jave watched in enthralled stillness. It was like watching a long lost country craft being rediscovered.

'There...er...can't be many people left who make their own tea,' he commented. 'I'm not sure I'd know how.'

'That's the trouble with today,' said Clerk Clarke Clark. 'Everything's instant. Food. News. Justice. It was bad enough in the eighties when I was born, but it's worse now.'

He handed Jave the tea which tasted wonderful and fresh and unlike the grey, pallid liquid that came through the food tubes.

'This is great!' said Jave. 'Where do you get this stuff?'

'Oh, there are still a few shops around that sell it to connoisseurs,' said Clerk Clarke Clark. 'Costs a bit, mind. But I think it's worth it.'

Jave sipped his tea and looked about him.

'Excuse me asking,' he said, 'but what do you do all day?'

Clerk Clarke Clark laughed.

'Oh, I sit and think and do a bit of writing. I don't do any work, as you might call it, but that's hardly my fault, sir. If they asked me, I'd do it. But there you go. They never ask.'

'Well, I'm asking now.'

Clerk Clarke Clark leaned back in his chair.

'Ah yes,' he said, 'Harris, Charles L. A strange case that, sir. A strange case. The young man concerned, as I recall, was a foreigner. Or at least he'd come from abroad.'

He sipped from a bone china mug in hands that looked

considerably more fragile. The tea left a slight fringe of condensation on the old man's moustache, like dew on a twig.

'But this must have been, oh, twenty-five, thirty years ago now,' he continued.

'You won't remember, sir, being too young, but at that time there was a great depression in Britain. It was just about the time of the change to ECUs and of course they managed to muck it up so we hardly got any of them for our old pounds. Criminal that was....'

The old man took an angry sip of tea and recalled himself to the topic in hand.

'Anyway, at that time I was working in what was the old police, see. I was a Sergeant in what they called the Black Economy Squad. It was our job to chase up on the black market situation. Terrible times they was, terrible. For a start there was hardly any work to be had, and where there was work you'd find a machine could do it better than you, cheaper and never have a tea break. Over three-quarters of the country was out of work then. Three-quarters! Think of it!' He slapped the arm of the seat on which he was sitting, sending up a little explosion of dust. 'Rioting on the streets,' he went on, 'no food in the shops. With the change to ECUs, no one had any money any more. People's savings wiped out in a single stroke.'

Jave studied him. The man was genuinely angry, even after all this time. Yes, thought Jave, and I know one person who lost everything.

Clerk Clarke Clark had calmed down a bit.

'Of course,' he said, 'that was when they called the Prime Minister back. Marvellous bit of science that. Anyhow, what with all this depression and unrest there was a flourishing black market. Now, my job was to chase up the drug dealers.'

'You mean narcotics?' asked Jave.

'No – drugs. Ordinary drugs: Aspirin, Penicillin,

monosodium glutomate. All the drugs that kept people alive. The whole system broke down, you see, and the hospitals couldn't get any drugs. But the black market dealers, they had plenty. Dreadful, it was. Dreadful.'

He leaned forward and extended a single, bony finger.

'People would go round to their doctor and he'd prescribe them something, but they'd stand no chance of getting it at the chemist. No chance. The only way would be to buy it from a black market dealer. Huge prices being charged, of course, but when it was a matter of the life of a loved one, people found the money somehow.

'And the prince of these drug dealers was Charlie Harris. At the time we only knew his name. We didn't know who he was, or what he looked like. We guessed he was foreign, or at least had foreign connections, because the drugs had to come into the country from somewhere. But he was the man to know.

'He had a network working out of Deptford at the time. Docklands somewhere. Made sense – the drugs would come in to the airport or through the Chunnel, straight into the heart of London.'

'So he only worked in London?'

'No, he had outlets all over the place. I first tracked him, or at least heard his name, in Swindonopolis. Not that it was Swindonopolis then. That came later. But it was the biggest city in England, even then, and that was where the drug trade went on.

'Charlie himself was nothing more than a jumped up con artist, if you ask me. Gift of the gab and all that, a real salesman, but a salesman with a gift for business organisation. A street thug made good.'

He laughed. 'Not that I ever met him, of course. But you get to know something about the man if you try to hunt him down.

'Anyway, after a while the situation cleared itself up. The Prime Minister cracked down on things and we got back on an even keel. If you can call this an even keel....

'But there was still a shortage of one particular drug, called Factor Seven. I don't remember rightly what it was. I think it was some kind of antibiotic or something. Fought off serious infections. Anyway, that's not important. What happened was that Charlie Harris had the monopoly of the stuff in this field. He had the whole supply. And when the calls came from the hospitals, Charlie tried to make a deal.

'He was clever. He knew that the thing couldn't last, that we were starting to crack the black market operators. He thought he'd go for one big effort. He held out for a while and things were getting serious. I mean, really serious. People were dying. Then he offered it to this hospital in return for 60 billion ECUs. Had it all worked out. Electronic transfer to Swiss bank accounts. Money passed along security protected lines and all that. Nothing traceable.

'Except, what he didn't know was that we had the hospital lines tapped when he made the first approach. No one knew we had lines tapped. This was the beginning of the Social Security stuff, you see. No one really knew how much they were controlled.

'We knew all about the deal and we followed it all the way. All that money buzzing along those telephone lines into all those little computerised bank accounts. The hospital paid up, the drugs were delivered – an ordinary courier firm of course, had no idea who they were working for or what they were delivering – and we traced the money all the way to its resting place in a bank in Geneva.'

He paused.

'That's in Switzerland,' he added.

'Thanks for telling me.'

The old man took a reflective sip of tea.

'Eight months I sat in Switzerland, holed up in a poky little hotel opposite some nondescript little bank. Eight months! We had the whole place wired, of course, ready for the slightest move, but we figured he'd come and get it in person this time.

'Finally, the alert went off. Someone walked into the bank and typed in the code details for that account.' The Clerk smiled. 'I tell you, sir, we were on him like a flash. The man never knew what hit him. You should have seen the expression on his face. Still, it didn't matter, because it wasn't Harris.'

'Who was it?'

'Now there you have me. I can't remember the name exactly – some petty criminal who had been working as a distributor for Harris' goods in Scotland. He was no good to us, anyway. He'd never seen his boss, only had contact on the phone. He knew all about the operation Harris had been running – the drugs, I mean – but he'd only been brought in at the end as a courier. We hushed the whole thing up. The courier went down for a longish stretch and the money stayed where it was, in the hopes that Charlie Harris would eventually try again. He never did though. Sixty billion ECUs.'

Clerk Clarke Clark sighed and gazed at the ceiling for a moment.

'Boring place, Switzerland,' he said. 'Just a lot of mountains and twits in lederhosen leaping around yodelling.'

'You never found him, then?'

'We never found him. And to this day they don't know what he looked like. Oh, we found a few people who had some dealings with him, but they only did stuff over the phone. He never saw anyone.'

'Why not?'

'Could be one of two things. One – he had some brilliant cover or disguise that he didn't want to blow.'

'And two?'

'He might have been very, very ugly.'

Jave thought for a moment.

'I think "one" sounds the favourite.'

Clerk Clarke Clark laughed a laugh that sounded like someone flipping through the pages of an old book.

'No, we reckoned he was wise to us. From the moment we grabbed the guy who ran his Scottish operation, he knew we were onto him. So, he never ran the risk. I suppose, by then, he had enough money. Anyway, he disappeared. We never heard of him again.'

'You remember this all very well,' said Jave, suspiciously.

'Not much else to do these days, is there?' said Clerk Clarke Clark. 'Anyway, it's a bit of a coincidence really. I've been thinking about Harris recently. I had this enquiry, you see, sir. An enquiry from way on high. Only came in a couple of days back. They wanted to make sure all the files on Harris had been destroyed. I was even told to go and check. Not that I bothered. I reckon that file was destroyed twenty years ago.'

'They destroyed it?'

'Orders from above,' said Clerk Clarke Clark. 'Very important, I seem to remember. Long time ago now.'

Jave looked at Clerk Clarke Clark and said, 'I don't believe in coincidence.'

The old man leaned back in his chair.

'You have to,' he replied. 'Why else would you be here? I mean, you come out of the blue and find the one man in the whole building who can remember the story, not only that but who worked on the case. Either it's coincidence, or someone is pulling your strings.'

'Yeah,' said Jave, 'I feel like that sometimes.' He thought about it for a moment. 'You know, I've felt like that for a while. Like someone is out there, pushing me around like a pawn on a chess board. Feels kind of creepy.'

'All depends on your point of view, I'd say,' said Clerk

Clarke Clark. 'Depends whether you think he's sacrificing you, or promoting you to a king.'

Jave shivered. Suddenly he felt uncomfortable here in this tomb of old records, millions of names and details on millions of forgotten people.

'Well,' he said, 'thanks for the tea and the information. I'd better be getting back upstairs.'

As they walked back out through the maze of files and papers, Clerk Clarke Clark turned to Jave. He said, 'Are you going to use that discount voucher?'

Jave hesitated before replying, 'What discount voucher?'

'The one you showed me when you tried to convince me you were still a Stamper.'

Jave's heart missed a beat. Several beats. Enough beats to make a drum track for a very long rhumba.

Clerk Clarke Clark looked at Jave, took off his grimy spectacles and wiped them on a sleeve. If anything, it made them more dirty than before.

'Jave Fleming,' he said. 'I remember you when you were a Stamper. Last time I saw you was what, three years back. You were always a cocky little skagger, even then.'

'You've known...'

'All along, sir,' interjected Clerk Clarke Clark.

They reached the outer office. 'See, you used to sit opposite me every day in the canteen.'

'I don't remember, I'm afraid.'

'Oh no, I don't suppose you do, sir. There are some people whom you can stare at and stare at, and never notice.'

They reached the outer office.

'Funny though,' said Clerk Clarke Clark, 'running into each other again in the midst of all the staff in this vast building. Must be coincidence.'

He smiled at Jave. 'Nice talking to you,' he said. And he turned and disappeared back into his mound of filing.

On his way back to his office, Jave stopped at a bar and sent Clerk Clarke Clark a bottle of Old Jock's Special

Reserve Highland Throbber Whisky.

He had to arrange a special delivery.

After all, Clerk Clarke Clark didn't have a food tube.

18

'So how'd it go?' asked Frid as Jave flew back towards his office.

'Pretty good,' said Jave. 'There's a guy in there who told me the whole story. Seems this Charlie Harris was a big wheel in the black market about twenty years ago.'

'Twenty years ago? So why would it matter today?'

'Well, the guy was never found and never even seen. So no one knows what he looks like.'

'Except us.'

'Yeah. Except us.'

He thought for a moment. 'Y'know, we're really going to have to be careful, here,' he said. 'That makes a very good motive for killing people. Abram Chones, and people who knew him, have been killed off. And they've probably been bumped off because they knew something about Charlie Harris.'

'Which implies that Charlie Harris is still around.'

'And doesn't want the past brought to light.' Jave swung his air car round a huge heli-transporter with a Garfield doll on the back. Ahead of him a Cortina C27 cruised along, a pair of furry dice waving in the wind.

'And what's more,' said Jave, 'this Harris, or someone he knows, is pretty powerful, because a long time ago, they ordered the old file at Social Security to be destroyed. Clerk Clark must be one of the only people around who remembers the story.'

Frid chewed a cashew nut. 'We is in a conspiracy, baby,' he said.

They arrived back at the office to find a note waiting for them.

'BORING, BORING, BORING!!!!' it said (in red crayon). 'Have gone out detecting.'

Jave looked at the scrap of paper in his hand and said, 'I don't know why it is, but a simple note like this fills me with complete horror. Where d'you think he's gone?'

'No idea, baby,' Frid replied. 'I shouldn't worry, though, man. He'll only get lost.'

They punched up some lunch. While he was chewing his marshmallow and ham sandwich, Jave spread the pictures out on his desk and looked at them.

There was Abram Chones and his young wife – Abram staring out into the camera with that challenging, almost mocking stare; his wife, fragile and delicate. She was porcelain; he, earthenware.

There was something about Abram in this picture; something that nagged at Jave. Not the stare, not the woman. Something much more basic. He thought about it, but the harder he stared the more difficult it was to define. Trying to reverse this process, he put the photo on his desk and tried to look at it out of the corner of his eye. Then he tried not to look at it at all. Nothing worked.

'You all right, baby?' asked Frid, his whiskers whirring as his brain did the accounts.

'I've got something...something on the tip of my brain.'

'Your brain hasn't got a tip,' Frid informed him. 'It *is* a tip, but it hasn't *got* one.'

Jave glared at the gerbil and said, 'Whoever programmed your comedy circuits should be sacked. I meant, there was something I was trying to remember.' He shrugged his shoulders. 'It's gone.'

He pushed the photo away from him and picked up the other one – the one of Charlie Harris and Abram Chones at school. With deep annoyance he felt himself assailed by the same mocking half-feeling. There was something here that he had seen before. He threw it down with annoyance.

'Bazz it!' he muttered. Frid looked at him quizzically.

'There are just too many echoes in this case,' said Jave. 'Too many little thoughts and not one single skagging big fact. Everything seems to revolve around these pictures.'

He picked up the photos and slipped them into an old plastic envelope. Then he rose from behind the desk and grabbed his coat and hat.

'Come on,' he said. 'Let's go and hunt facts.'

They flew across London, north again to the M25.

'Shoeban,' muttered Jave. 'He's especially annoying. We don't know anything about him. We don't know who he is. We don't even know if he has anything to do with this business at all.'

'Why else would the vicar go and see him?' enquired Frid.

'Maybe it was a social call,' Jave suggested. 'Maybe she just wanted a chat.'

'Maybe I'm a giraffe,' said Frid.

They landed in a small space beside the tumble-down lorry that Shoeban used as a home. Jave climbed out of the C27 and stepped gingerly through the piles of rubbish and the mud that surrounded the vehicle.

He was about to push open the door when Frid whispered to him.

'Someone in there!' said the gerbil, his whiskers scanning the building with tiny infra-yellow waves.

'Where?' asked Jave.

'In the main room,' said Frid. 'Probably male.'

'Shoeban,' muttered Jave.

Silently, he moved to the door of the van. It was open. From the inside of the lorry, Jave could hear the sound of someone turning over pieces of paper, humming slightly.

He leaned against the door. He pushed very gently. It creaked very loudly.

So much for surprise, thought Jave. He kicked the door fully open and rushed in. Unfortunately, he tripped up on the door ledge, fell head over heels and rolled with a sickening thump against the far wall of the lorry.

'Ouch!' he said, profoundly.

The figure sitting at the desk looked up.

'Hello, bruvv,' it said.

Jave rose very slowly, rubbing the base of his spine where he had smacked it against a rather unyielding wall.

'What are *you* doing here?' he demanded.

'I told you,' Kevving replied. 'Detecting.'

'You nearly got into serious trouble, there,' said Jave. 'I could have felled you with my ninja attack techniques.'

'What, you mean techniques like falling over and doing your back in?' asked Kevving. 'Yeah, that was frightening. I nearly died. Laughing.'

'For your information,' said Jave, 'I didn't trip. I dived into a commando roll.'

'I should try a ham roll,' suggested Kevving. 'It'd be more effective.'

Jave sat down on the shabby bed feeling his sore back.

'What have you been doing?' he asked.

'Looking around,' said Kevving. 'Thought I might find something.'

'How did you find this place?'

'You told me all about it.'

'And you remembered?'

'Of course.'

'Amazing. You were paying attention. It's a first.'

Kevving got up from the desk.

'And look what I found,' he said.

He was holding an old and tatty paperback book. Jave took it from him and looked at the cover. 'London A-Z,' he read, '2022 Edition, including full guide to Central London, M25 Housing Estate and Watford Shopping City.'

He looked at Kevving.

'Well?' said Kevving.

'Well, what?'

'Look!'

Kevving took the paperback from Jave's hands and turned it to the back. He held it out to Jave.

Jave peered at the pages. They were old and spotted with brown damp marks and the ring mark where a coffee cup had once been placed. The back two pages were blank, except for some scribblings in red ink. Whoever had been writing in the book had drawn a series of lines in some kind of pattern. Or it could just have been a doodle. But beneath this scribble, the owner had written a name, 'Vic Stockwell'.

'Well?' said Jave again.

'It's a clue,' said Kevving.

Jave looked at him.

'Kevving,' he said, 'this book is nearly thirty years old. At some time during those thirty years, someone scribbled in the back with a red pen and then wrote the name "Vic Stockwell". How is that a clue?'

Kevving looked disappointed.

'Well,' he said, 'perhaps it means something.'

'Of course it means something,' said Jave. 'Or, rather, it meant something. Otherwise whoever did it wouldn't have done it. But that doesn't mean that it means anything now. It's someone's name. At one time the owner of this book wrote it down to remind him of someone he had to meet, or talk to, or borrow money off. But that could have been years ago. What proof have you that it was made recently?'

'I dunno!' Kevving was staring angrily at Jave. 'I

thought it might help.'

'Well it doesn't.'

'Well *you* do better,' said Kevving, red-faced with annoyance.

'I shall.'

'Go on then.'

'Right.'

'Fine.'

Kevving stormed out, taking his book with him.

'Stupid bazzer,' said Jave, shaking his head.

They spent the next few minutes searching through different ends of the lorry. Jave took the desk again, but found nothing different from before. At the bottom of the pile, undisturbed from yesterday's visit, was Marc Shoeban's residential permit. The plastic card still showed the same blank, almost anonymous, figure with his black hair and his sunglasses and his painfully white face and chin.

'Well, whoever he is,' said Jave, 'he's gone.'

Under the residential permit, again where he had left it, was the photo of Abram Chones.

'And no one else has been here looking for him,' said Frid.

'Do you reckon he's gone?'

Frid buzzed.

'The place is cold, man. Difficult to say, 'cause the dude's latent heat wouldn't hang around. But I'd say he hasn't been back here since the vicar came two days ago.' He looked up at Jave and wrinkled his nose. 'Just a guess.'

'Yeah,' replied Jave. 'Just a guess.' Frid's 'guesses' were, of course, the results of thousands of millions of tiny impulses racing through his microchips in an intricate predictive computer sequence. In other words, they were pretty good.

'Well, he won't miss a couple of personal items, then,' said Jave, taking a pen from the desk and writing on the back of the photo 'Wardrobe. Marc Shoeban's Lorry-House' to distinguish it from the one that Chanis had given him.

Jave took a last look round the lorry.

'Whoever he was, he didn't have much and he didn't take it with him.'

'Think he's dead?' asked Frid.

Jave replied, 'Who knows? It seems to happen to almost everyone else. Have a last scan round, will you? I'm going outside.'

He found Kevving sitting outside in the C27 watching a programme on the vid screen.

'You all right?' Jave asked. Kevving nodded but didn't say anything.

'And now, CBC presents live from Swindonopolis, "The Cuddly Thought Hour" featuring your favourite Bishop Lou Blynell!' The voice of the vid announcer slid out of the screen like oil. The theme music from the vid unit filled the air.

'Listen,' said Jave, putting his hand on his brother's shoulder, 'I didn't mean to snap at you.'

'It doesn't matter.'

Jave sat back and looked vaguely at the vid screen where Kevving was watching.

The Bishop of Swindonopolis was just starting his Thursday afternoon show, a sort of mixture of church service, chat show and used car auction. The choir finished singing 'Choruses you have Loved', and the Bishop started talking to the millions of TV fans out there. Jave wondered if, just up the road, the screen in the Church of the Blessed Commuter was switched on.

'I just don't feel we're getting anywhere,' said Jave. 'There's some kind of connection here, something I almost get, but can never quite see. It's like trying to remember a name. It's like doing a jigsaw, only before you can even begin fitting the pieces together, you've got to sort out which pieces are part of the picture and which aren't. I guess I'm just tired.'

'It's OK,' said Kevving. 'Maybe it's not a clue. I just felt a bit useless back there, bruvv.'

'Brothers, sisters,' said the Bishop, pushing back his elegantly coiffured flaxen hair, 'there's no need to despair or worry. Take the love that God offers, accept him and you'll have all the money you need. God doesn't want you to be poor! God doesn't want you to suffer! God wants you to have blessings and abundant wealth, and the Bible is clear on this, my friends. The worthy are always wealthy.' As if to illustrate his sermon, the glint of a gold-plated wrist unit flashed out from beneath his immaculate dark grey suit.

'What a bazzer,' said Jave.

His brother replied, 'Lou Blynell is very popular.'

'This the kind of religion you go for?'

Kevving turned to his brother and smiled.

'No,' he said. 'I go for the real stuff.'

'Yeah, but how do you know what's real?'

He looked down at his feet and kicked a ball of newspaper out of the way. There was a pause.

'Real is what you find in the Bible,' said Kevving suddenly. 'Jesus is real. Not this snorking great pilchard. I mean, Jesus never had any money. According to the Bish-boy, that makes him a failure.'

They turned and looked at the screen.

Jave realised he was still holding the photo of Abram Chones and the residential permit. From his pocket, he pulled the plastic envelope containing the photos. In his haste in leaving the office, he had not sealed the envelope correctly and, as he pulled it from his coat, the other two photos fell to the ground.

'Skag it!' exclaimed Jave.

He knelt down and retrieved them.

'Want a hand?' asked Kevving.

'No, it's just all these photos,' said Jave. 'That's the trouble with this case. There are too few facts to go on. All we have is images, pictures, photos from the past.'

'Isn't that all we ever get?' asked Kevving, biting his nails as he watched the Bishop acting his heart out. 'Impressions from the past. Pictures from some other zeke's life. Thing is, sooner or later you have to make your mind up. And all you ever get for proof is old pictures.'

'Are you getting metaphysical?' asked Jave. 'Or are you back on the hard stuff?'

Kevving grinned. 'Just thinking, aloud,' he said.

'All it takes is belief,' said the Bishop on the vid screen. He was obviously building up to his big appeal. 'That's all it takes. Belief in God.'

Kevving gestured towards the screen. 'That's what's wrong about this zeke. He wants to give you rewards for believing. But you don't get that. Not that kind of reward anyway.'

'What do you get then?'

Kevving looked at Jave.

'Same as you get when all the jigsaw pieces fall into place. Same as you get when all the photos make sense. You get the truth.'

Jave looked away. He looked around him at the muddy street on the M25 Estate; at the tumbledown, semi-decrepit lorries and container vans that housed the goods that no one ever wanted; at the equally decrepit van that had once been home to Marc Shoeban, perhaps another piece of merchandise that no one wanted. It was a weird place to be discussing the truth.

'How can you be sure, though?' he asked. 'And anyway,' he whispered, 'what does it matter?'

Kevving replied, 'The truth always matters, doesn't it?

I mean, when you find out the truth about this business, that will matter, won't it? It'll matter to Chanis, apart from anyone else.'

'But is that it? You...you've changed. But there must be something you get. I mean, all right, so the Bishop's a complete skag-head, but there must be some rewards. After all, when I find out the truth, I get paid.'

'Oh, there are rewards, sure,' said Kevving. 'Don't get me wrong – it's great. Rescued me, man.' He shrugged. 'But you don't go into it because it's going to give you more money than you've ever had. When you first come to it, faith has only one promise: the truth. The rest comes later.

'And sometimes the rest is painful. In the Bible, there's this zeke called Paul. He wrote about the "prize". You know what prize he got? He was executed. Like a complete headectomy. Some prize, that. No, the rewards are all different.'

He pointed a thin finger at the Bishop. 'That's why this dude will fade away in the end. The kind of religion he's peddling just isn't real. In the real thing there's no money-back guarantee.'

On the vid screen, the Bishop was bringing his oration to an eloquent conclusion. The lights were lowered, close-up cameras filled the screen with his classic, clean-cut, sincere features.

'You see, people,' he said, 'God wants to reward the righteous. And, brothers and sisters, I don't mean reward in some vague, mystical way. I mean, really reward.' He paused and smiled into the camera. 'Easy, isn't it?' he said.

There was a brief silence, then the tumultuous, tinny applause of the studio audience burst into life and the Bishop's smile grew even wider and more welcoming.

The picture was frozen on the screen and some text advertising the Bishop's latest book *How to Pray for a*

Million a Day began to roll across the smiling face, along with an address in Swindonopolis to write to.

Kevving said, 'I'd like to buy that book, just for the sheer joy of ripping it to shreds.'

But Jave wasn't listening. He was staring at the frozen image of the Bishop. The hair was golden. The face was peach-pink and glowing with health and prosperity. Teeth gleamed white in a smile of warmth and reassurance.

And suddenly Jave was thrown back thirty years and the face which filled the vid screen was no longer that of Lou Blynell, Bishop of Swindonopolis, but of the young, brash classmate of Abram Chones, 'Harris, Charles L'.

19

'Are you sure?' asked Kevving.

'Can't you see it?'

'Well, there is a slight resemblance.'

'Slight!' Jave looked skyward in despair. 'It's as plain as the noses on your face,' he said. 'Look at the hair, the grin, everything. I mean, the guy has "con-man" written all over him.'

'Con-man?' said Kevving.

'Oh, hey, I forgot. I didn't tell you what happened this morning.' And Jave recounted to Kevving the story of his meeting with Clerk Clarke Clark and the tale of Charlie Harris, black marketeer, drug dealer and fugitive from justice.

'But, I mean...' Kevving scratched his noses thoughtfully, 'how does all this fit in?'

'Don't you see? Abram Chones comes to work here.

Don't forget he's never had a TV in his life. He goes into church one day where they've got these massive vid screens up and there it is before him – the face of Charlie Harris, now Bishop of Swindonopolis. A man who has found a new way to make money.'

Jave was pacing round the C27 in a frenzy of speculation. 'He can't have known about Charlie's history. He must have let slip the name to the vicar, not knowing that she was helping to mastermind the Bishop's campaign for the Archbishop's post.'

'But would she have known that the Bish was an ex-criminal?'

'Probably not. But she wouldn't have to. All she'd have to do is report it back to her bosses. Someone up there would have known the truth.'

'Well, why haven't we heard?'

'Heard what?'

'That the Bishop is really Charlie Harris.'

Jave looked at his brother in amazement.

'You are really naive,' he said. 'I mean, have you got any idea how much it costs to make TV programmes? And look at this guy – wrapped from head to toe in marketing deals and merchandise agreements and whatever. He is worth a fortune. If you let on that your beautiful Bishop is an ex-black marketeer then bang goes his street-cred for a start. No more true believers. No more T-shirt sales or book deals. They're not likely to let all that go.'

'Are you telling me that these people had Abram Chones...'

'Firebombed.'

Kevving looked shocked. 'Wow! Talk about over-reacting.'

'This is big business,' said Jave. 'And that makes sense of the vicar. Why was she going to visit the head of a vid corporation? Because the same corporation put out this rubbish.' He gestured to the programme still playing on the vid screen. 'You told me yourself that Anson Enterprises had branched out into religious programmes. They own the rights to Bishop Lou Blynell, you see.'

The brief commercial break had ended and the Bishop was once again exhorting the faithful to 'pray up and pay up'.

'I see,' said Kevving. 'You reckon she was going to warn them that someone was looking for Abram Chones?'

'Something like that. She was heavily involved with Lou Blynell, and she wouldn't have wanted anything to get in the way of his career. As for the rest of it....' He shrugged. 'Maybe she was in on it, maybe not. Probably not, as far as the murder of Chones was concerned. I mean, she never seemed like a killer to me. Just an overgrown groupie. But she must have had her instructions – to report to them whenever anything suspicious occurred.'

'Meaning you.'

'In this case, yes.'

Kevving thought for a moment.

'All right,' he said, 'but where does Shoeban fit in?'

Jave stared at him and opened his mouth to say something. Then he shut it again. Then he opened it.

'Haven't the foggiest,' he said.

Kevving looked disappointed.

'Oh, come on,' said Jave, 'I'm not infallible. Just a genius, that's all.'

Frid came out of the lorry.

'Nothing more,' he said. 'Mostly old newspapers and food packaging. The only bits with any writing on, you got.'

He looked at the brothers.

'You guys bin doing some thinking,' he said. 'I always know when you guys bin thinking. The backs of your ears goes red.'

'So where does Shoeban fit in?' asked Frid, after Jave had run through his explanation for a second time.

'Oh, don't *you* start!' exclaimed Jave. 'How do I know? Maybe he was a friend of the family. Who knows?'

'The vicar knew,' said Frid.

'Yeah, and look what happened to her.'

'So what happens next?' asked Kevving.

Jave looked at his wrist unit.

'Fourteen hundred,' he said. 'How long will it take us to get to Swindonopolis, Frid?'

''Bout half an hour.'

'Right. I think it's time we called on the powers that be.' He turned to Kevving. 'I want you to do two things,' he said.

'What?'

'One – go home.'

'Wow,' he said. 'Boresville.'

'I haven't finished.' Jave looked down at his feet as if he were embarrassed. 'Two – write down everything we've just talked about,' he continued. 'Take these.' He handed over the photos and the documents they had found. 'No, hang on. I need a copy.'

He leaned into the C27, flicked open the glovebox and pressed a button on the communications console. A flap over a small opening flipped up and Jave fed the photo of Abram Chones and Charlie Harris through the slot, re-emerging through another slot as two photos, the bottom a copy of the original. Jave took the copy, folded it and put it into his pocket. He turned back to Kevving and gave him the original.

'Make your story as thorough as possible and then send it and the photos somewhere safe. Send them to a friend you trust and who can't possibly be connected with all this. If I don't come back tonight, get in touch with the friend and tell him to send them to a national newspaper. Pick one that will actually report on it.'

'OK,' said Kevving.

'And tell your friend that if he hasn't heard from you within twenty-four hours he's to send them anyway.'

Kevving looked at his brother. 'You really think this is going to be dangerous?' he asked.

'I don't know,' said Jave. 'I hope not. But I think it might. I don't want you to take any chances. Once they know about me, they'll find out about you. That's why we need to use one of your friends. Someone whom you can really trust.'

Suddenly, and without warning, Kevving hugged his brother.

'Hang loose, bruvv,' he said.

'Yeah,' said Jave, suffocating.

Kevving turned and shrugged.

'Still a bit up-tight,' he said. 'You really gotta loosen up.'

He turned and sauntered off up the street towards the transporter cars that hovered in the distance.

'He gonna be all right?' asked Frid.

Jave watched the retreating figure, his cropped blond hair bobbing as he skipped between parked air cars. At that moment he felt what could only be called affection for his brother.

'Oh, Kevving will be all right,' said Jave. 'He always muddles through somehow.'

He turned to the gerbil.

'It's us I'm worried about.'

20

Even in a country full of huge cities, Swindonopolis was massive.

From twenty miles out, it sprawled in front of Jave like a giant splash of silver paint, thrown against the green English landscape. As he travelled nearer he began to make out buildings: huge towers with steel walkways thrown like ropes between them; the massive air terminal to the north with its control mast that soared over three kilometres into the sky; the squat, butter-yellow glint of Parliament to the south, reflecting in its golden walls the dull blue of the River Thames (artificially redirected fifty miles south of its original course to make the new capital feel more like the old one); the airways, teeming with life and movement, cars flying hither and thither, huge air transporters hovering like giant, overweight humming bees as they unloaded their goods into the gaping maws of the shopping precincts; the pyramid-shaped Bank of Europe building with its eighty storeys topped by a ten-storey, golden, revolving office suite shaped like an ECU coin.

Below, lapping against the bases of the giant office blocks, were the shopping malls and the leisure arcades, the vid-palaces and the tube-restaurants, the virtual-reality theatres and the hyperdrug joints. In between, humanity swarmed, rushing like insects from building to building in their endless pursuit of something to buy, something to experience, something to consume.

Jave sighed. He hated Swindonopolis.

The trouble was, one of the *many* troubles was, that Swindonopolis was transparently, totally, artificial. And, what's more, it didn't care.

When Swindon started to burst into new life at the tail end of the twentieth century it could scarcely have foreseen the glorious future that awaited it. The old railway town that one day found itself to be the fastest growing town in Europe, soon turned into the fastest growing city in Europe. And still it grew.

It was greatly helped by the motorways, of course. Initially, in the twentieth century, there was the M4. Then there was added the M4.5, which ran parallel to the M4, but about three miles north, taking it straight into Swindon from the east. It was soon joined by the M4.6 (running south into Swindon from the M6) and the M4.7 (running north into Swindon from the M3). These were speedily followed by the M4.8 (east into Swindon from the M5) and, most amazingly, the M4.9 (running up into Swindon from below. This was the world's first underground motorway, running through a long tunnel that led, eventually to France).

So, Swindon grew. In a way, it couldn't help itself, because others were almost force-feeding it. The European Council began to switch all of its British investment into Swindon and away from other cities such as Glasgow, Birmingham or London. As success bred success and investment attracted more investment, Swindon's growth resembled that of a snowball rolling down a mountainside.

By 2030 it had rolled on to become Swindonopolis, a massive sprawl of buildings running from Oxford to Bath. And, once absorbed, both of these cities were completely transformed by the authorities of the ever growing city, whose motto seemed to be 'If you can't beat them, sell them'. They became 'theme shopping towns', a development of which the Swindonopolis Marketing Staff were particularly proud.

'Ye Medieval Shoppes of Oxford' had staff dressed as students of the sixteenth century and guides who wandered the streets dressed as professors. The colleges,with their elegant quadrangles and stately fronts, proved ideal for conversion into shopping arcades.

Bath, likewise, became 'The Regency Shopping Experience' complete with beaus, sedan chairs and, for those visitors who really cared about historical accuracy, the pox.

Eventually, the growth of Swindonopolis and its increasing financial power gave the European Council the excuse they had been looking for to alter the structure of Britain completely. They decided that Swindonopolis, with its clean, plastic smile, made a much better centre of operations for Great Britain than shabby, crumbling, dirty, old London. Euro-Council directive 28994/B, therefore, decreed that the nation's capital should be moved to Swindonopolis.

A few members of the Government in London raised some objections, but most of them happily conformed to the directive. After all, they were indirectly responsible. Initially, it was their massive investment and incentive programme that had sown the seeds of London's demotion, and once they had handed over the economic control of the nation to the European Council, full of people who cared little for history and even less for tradition, the demise was assured.

So, in 2032, the nation's capital was officially moved to Swindonopolis. Parliament was rehoused in stately new buildings, the Bank of Europe, the Stock Exchange, the British Museum even, they all moved to Swindonopolis. It had taken over.

It somehow seemed fitting to Jave that the heart of the nation was no longer deemed to be London, grimy and old and throbbing with some kind of life. It was Swindonopolis – plastic, huge and successful and wearing its wealth with pride. It was a symbol of the changes that had overtaken England as far back as the 1980s. It was an artificial heart, transplanted by people who no longer cared if the patient lived or died.

The building at the end of the walkway in front of Jave was typical of Swindonopolis.

He had parked his air car in a huge car park labelled 'NCP Air Park – Mortgages Available' and had strolled across a shiny steel walkway that seemed to hang in the air with all the fragile beauty of a spider's web. The building to which he was walking was sheathed in shiny chromium steel and glinting in the pale light of the afternoon sun.

Jave approached a pair of huge chromium and glass doors bearing the legend, 'Anson Enterprises Inc.'

'Are you sure she was coming here?' he asked.

'Positive, baby,' affirmed Frid, sitting on Jave's shoulder. 'The co-ordinates were precise. And she was heading for the Anson dude himself.'

'Yeah,' said Jave, grimly.

'Anson,' repeated Frid. 'The main man. He is the top dude. The head honcho. The boss. The chief.'

'Yes, all right,' said Jave.

'The big cheese, numero uno, the crême de la crême...'

'I've got the point, thank you.'

'Top of the pile, number one, mmmphhfffggfhhgffggphhhm...'

Jave walked through the doors, stuffing the gerbil into his pocket.

Inside the doors was a light and spacious reception hall. People were milling to and fro beyond a security barrier that lay straight ahead of Jave. He walked up to it. The barrier stretched across the width of the reception hall and was broken by three entrance points and three exits, not unlike the old toll booths on the now disused Severn Bridge. Jave stood at one of the entrances. Beyond the barrier, at head height, was a free standing speaker grille. On Jave's side of the barrier, just to his left, was a pillar, on top of which was a small steel panel.

'Hello, visitor,' said the grille. 'Please place your hand on the panel. Your entry will be automatically logged against your National Identity Data.'

Jave sighed again. How he hated Swindonopolis.

In 2045, despite objections by Civil Rights Organisations, Consumer's Groups and something that called itself 'The Committee to Stop Really Stupid Things Happening', the Government introduced National Identity Data.

Each person's data, including such details as name, date of birth, identity number, criminal record, credit rating, shoe size, IQ, dandruff count and palm print, were all logged. The Government didn't, of course, have to ask for this information as Social Security already had it. All it did was transfer the information into one, enormous database run by one, extremely hot computer.

This led to massively increased security. Everything, for example, could be coded into credit cards, allowing credit-scanners to assess whether the person using the card really was the rightful owner. Retinal scanning could check for identities by matching the data in the National Identity Database against the retinal patterns of the person in front of the machine. One especially useful application was the development of the Palm Print Entry System, which allowed entry to any public building to be effected only through logging the visitor's palm print on entry. Once their palm print was logged, their names were registered and all their credentials checked. Or at least that was the theory.

In practice it never worked out this way and, by 2050, few businesses were still actually employing the entry security system.

The problem was that the computer holding all this information was based at Swansea. Its proud boast was that it kept up the same standards of accuracy that it had when it was called the Driver and Vehicle Licensing Centre....

Jave put his hand on the metal panel.

'Your palm print has been logged and identified against National Data,' said the grille. 'Welcome, Mrs Doris Blastgirdle.'

'I'm not Doris Blastgirdle,' said Jave.

The grille beeped.

'National Data identifies your palm print as that of Mrs Doris Blastgirdle of Royal Milton Keynes,' said the grille.

'Well, I'm not.'

The grille beeped stubbornly.

'You are now,' it said as the barrier swung upwards.

Beyond the barrier was a further reception area. Jave

waded through the deep carpet to a desk with a real, live human receptionist. She looked up and smiled a dazzling smile.

'Hi,' she said. 'You must be Mrs Blastgirdle. I've received your data from the door.'

'I'm not Mrs Blastgirdle,' explained Jave. 'It's the National Data Registry. It's always happening. These skagging doors never work. Last week I was called Eric Mossfumbler of Newcastle. The week before that I was Lord Chalke of Peckham.'

'I'm sorry,' smiled the receptionist, 'but we always go by the name given us by the door. Now, what can I do for you, Mrs Blastgirdle?'

Jave tried again.

'I'm not Mrs Blastgirdle.'

'According to our files you are.'

'Do I look like Mrs Blastgirdle?' asked Jave, exasperated.

'That's not for me to say,' replied the receptionist sweetly. 'If you choose to look like a badly-shaven man with a dirty trenchcoat, that is up to you. You are an individual with a right to look like what you want. That's in the constitution.'

'Thanks. I'll remember that.'

'So, what can I do for you, Mrs Blastgirdle?'

Jave gave in.

'I'd like to see Mr Anson.'

'I'm sorry, Mr Anson never sees people.'

'What is he, blind?'

The receptionist laughed insincerely.

'No, he's just very important,' she said. 'He's in charge here. The boss. The big man...'

'El supremo,' came a voice from Jave's pocket. 'His nibs...'

Jave hit his pocket.

'Sorry, did you say something?' said the receptionist.

'My pocket was thinking aloud,' said Jave.

'So I'm very sorry, but your request is impossible,' smiled the receptionist. 'Perhaps one of our junior staff will do? One of our extremely junior staff?'

'You don't understand,' said Jave. 'I have an appointment.'

'You do?' said the receptionist, suspiciously.

'Of course.'

'Well, what's it about?'

Jave stared at her.

'Tell him I want to talk about Charlie Harris.'

'Well – I'll try,' said the receptionist.

'And don't let this trenchcoat deceive you,' said Jave. 'I'm actually an eccentric billionaire.'

She pressed some buttons.

'Hello? Mr Anson? There's a Mrs Blastgirdle to see you.'

There was a pause. The receptionist looked upset.

'But he said he had an appointment,' she almost whispered. 'He said it was to talk about Charlie Harris.'

There was an even longer pause. A silence, even.

'Right...yes, Mr Anson, sir.'

The receptionist clicked off the switch and looked at Jave, her composure completely restored.

'Mr Anson will see you now,' she said.

Melling Anson was the fattest man Jave had ever seen. He was not so much a man, more a small planet. Jave had no need to walk towards him. He just relaxed and let gravity do the rest.

At the top of his body was a totally hairless lump that looked like a badly inflated football. Judging from the position it occupied, Jave guessed that this was Anson's head. This opinion was confirmed by two pendulous eyelids opening to reveal small, gleaming black eyes. It looked like someone had pushed two marbles into a ton of dough. His vast, obese body was dressed entirely in white, making him look like a snowman who had put on a lot of weight.

'Mrs Blastgirdle?' enquired Anson, his chins wobbling.

'I'm afraid not,' said Jave. 'The name's Fleming, Jave Fleming. It's Swansea, you see...'

Anson laughed, his jowls flapping like vast balloons.

'Quite so,' he said. 'Computers. Never trust 'em.'

'You don't?'

'Too literal minded,' said Anson. 'Can't recognise mistakes, can they? No idea of what constitutes reality except what's in their programming. Far too limited.'

Jave looked around him. He was in a big, plush office suite. It reminded him of his room at home. Had the room-cleaning computer gone completely berserk? It was sparsely furnished – just two chairs each side of a massive, mahogany desk. Behind Anson's desk the wall was filled with a vast glass window overlooking the Swindonopolis cityscape. Behind Jave's chair, the wall opposite the desk was filled with fifteen or so vid screens, all showing different stations and emitting a low babble of sound. Their flickering images filled the white room with lights and shadows.

Two black eyes fixed on Jave. 'Fleming, eh?'

Anson flapped an enormous hand into the middle distance. Jave guessed he was indicating the black leather chair that stood in front of Anson's vast mahogany desk. He sat down on it, and was surprised to find that the chair was covered with a thin film of plastic.

'Nice place you got here,' Jave commented. 'Nice view.'

'Yes,' said Anson. 'I suppose it is. Never look at views meself. Waste of time. Please excuse the plastic on your chair, by the way. It's a matter of general hygiene. Nothing personal, you understand.'

Anson pressed a button on his desk and the sixteen video screens that filled the wall behind Jave went mute.

'But, Mr Fleming, you don't want to hear my admittedly

extreme views on hygiene. You want to talk about something else, I believe.'

'About Charlie Harris.'

'Quite so. And who, exactly, is this?'

Jave looked at the man. He was very slow, very relaxed and very, very sharp. Behind the folds of flesh that hung like sallow porridge from his enormous frame there was a lithe, needle-sharp mind. He reminded Jave of a very fat crocodile. Slow, but lethal.

'Charlie Harris is a name without a face,' said Jave. 'A black-marketeer who made profits during the great recession. He sold drugs to desperate hospitals. Sometimes he didn't sell drugs to desperate hospitals. It all depended on whether the hospital was desperate enough.'

'Most reprehensible,' murmured Anson.

'The authorities never caught him, for a number of reasons, not least of which was the fact that they didn't know what he looked like.' Jave paused and stared at Melling Anson. The man returned his stare. With interest.

'But I,' said Jave, 'know what he looks like.'

Melling Anson brought the tips of his fingers together and blew on them gently.

'And what makes you think this will interest me?' he enquired.

'Because he looks like someone you are deeply involved with,' said Jave. 'Someone you have a lot of capital riding on. Someone you really wouldn't want to lose.'

'I am intrigued.'

'Yesterday,' Jave continued, 'a member of the clergy was killed in an air car accident. I have reason to believe that she was coming to see you about this. The day before that, a man called MacWhirter, an old associate of Harris, was also killed. Some days before that a man named Abram Chones was burned up by a firebomb. They all knew about Charlie Harris. Someone, it seems, is trying to stop that information getting out.'

Anson smiled. 'I hope you're not accusing me, Mr Fleming. I have excellent alibis for the last few days.'

'I'll bet you do,' said Jave. 'The point is that the only thing that links these people is the fact that they knew the identity of Charlie Harris. They knew what I know, Mr Anson, but I've got proof.'

'Proof?'

'That Bishop Lou Blynell, your media mega-Bishop, was once known as Charlie Harris.'

21

The fingers drew slowly apart, and Melling Anson said, 'I'm not sure I like your manner, Mr Fleming.'

Jave smiled.

'I don't blame you,' he said. 'Even I don't like my manner, and I'm used to it.'

Anson did not smile. 'But, leaving that aside, I am intrigued. What kind of proof could there be?'

'It's an old photo. It's clearly labelled. It comes from Abram Chones' past, when he was at college in Italy with a boy called Charlie Harris. The face is quite unmistakable.'

'Not much proof,' murmured Anson. 'People change as they grow older. The photo must be thirty years old.'

'More like twenty-five. I agree. It's not much proof. But enough. Especially when you take into account how well the Bishop has retained all his boyish charms. And then when you tie it in with all these murders....'

'Mr Fleming,' said Anson, 'I hope we're not going to dislike each other. I don't like disliking people.'

'Nor me.'

'So,' said Melling Anson. He leaned forward on the desk and stared at Jave. 'What is it you want from me, Mr Fleming?'

'Information,' said Jave.

'What kind of information?'

'Oh, little things. Things like who killed Abram Chones. And MacWhirter. And Reverend Shamworth. Little things like that.'

'You seem very sure that I know.'

'You're the obvious person,' said Jave. 'I don't mean that you did it, but you have the motive, you have the ability. You have enough power to get these things done. You have someone to protect.'

'Ignoring the insulting nature of your assertions, what if I am unable to tell you all you want to know?'

'Then the facts I have get sent straight to a news vid station. They'll be delighted to run a story on it.'

Melling took a paper hankie from a packet on his desk and wiped his forehead with it.

'And what if you're in no fit position to send this information?' he asked, very quietly. His pudgy finger flicked a button, a panel slid open on the top of the desk and he dropped the used hankie into it with scrupulous care.

A trickle of cold sweat ran down Jave's spine.

'Meaning?' he said.

'Do I have to make it clear? Meaning I could have you dropped out of this window here and now. It's a long way down. You'd have plenty of time to admire the view.'

'Two things,' said Jave. 'First, harming me won't stop the information getting to where it's intended to go. I've made sure of that. Secondly,' he glanced down at his pocket, 'this gerbil is loaded.'

Frid's head poked up out of the pocket of Jave's trenchcoat. His nose glowed red for a moment before emitting a wire-thin, bright red line that vaporised a letter opener.

'I is a dangerous dude,' he said, before disappearing back into the coat.

Melling Anson looked very angry.

'How dare you come into my office, threatening me!' he yelled. 'How dare you walk armed with a dangerous gerbil!' He *was* angry.

Jave grinned.

'I'll go then, shall I?' he said, getting up from his chair.

'Sit down!' roared Anson. 'And don't be such a fool. Look at the dirt!'

From a drawer beside his desk he drew out a small brush and a plastic bag and carefully swept the remains of the letter opener into the bag. Then, sliding back a metal hatch, he popped the bag into a small chute that ran down the left hand side of the desk into the floor.

Jave sat down.

There was a moment's pause while Anson calmed down. His huge jowls lost a little of their red colour and ceased to billow up and down like the spinnaker of a large yacht. Finally, he said, 'Well, that was most disagreeable. I dislike getting hot and bothered. And, surprise you though it may, I dislike violence intensely. Even if it is aimed at inanimate objects.'

'If it's any comfort to you,' said Jave, 'I'll make a donation to the deceased letter opener's trust fund.'

'And, above all of these, I dislike mess and dirt. You may have noticed, Mr Fleming, this room is clean.'

'Almost antiseptically.'

For a moment Anson looked pleased.

'Precisely,' he said. 'Germs, Mr Fleming, germs. Those are what we have to guard against. And where do they lurk? In dirt and mess.'

'You must meet my brother sometime,' said Jave. 'He has the biggest dirt collection in the northern hemisphere. Most of it is up his noses.'

'He sounds a most distasteful person.'

Anson flicked a finger in the direction of Jave's raincoat.

'I hope that rodent in there isn't verminous.'

A muffled oath came from Jave's pocket.

'He's perfectly healthy,' said Jave. 'Apart from the rabies.'

Melling started. Then he scowled at Jave.

'That was a joke, I trust.'

Jave leaned across the desk and smiled.

'Wouldn't you like to know?' he said.

Anson pulled another handkerchief from the dispenser on his desk and mopped his brow again.

'Most distressing,' he said. 'I need a drink.'

He punched a number, and from somewhere within his desk a glass of clear liquid appeared.

'Will you join me?' he asked.

'Thanks,' said Jave. 'I'll have a whisky.'

Anson grimaced.

'No alcohol, I'm afraid,' he said. 'I don't drink alcohol.'

'What do you do with it then – inject it?'

'Very funny.' Anson punched the number again. 'Here – try this.'

A glass of pale, clear liquid appeared, identical to the one that Anson was drinking.

Jave sipped it. It tasted good – fresh, clean and bright.

'What is it?' he asked.

'Water,' said Anson.

'Water? Like out of the taps?'

'No, Mr Fleming, definitely not like that which emerges from our taps. This is pure water. Not water that has been chemically treated by the many and varied strains of effluent that bob gaily up and down the reservoirs of this country. This is one hundred per cent pollutant free water. However, I believe our Prime Minister has steps in hand to help the water supply.' He drained his glass. 'Pure,' he said. 'Unlike so much of the business I have to deal with.

'Which brings me once again to the business in hand.'

He placed a small tissue coaster on the desk, on which he put, precisely in the middle, his glass of water.

'This photo. You have a copy, I presume?'

Jave took the copy of Abram Chones' school photo from his inside pocket and pushed it across the shiny surface of the desk towards the two bunches of pale, white bananas that Melling Anson would have called his hands.

Melling Anson stared at the photo for a moment, his tiny eyes glittering. He slid the copy back across the desk.

'And if I tell you what I know?'

Jave shrugged.

'The programme won't be featuring the Bishop, I guess.'

'I see.' Melling Anson stared at Jave, his eyes, tiny black balls, hard as iron. 'It appears I have no choice,' he said.

'Do you know what kind of business we have here, Mr Fleming?' he said. 'We sell ideas. We started very simply, many years ago. Started with game shows. You might not think them the most cerebral of entertainment. You might think ideas are alien to such shows as *Blind Chance* and *Who'll Whitewash Granny?* but each one was selling a consumerism that the viewers found most attractive.'

His huge hands opened a drawer in his desk, took out a glossy brochure and flipped it across the table.

'After a while the viewers seemed to tire of such gross, unbridled materialism, even though the prizes were, by any standards, impressive. The audiences grew bored with seeing two contestants fight their way through a series of rounds to win a small town in Belgium. They wanted something else.'

He paused for a moment.

'We found that something,' he said. 'Religion. Religion was what they wanted. Not actual religion – that only tends to get in the way of life. Real religion upsets things. No, what people wanted was a religion that helped them to live the way they wanted to live. A religion that enabled them to keep everything they earned. A religion that made them feel better about guilt.

'Bishop Lou Blynell has been at the forefront of such a movement. He has revolutionised the image of Christianity in this country. What was seen as a dull, fading, irrelevant faith for fanatics has, once more, been elevated to the status of this country's official religion. And all because of Lou Blynell. Don't you find that impressive?'

Jave swallowed a sip of his water.

'Personally,' he said, 'I can't stand the zeke.'

Anson laughed.

'But you, Mr Fleming, are so very unusual. You strike me, if you will forgive me, as a bit of an anachronism. The way you dress, for example. Your role models are approximately one hundred years old. I suspect your mind-set is similarly anachronistic. If, for example, I offered you many millions of ECUs for that photo, you would refuse, wouldn't you?'

'Why don't you try it?' asked Jave. 'I might surprise you.'

'No, Mr Fleming, you wouldn't surprise me one iota. I know people, you see. And I know that tucked away in that out-of-date mind-set that fills the space between your ears, you have a concept of honour. It is curious that you should come here looking for Abram Chones. You have so much in common.'

'You met him then?'

'Oh yes,' said Anson, very quietly. 'I met Abram Chones.'

'When was this?'

'Some days back. I forget the precise date, but I can find it if you want.' Jave shook his head and Anson continued. 'Mr Chones was brought here by the Reverend Shamworth. He came to me with the same story as you have just told me only, unlike you, Mr Fleming, he was a little more vague about the proof. All he would say was that he had known Lou Blynell as a boy. Before he called himself Lou Blynell.

'You understand my position, of course. I have hundreds of billions of ECUs riding on the promotion of the Bishop of Swindonopolis to Archbishop. He is already a much watched, much merchandised figure, worth a great deal of money. That value would triple if he were to become, what one might term, the "top man".'

'Head honcho, top banana...ouch!' Anson didn't appear to notice Jave strike the lump in his pocket.

'Naturally, I couldn't let a man like Mr Chones wander around damaging valuable property,' he continued. 'So I tried to bargain with him.'

There was a pause. With not a little effort, Melling Anson lifted himself from the chair and waddled the couple of paces to the window. He gazed out over Swindonopolis.

'You know,' said Anson, 'I don't think Abram Chones did know the whole truth. He knew that the Bishop had once been Charlie Harris, and he knew that was somehow important. But he knew nothing more than that. I don't think he knew why we wouldn't want that out in the open.'

Jave stared at Anson's back.

'You mean he didn't know that Harris was involved in the black market? He didn't know all that stuff about the drugs?'

'I think not,' Anson replied. 'Of course, I can't be certain.... But Mr Chones was not the type of man who would have kept that to himself. He would have told everyone.'

'So why did he come here?'

'The Reverend Shamworth persuaded him to come. He had gone into her church, you see, and seen our Bishop on the huge screen during one of his television spectaculars. I believe Mr Chones mentioned to the clerical lady that the man's name was really Charlie Harris. The Reverend Shamworth immediately contacted me to ask what this meant.'

'So she didn't know about Harris either?'

'No. And she, you must understand, was a keen supporter of the Bishop.'

'Yes, I know.'

'She reported this occurrence to me and I asked her to bring Mr Chones along. Naturally, I played my cards close to my chest. I did not let on what the Bishop's past had been. I explained to Mr Chones that the Bishop had reasons for wanting to keep that side of things hidden.'

Melling Anson turned away from the window and faced Jave. He clasped his hands behind his back. Jave wondered how he could reach.

'A remarkable man, Mr Chones,' Anson continued. 'Quite remarkable. I offered him a great deal of money to keep the fact to himself. But he refused. He told me that he was not concerned with money, but the truth. He didn't think that the Bishop was telling the truth in his sermons. I don't mean the truth about his identity, but the truth about Christianity. That was all that concerned Mr Chones.'

'So what happened?'

'He left. With the Reverend Shamworth.'

There was silence.

'That's all?'

'If you mean, did we come to an agreement, we did.

Abram Chones promised not to let people know what the Bishop's real name was.'

'How did you make him promise?'

'I asked him to.'

'What?'

'Mr Fleming, you don't understand the type of man Mr Chones was. He was a devout Christian; a Christian of a type which is rarely seen today. You have no doubt seen pictures of him. He has about him – had about him – an air, almost of a prophet. A monk of some sort. To him it was simple. He had seen his old school friend Charlie Harris on the screen. He had been taken to meet me. I told him that the Bishop had painful reasons for changing his name and Mr Chones accepted that. He was not interested in money.

'Mr Chones seemed content. He told me that he thought the Bishop's teaching was wrong and that he would do all he could to tell the truth as he saw it. But he seemed to think it an act of charity to keep the name of Charlie Harris to himself.'

'Let me get this straight,' said Jave. His mind was whirring around and all the theories that he had been building were slowly disintegrating. 'He just left it at that?'

'At that stage, yes.'

'What do you mean "at that stage"?'

Melling Anson walked slowly back to the chair. He lowered himself into it and pulled open a drawer at the side from which he took a brown envelope.

'Once Mr Chones and the vicar had left, I took immediate action. I am not without influence, so I sought to protect myself from further harassment of this sort.

'I checked that all documentary evidence had been destroyed. There had once been a file at Social Security, but my contacts assured me that it had been destroyed many years ago. I thought it very likely that the matter would be closed. You must understand that there was something about Abram Chones that was...well, unusual. It may be a kind of madness. But for the moment I had no reason to distrust him.

'Some days went by and then I received a communication from the Reverend Shamworth. She seemed upset. She told me that Mr Chones' lorry had been firebombed. She seemed to think I had something to do with it.'

'And had you?'

'Ah.' The dead black eyes glittered. 'The sixty-four thousand ECU question. No, Mr Fleming, I had no hand in that. I neither ordered such an action to be taken nor did I approach Mr Chones' abode in the dead of night with a molotov cocktail and some blue touchpaper to light. Of course, you are unlikely to believe me, whatever I say. After all, if I *had* taken action against Mr Chones, I would hardly admit to it now, would I? But I believed him, you see. And anyway, firebombing people is hardly my style. A little too "urban guerilla" – don't you agree?'

He chuckled drily, cheeks flapping.

'That being so, I reassured the good lady that I had nothing to do with it. But that was not the end of the story. A few days after that the Reverend Shamworth appeared again. This time she had a demand with her. A written demand. It was for money. To be precise, the very amount of money I had offered Mr Chones some time before.'

'She wanted the money?'

'No. She had been approached by someone else.'

Jave thought for a moment then said, 'Marc Shoeban.'

'The very same. Apparently, this Mr Shoeban had written to the Reverend Shamworth, only this time with more information that Mr Chones had. Mr Shoeban, it appeared, knew all.'

'What did you do?'

'Do? I paid. A one-off cash payment. I needed to buy some time, you see. I told the vicar to find out what she could about Marc Shoeban; to keep an eye on him. In the meantime, I paid him a substantial sum.'

He turned his eyes on Jave again.

'Despite what you think, Mr Fleming, I am not a thug nor a mobster. I am the head of a corporation.'

'Is there a difference?'

'Oh yes. Very much so. Our ways are so much more subtle than murder.'

'So – Shoeban got the money. How was it delivered?'

'I did not worry myself with that.'

'Shamworth took it.'

'As you say. She was in charge of the delivery.'

'And have you heard anything since?'

'I am glad to say not. I did, however, ensure that our technicians took the opportunity to place a simple tracing device in the cash payment. Other operatives were then directed to follow this signal once Reverend Shamworth had delivered the money.'

Jave held his breath.

'So you know where he is?'

Anson looked angry.

'I regret not. The tracing device was tracked to a certain area and then it just disappeared.'

'You lost him?'

'I am afraid so. Believe me, the responsible parties were made aware of my displeasure.'

Yes, thought Jave. I imagine they were.

'So whereabouts did you lose him?'

'Mr Shoeban, it appears, went to ground. In inner London.'

He opened the same drawer again and pulled out a report. He turned a few pages with his thick fingers until he reached the relevant paragraph. 'Co-ordinates J23/45. The area once known as Belgravia.'

'But on the ground level.'

'Indeed. Our technicians believe he must have checked the package there and found the device. Since that device was most carefully hidden, we must assume that Marc Shoeban was a resourceful man, with a lot of experience at this sort of thing.'

'And that was the last you heard of him?'

'Absolutely. That was the last time I heard of the entire matter. Until, that is, you came with the most unwelcome and distressing news about the poor Reverend's untimely demise.' He looked distressed. 'You are certain it was not a mechanical accident?'

'Pretty certain,' said Jave. 'There's nothing on a C27 to blow up. It doesn't carry any combustible fuel. There's nothing more you can tell me about Shoeban?'

'I am afraid not. I never met the man. He dealt purely with the Reverend.'

There was a pause. Again, Anson brought the tips of his fingers together and blew on them gently. For a big man, a very big man, he had a surprising delicacy of movement – precise and almost clinical. Everything in his office was neat to the point of sterility. Dressed as he was, entirely in white, it was like meeting an iceberg.

'I trust I have fulfilled my part of the bargain?' he enquired, eyeing Jave through half-closed eyelids.

'For the moment,' said Jave. 'Unless I can think of anything more to ask.'

'And the pictures?'

'What about them?'

'I want them. All of them.'

'They're not mine to give. Don't worry. They won't be sent anywhere. You have my word.'

Anson looked coolly at Jave.

'You had better be telling the truth, Mr Fleming,' he said. 'I don't like people who lie to me. And I hate to lose.'

Framed by a gentle smile, the words were painted over the top of a harsh cruelty. Melling Anson was obviously a man who never forgot, or forgave, an injury.

'You have my word,' said Jave again.

'So, will you go after this elusive Marc Shoeban?'

Jave thought for a moment. The obvious move would be to lie. Anson wouldn't want Jave to muddy the water. As far as Anson was concerned, Shoeban was safer underground.

'Well,' said Jave, 'it sounds like he's a professional. When a professional doesn't want to be found, that's a pretty difficult job. And anyway, I don't suppose you'd really want the man brought to justice.'

'On the contrary,' said Melling Anson. 'I would welcome the chance to mete out some justice to Marc Shoeban. But not, of course, in public. If you do intend to find him, then I would urge you to be careful, Mr Fleming. You have given me your word about the Bishop and, for some strange reason, I believe you. But I would be very displeased if you handed Shoeban over to the authorities, only for him to reveal all he knew. Yes...' Anson released the word like a hiss. For a moment Jave thought he had a puncture. 'I would be very unhappy indeed.'

'I see. Well, if I ever bump into him, I'll let you know.'

Melling Anson smiled.

'Do that,' he said. 'I would see you were well rewarded.'

Jave rose from his chair. He turned and waded back through the carpet to the plexi-glass door at the other end of the room. As he walked towards it the massed banks of vid screens flashed into life again, flooding the white room with colour and light and noise.

'You know, Mr Fleming...'

Jave turned in the doorway and looked back at the huge man slumped in the vast leather chair, his massive fingers resting delicately on the controls of a video console.

'You are very like Mr Chones. You remind me of him. You, like he, do not seem to belong to this era. Take care that you do not suffer the same fate.'

The volume rose from the vid screens and the door hissed shut. Melling Anson was once again alone in his clean, clean room.

22

'So what do you think?'

Jave sat in the flat, the photos in his hand. He was drinking a cup of syntho-coffee.

'Think about what?'

Jave sighed and said to his brother, 'Haven't you been listening? About all that Anson said.'

'I think he sounds like a real bazzer. Anyone who makes money out of the barff Bishop has got to be a 24-carat creepoid.'

'Sometimes,' said Jave, 'I can't understand a word you say.'

'That's just my natural linguistic creativity.'

'No – it's because you're a prat.'

Frid sat in a corner, chewing a large monkey nut.

'The guy weren't lying. Not as far as I could tell. Heartbeat steady and all that jive.'

'I shouldn't go by that necessarily,' said Jave. 'Anson could lie his way out of anything. He's had years of practice.'

He drained his coffee.

'Nice water though,' he added. He closed his eyes and tried to think back to the facts that Anson had given him.

'What does it all boil down to?' he murmured.

'Steam?' suggested Kevving.

'What?'

'I thought you were still talking about the water.'

'Listen,' said Jave, ignoring him, 'it's got to be this Shoeban guy. He's the key. Here's how it goes. Somehow, he hears about Charlie Harris from Abram Chones. Realising what the implications are for blackmail, he kills Chones and proceeds to work through Shamworth. Then, when Shamworth has done her job as message boy, he kills her as well and disappears.'

'What about MacWhirter?'

'Yes, what about him?'

Kevving screwed his eyes up tight and wrinkled his noses.

'I've just had a thought,' he said.

'Good grief.'

'That old bazzer you talked to in the Department this morning. Didn't he say something about the guy whom they nabbed for Charlie Harris' deals? The guy who distributed the stuff?'

'So?'

'So, wasn't this guy–this distributor–wasn't he Scottish?'

Jave stared at his brother, thunderstruck.

'Yes!' he said. 'That's right. What if that had been MacWhirter? He'd have been in on the deal. He'd have been able to fill in the missing details on Harris' career. He and Shoeban must have been working on this together. And then Shoeban got greedy.'

He shrugged. 'Oh, what does it matter, anyway? We don't know where Shoeban is, do we? I'm not even sure if we want to find him.'

'What?' squealed Kevving, leaping to his feet. 'And waste all these hours of detective work?'

'All right, Sherlock Holmes, let's say we do want to find the guy; where do we start?'

Kevving pulled the A-Z out of his pocket and said, 'I've been thinking about that.'

Jave laughed. 'You're not still on about that book, are you?'

'Well, it's a clue.'

'Not necessarily. It could be years old.'

'It could still be a clue.'

'All right, have it your own way. Let's pool what we've got about Shoeban. You got the photos back?'

'Yeah.'

'Whoever you sent all the stuff to must think you're mad, giving the stuff and then taking it back.'

'Nah, she's used to me doing weird stuff. It goes with the noses.'

He dragged over the low plastic coffee table and put down on it a plastic file from which he took the residential permit of Shoeban, pale, with dark hair and dark sunglasses, the photo of Abram Chones they had found in the lorry and the picture of Abram Chones' college class.

Kevving picked up the gram of Chones.

'Where'd you find this?' he asked.

'In Shoeban's lorry,' Jave replied, 'in the wardrobe. I made a note of it.'

He turned the photo over to reveal the note he had made on the back.

Kevving held it in his hand and stared at the words 'Wardrobe. Marc Shoeban's Lorry-House' as if in shock.

'When did you write this?' he asked.

'This afternoon. In Shoeban's place.'

Kevving leaped to his feet and gave an ear-splitting yell.

'I knew it!' he shouted. 'I knew it!'

'What? What is it?'

'Look!'

Excitedly he pointed to the writing on the back of the gram.

'What about it? Have I spelled something wrong?'
'The pen!' said Kevving.
He picked up the A-Z and opened it at the page where he had found the name.
'Look!' said Kevving. 'You see?'
Jave looked at the page and then at the photo.
'I don't...' he began. Then he realised. 'The writing,' he said. 'It's the same ink.'
'Exactly. Which means that Shoeban himself marked on this A-Z recently.'
Jave took the A-Z and stared at the name. 'So who is Vic Stockwell? Frid?'
'Not me,' said Frid.
'No, I meant, do you know?'
Something in Frid whirred slightly.
'No such person registered in London,' he said.
'Vic. Old-fashioned name,' commented Jave. 'Short for Victor.'
'Could be short for Victoria,' suggested Kevving.
'Could be...but Victoria is usually shortened to Vicky. No, I think we're looking for a Victor here. Not that that helps as there's no such person in London.'
He threw the book down on the table.
'What's the use?' he said. 'All the evidence seems to suggest that Shoeban is a professional blackmailer. If that's so, then he wouldn't be likely to have left anything around which would allow us to trace him. The name probably doesn't mean anything at all.'
There was a buzz at the door of the flat followed by a grating noise.
'Your door sounds rusty,' said Kevving.
'That's not the door. It's Chanis' voice at the entry phone.'
Jave said, 'OK,' and the flat automatically opened the door to allow Chanis in.
She was wearing a dark green disposable plasti-dress

with the obligatory gold twenty-four hole Doc Marten's. Her long dark hair hung down over one eye.

'Veronica Lake,' said Jave.

'Sorry?' she asked.

Jave went bright crimson.

'Just thinking aloud – you, er, you looked like Veronica Lake. She used to be a star a long time ago. When they had films instead of vids and all that.'

'I see.' Chanis laughed. 'No one's ever called me Veronica Lake before. I thought it was the name of a place.'

'No, no, she was a film star. Very beautiful.'

Chanis looked down for a moment.

'Thank you,' she said.

'Never mind Veronica Lake,' interrupted Kevving. 'It's Vic Stockwell I'm worried about.'

Chanis looked confused.

'Who?' she asked.

'It's perfectly simple,' said Kevving. 'Vic Stockwell is in this book. Written. And the colour he is is exactly the same as the colour on the back of the gram. So that makes him recent. So he must mean something. See?'

Chanis sat down.

'No,' she said.

'I'll get you a coffee,' said Jave.

While punching in the numbers on the tube, he explained to Chanis what they had been doing during the day.

'So you see,' he said, 'it very much looks like your father was killed by someone because he knew Charlie Harris. That someone is probably a man named Marc Shoeban. He is, in all likelihood, a professional criminal, judging by the methods he used, and the way he disappeared.'

He handed the cup to Chanis. Her hand shook slightly.

'I'm sorry,' he said. 'I shouldn't be putting it like this. Stupid of me.'

'No, I'm all right,' croaked Chanis. 'It's just, well I didn't know it was all going to be like this. I suppose I thought it would be sort of cleaner, you know? Instead it's all about blackmail and big money. It just seems so unfair. They killed him just because he went to school with someone.'

She started to cry. Soft, silent tears that dribbled down her face to drop onto her lap. 'I'm sorry.'

'No, no, it's perfectly all right,' said Jave. He went to the kitchen and found a tissue for her.

'Here.'

Chanis dried her eyes.

'Where do we find this Marc Shoeban?' she asked.

'Are you sure you really want to?'

'Why shouldn't I?'

'Well, for a number of reasons. First it's going to be very difficult. I don't know exactly where he is and I'm not even sure how to go about finding him. Secondly, even if we do find him, he could well prove to be dangerous. Thirdly, what would we do with him?'

Chanis dabbed at her eyes with the now extremely soggy lump of Kleenex.

'We don't have to do anything with him,' she said. 'I just want to see him. I don't know....' She looked up at Jave appealingly. 'Is that stupid?'

'No. Not necessarily. Not if it will help you come to terms with the situation. If it's catharsis you're after, meeting him would probably give you a bucketful of the stuff. It's just that, well, Shoeban is pretty likely to be some kind of criminal. Your father won't be the first person he's killed in his life, no doubt. Even if we can find him, I doubt you'll find it a very satisfying experience. I'm just worried it would leave you worse off than before.'

'It won't,' said Chanis. 'I can feel it.'

'Yes, well. Anyway.' Jave struggled on. 'Then the only clue we've got to his whereabouts is the co-ordinate that Anson gave us.'

'J23/45,' said Frid. 'The turf used to be called Belgravia.

Just south of the old Palace Museum of Monarchy.'

'Right. He went to ground somewhere down there. I'll go down there and ask around. See if we can pick up some traces of this Stockwell guy as well.'

'So that's where we go,' said Kevving.

'We?' enquired Jave.

'Well, yeah,' said Kevving. 'I mean you're going to need some protection, aren't you?'

'I have protection. I have a sawn-off gerbil.'

'Well, more protection then.'

'Kevving, you are about as much protection as a Plasticine crash helmet.'

'Don't worry, we'll be all right,' Kevving assured him.

'Yes,' agreed Chanis. 'We'll be all right.'

'Oh all right, I suppose so....' A thought hit Jave like a bullet. 'What do you mean "we"?' he asked, wheeling round to face Chanis.

'Is there an echo in here?' said Frid, in the corner.

Chanis looked at Jave with wide-eyed innocence and asked, 'Well, you don't think that I'm going to miss out on this, do you? I've got to meet him down there, or it won't be cathartic.'

'No,' said Jave, resolutely. 'No, no, no, no, no. Definitely not. Absolutely and totally and utterly not. It's bad enough having Super Nostril along for the ride, without his sidekick as well.'

Chanis looked defiantly innocent.

'Look – this is the ground level we're talking about here. It's dangerous! It's not a nice place to visit.' He crossed his arms resolutely. 'No. You are not coming to the ground with me tomorrow. Either of you.'

He stared at them grimly.

'And that's final.'

[illegible] south of the old Palace Museum [illegible]
"Right, the [illegible] to [illegible] somewhere [illegible] I'll [illegible] down there and ask [illegible]. See if we can [illegible] something [illegible]. [illegible] will [illegible] you."
"[illegible] when [illegible]," said [illegible].
[illegible]
"Well, [illegible] the [illegible] to [illegible] to [illegible] [illegible]?"
"I have [illegible] and I have [illegible] to [illegible]."
"Well [illegible] [illegible] then."
[illegible] as [illegible]
[illegible]
"Don't [illegible]," [illegible].
"Yes, [illegible] home. [illegible] all right."
"On all [illegible] [illegible] [illegible]
[illegible] the [illegible] he asked [illegible]
[illegible]
"[illegible] in [illegible] [illegible]."
[illegible] and [illegible] and
[illegible] [illegible] to [illegible]
on [illegible] [illegible]
with the [illegible]."
"No, [illegible] [illegible]. Both
[illegible] and [illegible]
[illegible]
[illegible]
[illegible]
[illegible]
[illegible] his
[illegible]
[illegible] other days."
He [illegible].
"And [illegible] fool."

THE FIFTH DAY

23

'Why is she here?' hissed Jave. The boy next to him scratched his noses.

'Relax, bruvv,' said Kevving. 'She's looking for adventure.'

'This is a dangerous part of London,' said Jave. 'Round here they spell adventure "D-E-A-D". That's if they can spell anything. That's if they can even write.'

'All right, then maybe it's some kind of pilgrimage or something. Catharsis and all that.'

Jave looked at the slim, beautiful girl hunched up in the back of his air car.

She smiled at him.

'Where do we start?' she grated.

He winced slightly. Not for the first time, Jave cursed the faulty genetic engineering kits.

'So near and yet so far,' he muttered to himself.

'I'm sorry?' said Chanis.

'Don't keep saying that,' said Jave. 'You keep saying, "I'm sorry." There's no need.'

She laughed.

'Look,' he said. 'I'm serious. You shouldn't be here. Frid and I should be handling this.'

The gerbil, who had been sitting on Jave's shoulders

listening to his laser-disc walkman, nodded.

'Right on, baby,' he said. 'When the going gets tough, the tough get going.'

Chanis looked appealingly at Jave.

'But he killed my father,' she croaked.

'Exactly. The man we're after is a killer. A vicious, greedy killer. Which is precisely why you shouldn't be here.'

Jave turned to his brother, who was grinning broadly.

'This is going to be an experience,' said Kevving.

Jave groaned, 'Oh, I hope not.'

They had landed on a platform about ten metres above the street.

The platform was metal and square – a security post, where the state police came to shoot people during riots. (They tended to come and shoot people when there wasn't a riot, as well.) From the platform some retractable metal steps led down to the ground.

'Right then,' said Jave, making towards the metal steps. 'Let's go.'

London in the mid-twenty-first century was an OK place to live, as long as you were at a certain height. If you were not at that height, it was a very nasty place to live.

The height in question, was somewhere about thirty metres up, where the perspex and concrete walkways started crossing from one gleaming tower block to another; where the lifts always stopped; where the Sinclair C27s hovered outside windows waiting to whisk people away to another high-altitude location.

Up there, it was a very nice life. Of course, property prices were high, especially the higher you went. So if you couldn't afford it for some reason – sickness, old age, misfortune – you went the way of all rubbish. Down to the ground.

On the ground, London was a dirty, squalid ghetto fifty miles wide, where people lived in houses constructed from whatever they could find. The rubbish that cascaded down on them each morning was used to build their homes – shanty towns of cardboard cartons and plastic bottles; villages of refuse; whole communities living in other people's waste. The ghetto had once been packed to overflowing with people, but disease, hunger and old age had inevitably taken their toll, and nowadays the ground was, if not sparsely populated, then less heavily populated than it had been. Consequently, many of the make-do hovels that Chanis, Jave, Frid and Kevving were passing were empty and cold.

Of course, there were still some actual buildings at ground level – historical buildings like the Palace Museum of Monarchy, or the Ex-Houses of Parliament. But they were protected from the squalor around them by huge plexi-glass domes which completely encased them, and into which walkways entered at a thirty metre height, to be met by lift-shafts which would whisk people down to visit. But these historical buildings were the exception. The rest of the ground level was shunned by most of the city-dwellers. It was not their patch. It was the country below them. It was a wildlife reservation for the poor.

Jave splashed his way through another puddle of something he preferred not to think about.

Squeezing through a gap between the concrete and steel of a tower block and a shack made mostly from packing cases, they started up a muddy street.

They had been walking through fetid streets for some hours now. Even though it was midday, it was dark. Little light filtered down to this level. What light there was, had to squeeze between the walkways that formed a roof ten storeys above them. The first time Jave had visited the ground level, he had been reminded of old vids of the tropical rainforest. Here, there were the same effects of weak light filtering through to the ground; the same heat and sweltering humidity. The only thing missing was the wildlife. Down here, there were only rats, insects and the poor.

'Are these tower blocks?' asked Chanis as they rounded another huge, concrete and steel frame.

'The bases of tower blocks,' explained Jave.

'But they're falling apart. They're rotting!' exclaimed Chanis. 'And up there, the buildings are so clean!'

'Yeah, but up there, there are robots to attend to that sort of thing. Down here, no one cares. Down here, no one bothers to paint over the cracks.'

Indeed, down at ground level, the buildings that gleamed so brightly could be seen from an entirely different perspective. As the small group made their way through the cramped streets that wound round the bases of the huge tower blocks, they could see quite clearly that the buildings which looked so clean higher up, had rotten, filthy foundations. The concrete walls, against which many wood and cardboard shacks leaned, were greened with mould and slimy with water. Some of the buildings had steel girders visible, where the rotting concrete had fallen away from the metal frame. The rusty red girders gaped out from beneath the plaster like broken and diseased bones jutting out through rotting skin.

Jave looked up. Somewhere above him the world was bright and clean and spacious. But not here.

They splashed on, through streets that were dirty, stinking, dark and oven-hot. Steam rose from drains and gutters. Water dropped from the lips of the walkways in thin, glass-like sheets.

A hand reached out and grabbed Jave's coat.

'Please...' said a voice.

The thin, emaciated woman squatted at the side of the street in a shelter made from an old piece of cardboard and a sheet of thin plastic packaging material.

'Give us some money,' she said, through cracked lips. 'I'll do anything you want.' She was clutching a baby and both of them were dressed in filthy, oily rags. The woman's hair was thin and dry, and there were large bald patches on her head through lack of nourishment. It was impossible to tell where her clothes ended and her skin began; both were equally begrimed and blackened.

As she looked up, Jave found himself staring into her eyes.

There was nothing there. And her baby didn't move.

Jave pulled his coat out from her grasping, twig-like fingers and walked on.

'Oughtn't we to do something?' said Chanis, looking behind her at the figure still squatting on the ground.

'What?' asked Jave.

'Help her, or something....'

'We can't.'

'Why not?'

Jave turned and looked at the girl.

'A very simple reason,' said Jave. 'She's a drop in the ocean. Help her and there's another load behind her, forming the queue. Helping her doesn't solve the problem, because you can't solve the problem. It's too big.'

Chanis looked at him.

'That's not a reason,' she replied. 'That's an excuse.'

Jave wiped the sweat out of his eyes. 'We're wasting time,' he said.

From his pocket he took out the A-Z. The moisture in the air made the pages sticky and limp and difficult to separate. He turned to the page with the writing on. The dampness in the air had caused the writing to run. In the darkness it looked like a stain. In the darkness it looked like blood. Jave closed the book and put it back into his pocket.

'Difficult to tell where we are,' he said. 'Everything's changed in the past thirty years. None of the old street patterns are the same. You got any idea, Frid?'

'No problem, dude-baby,' said Frid. 'I is on the case. Just a matter of marking co-ordinates. Next street up and then left should take us where we want to go.'

'Which assumes that there's anything at all to find at those co-ordinates.'

'You gotta think positive, man,' said Frid. 'Ac-cent-chew-ate the positive, ee-lim-in-ate the negative, like the man said.'

'Yeah. Think positive,' said Jave grimly. He looked back at Chanis and his brother. Kevving was looking about him with almost a look of wonder on his face. Chanis just looked sad. 'Come on,' he said.

They fought their way further up the street until they came to a place where the pathways thinned to pass between two broken down caravans that had once, according to the legends on their sides, sold 'the best kebab in South London'. Behind them a grille was belting out steam. Somewhere, deep within the gargantuan building the heating system was hard at work, providing hot water for the Shower-o-Matics and warmth for the flats that could be found ten storeys above them. Down here, all they got was hot, stinking steam.

Jave turned. Their way was blocked by two figures. The first was a small, weasel-like man, who appeared to be dressed in the remains of a dog. Over his shoulder, the head of the animal gaped, like a grotesque on a cathedral, its eyes filled with two large, glass jewels. Next to him, nearly seven feet tall, there stood a monster with the muscles of a gorilla.

A prickle of fear raced down Jave's spine as he real ised, with horror, that Kevving was talking to them.

'We go to this great church, see?' said Kevving. 'You ever thought about Christianity?'

The gorilla looked at Kevving. It was obviously some

time since he had thought of anything at all.

'What?' he said.

Jave rushed to the rescue.

'Ha-ha,' he laughed. 'Just his joke.'

'I'm telling them about church,' said Kevving.

'This is not the time,' hissed Jave.

The men looked at them.

'Nice,' said the small man. 'Very nice.' The tip of his tongue flicked across his thin lips leaving tiny bubbles of saliva. He was not looking at them.

'How much?' he said to Jave.

'What?'

'The girl. How much?'

Jave felt Chanis move behind him.

'There's been some mistake...' he said.

'There certainly has.' The weasel had a voice that whined like an insect in flight. 'This is my patch. You're trespassing. Isn't that right, Mikey?'

'Er...yuh,' said Mikey. 'His patch.'

'Nice girl,' said the weasel. 'Nice merchandise. Top dweller, ain't she. Plenty of meat. Ain't that right, Mikey?'

'Yuh. Meat.'

'We don't want any trouble,' said Jave.

Suddenly, there was a fluid movement from beneath the weasel's coat and he was holding a knife. 'No trouble at all,' he said.

'Look,' said Kevving. 'There's obviously a lack of communication here. Why don't we sit down and talk about it?'

He smiled his best smile and wrinkled his noses endearingly.

The gorilla responded to this loveable sight by grabbing Kevving's throat and lifting him off the ground.

'Uggghhkkkknnnnnnnck!' said Kevving, not really at his most eloquent.

'Frid!' said Jave. There was a hum from the gerbil on his shoulder and Frid's nose glowed red. A thin band of light shot out and burned into the weasel's hand.

'Owwwww!' yelled the weasel, dropping the knife and rubbing his wrist. Just to annoy him, Frid shot the other wrist as well, leaving the injured man nothing to rub with. Bellowing with rage, he charged at Jave, head down. Jave waited till the last moment before sidestepping and allowing the man to collide with a pile of garbage, behind which was a large concrete wall.

Jave picked up the knife.

'Oi!' he called. 'Ugly.'

The gorilla looked at Jave. Then he looked at the knife. Then Jave kicked him in what he judged to be the place where it would hurt the most.

It took a few moments for Mikey's brain to transmit the pain from his lower abdomen to his brain.

'Uh...ouch!' he said. Dropping Kevving on the ground, he moved towards Jave, one hand flailing dangerously, the other clutching his groin.

He had almost reached Jave when Frid lasered him in the foot. This caused Mikey to stop dead in his tracks, while he attempted to come to terms with the fact that his right foot was on fire. Then he fell over.

'Amateurs,' said Jave. He grabbed the weasel by the collar of his dog coat and pulled him from the garbage where he had crashed.

'That's not fair!' the weasel complained. 'You had lasers!'

'You all right, Kevving?' asked Chanis.

'He certainly wasn't very open to the gospel,' said Kevving, trying to push his neck back into shape.

The weasel looked up.

'So, all right, she's not for sale,' he said. '"No" would have sufficed.'

'All right, peabrain,' said Jave. 'Let's have a bit of help, now you've calmed down a bit. We're looking for someone.'

'Why should I help you?'

Jave twisted his collar and the man's eyes bulged.

'You are getting on my nerves,' he said.

'All right, all right!' said the weasel. Jave let the collar un-twist and the man rubbed his neck with his still sore hands. 'Skag me!' he said. 'Even the pansies are tough guys these days.'

Suddenly, behind them, Mikey gave a yell and staggered to his feet.

'Dat hurt!' he said, rushing towards them. Frid shot him in the other foot and the big man sort of swerved, like a car out of control, to crash into another pile of rubbish where he lay clutching his other foot now.

'The boy never learns,' said Frid.

'OK,' said Jave. He fished into his pocket and pulled out the residential card. 'We're looking for someone and we think he hangs out somewhere around here. His name's Shoeban. Marc Shoeban. Know him?'

The weasel licked his lips.

'Can't say I...' he began.

Jave twisted the collar again, and said, 'Don't even think of lying.'

'I...I never heard about the guy,' gasped the weasel. 'I don't know nothing!'

Jave thrust the residential card in the weasel's face, so that he could clearly see the picture of Shoeban.

'Ring any bells?'

'I never seen the bloke. I never heard of him.'

Jave let go of the weasel's collar.

'OK,' he said, 'that's all.'

He turned round and blinked, hard.

Mikey was sitting up on a packing crate and Chanis was rubbing his foot.

'How does that feel?' she said. The gorilla mumbled.

'Better?' asked Chanis. The gorilla nodded.

'Frid,' said Jave, 'what is she doing?'

'Man,' said the gerbil, 'I think you is not her favourite dude.'

'What are you doing?' asked Jave.

Chanis gave him a look of scorn.

'I suppose you're proud of yourself,' she said.

'What?'

'Kicking and shooting and nearly choking people to death. I suppose you enjoy that.'

'What do you mean? These guys attacked us! With a knife. And a complete and frequently used set of muscles. What was I supposed to do?'

'I don't like violence!' said Chanis.

'Lady's got a point,' said the weasel, from his seat among the garbage. 'Can I have my knife back?'

'Shut up!' Jave turned back to Chanis. 'I don't believe you,' he said. 'I just saved you from a fate several times worse than death. Do you know what this guy uses women for?'

'Hey, hold on a bazzin' minute,' said the weasel. 'I'm just a dealer. I never touch the merchandise!'

'I can guess,' said Chanis. 'But two wrongs don't make a right.'

'Oh great!' said Jave angrily. 'Brilliant. Skagging marvellous!'

'And don't swear.'

'Listen, girlie,' shouted Jave. 'I'll skagging swear if I skagging well want to. I never asked you to come with me. I didn't want you here in the first place. You and the phantom nose over there just get in the way. But, if you want your dad's murder solved, then we do it my way. My way, do you hear? Swearing and violence and all.'

He stood staring at Chanis, breathing heavily. There was a strained silence.

'Er...can I have my knife back?' asked the weasel.

'No, you cannot have your snorking knife back!' yelled Jave.

'I only asked,' said the weasel. 'No need to shout.'

Chanis turned away and gave the gorilla's foot a final rub.

'You know,' she said to him, 'your feet are in a terrible condition. You ought to see a chiropodist.'

'I don't believe this,' said Jave. He turned to the weasel. 'Can you believe her?' he said. 'This is ground level, sweetheart,' he said. 'They don't even have doctors here, let alone chiropodists. When it's an everyday struggle to keep alive, the odd hanging toenail doesn't seem to matter much.'

'Well there ought to be something done about it,' said Chanis. 'It's basic health care.'

Mikey muttered something.

'What did you say?' said Chanis.

'Health.' said Mikey. 'Doctor. Shoeban.'

Jave stared at him. His brain juddered to a halt. Then, very slowly, it started up again.

'Did he just say Shoeban?' he asked.

The weasel shrugged his shoulders, causing the dog's head to execute a couple of quick nods.

'He's just repeating things,' he said.

Jave went to Mikey. 'Did you just say Shoeban?' he enquired.

Mikey looked sullenly at Jave.

'Not talk to you,' he said. 'Burned Mikey's foot.'

'Now listen, brain cell,' said Jave.

'Take no notice of him,' said Chanis to Mikey. 'You talk to me. Do you know this Shoeban?'

Mikey looked uncertainly about him for a moment.

'Helped Mikey once. Mikey's tooth.'

Chanis smiled at him.

'Your tooth was hurting, was it?'

Mikey nodded.

'Shoeban in street,' he said. 'Gave Mikey pill.' He pulled back his lips to reveal the most disgusting set of teeth Jave had ever seen.

'Oook!' said Mikey.

'Very nice,' said Chanis. 'You have got good teeth now. I hope you brush them.'

Mikey nodded. 'Shoeban say brush. Mikey brush.'

'This Shoeban,' said Jave. 'Is this him?'

Mikey looked at the card and laughed. He said, 'Mikey not talk to you. You stupid.'

'That's the pot calling the kettle black,' murmured the weasel.

'Anyway. Picture all wrong.'

'Wrong?' said Jave. 'What do you mean wrong?'

'Shoeban not look like that,' said Mikey. 'You stupid.'

Jave stared at the picture on the card: the black glasses, the pale lips on even paler, drum-tight skin. Wasn't this Shoeban? Was this the wrong man?

'What did he look like, then?' said Jave.

'Mikey knows,' said the gorilla. 'Man in picture got black. Shoeban not got black.'

Jave looked at the picture again and a wave of anti-climax surged over him. The sunglasses! Of course. When he met Mikey, Shoeban hadn't been wearing sunglasses.

'Did you talk to him at all, Mikey?' said Chanis, helping the Neanderthal back into the huge shapeless lumps of plastic that he used as boots.

Mikey nodded. 'Mikey ask Shoeban where he come from. Shoeban say he a mixture. Then Shoeban go.'

'Mixture? What did he mean?'

Mikey shook his head. 'Dunno. Then he go.'

He finished pulling on his boots and looked up at Chanis and grinned triumphantly with teeth set at odd angles like old and broken gravestones.

'But he fix Mikey's tooth,' he added.

24

'Where have you been?' said Jave.

Jave, Chanis and Frid had forged their way, bad temperedly, past the decrepit caravans, and then turned left down a small alleyway. There, waiting for them, was Kevving.

'Well, I came on ahead a bit while you were chatting.'

'Chatting?' said Chanis. 'Only in between punches.'

'Chanis...' said Jave, but he couldn't say what he wanted to say. He was aware that his violence had angered her, but he couldn't think of anything else he could have done. Was it true what she said? Did he enjoy it?

'Oh,' said Kevving, plainly at a loss.

'Anyway, how are you now? Is your neck all right?'

'Yeah, no trubbs.' Kevving gestured around him. 'Great, isn't it?'

Ahead of them, there was a clearing between massive square bases of tower blocks. The light from above filtered down between the walkways in thin, sheet-like beams that flickered as, ten storeys above them, people walked across the walkways.

Ahead of them was what had once been a large canopy of steel and glass. It had since been vandalised or collapsed of its own old age, so that only remnants of the original structure remained. Underneath this a small village had grown up, cardboard and corrugated iron houses nestling unevenly against each other in a pile of shanty housing. Through the gloom, Jave could see people sitting outside the houses. Some were hanging out washing. Some were cooking over open fires. There were small knots of children playing on a pile of garbage over to the left.

'Poor people,' said Chanis.

'Do you reckon?' said Kevving. 'Yeah, maybe. But look – they're actually cooking and all that. They, like, know each other. I mean, radical.'

Jave saw what he meant. For all its poverty and squalor, this place had a sense of community. A sense of a people living together. A sense that had been lost for ever in the hermetically sealed, pre-packed life that was going on way above them, where everyone stopped outside their own window and where all goods were available at the touch of a button.

He looked beyond the cardboard village at the building which overshadowed the tiny community. The remains of this edifice were squeezed in between the bases of two enormous towers. The ruins had several entrances at ground level, or what had once been entrances – arches that led into the dark interior. Through the collapsed walls, Jave could see piles of rubbish and old, ruined masonry, above which there hovered the remains of a steel-framed roof. Now, the frame stood empty and rusting, the glass which had once covered it shattered and fallen. It looked like the branches of a tree in winter.

On the front of the building there were the remains of old signs. The biggest, now old and battered and weather-faded, read 'Victoria Station'.

'Where are we?' he asked Frid.

'We is where we is,' said the gerbil, enigmatically. 'We is where we's supposed to be.'

'You mean this is the place where Shoeban disappeared?'

'The very spot,' replied Frid.

Jave looked around him.

'He could be anywhere,' he said.

'What about in the shacks over there?' suggested Kevving.

'Could be. They might know something, at least. We know he's been seen around here.' Jave described to Kevving the information that Mikey had given them. 'Not that that's reliable,' he said. 'I mean, the guy had the attention span of a hat rack.' He looked at the huddle of buildings across the square. 'So, I guess we try over there first.'

'What are you going to do this time?' asked Chanis. 'Shoot or strangle? Or maybe you'd prefer something more refined like ripping off their ears.'

'Oh, for skag's sake!' exclaimed Jave. 'Don't start all that again. Why can't you understand? They wanted to buy you. I wish now I'd taken them up on their offer.'

'Ease up, bruvv,' said Kevving.

'And you were just as bad! The ape-man was warmly shaking you by the throat and what happens? I rescue you. The next minute you're off on another trek into the unknown. I mean, don't you ever think about me? About how I feel?'

Kevving looked shamefaced.

'Sorry, bruvv. Didn't know it would worry you.'

'Of course it worries me. It scares me stupid. This whole area scares me stupid. If it doesn't worry you two, that's because you don't know enough about it.'

'I didn't know you felt that way,' said Chanis.

'What way?'

'Well, so concerned.'

Jave turned away. 'I'm not concerned. It's a professional relationship, that's all.'

'Yes, well, I'm sorry I shouted at you. I know now that you were only doing what you thought best.' She laughed. 'And as for professional relationships, do you call all your clients Veronica Lake?'

There was a pause. Jave didn't answer her. 'Well, there's no need to sulk!' she said.

Jave waved his hand at her, and said, 'Shut up!'

'Charming!' she grated.

'Veronica Lake,' said Jave. 'What was it you said to me?'
'I said, "Do you call all of your clients..."'
'No, not just now!'
'Well, when?'
'Yesterday. When I called you Veronica Lake. You said something.'
'I don't know.'
'Well – think!' shouted Jave.
'All right, all right, I said, "Sorry?" I didn't understand you.'
'And then what?'
Jave was standing, staring into the distance, almost straining at the leash.
'I...I'm not sure. I think at first I thought you were talking about a lake. You know a place. Water.'
'That's it!' said Jave. 'I called you a name, and you thought I meant a place. Don't you see?'
'No. Should I?'
'That has to be it,' repeated Jave. He turned to his brother. 'Kevving, you're a genius,' he said.
'What took you so long to realise?' responded Kevving.
'Now come on.'
Jave grabbed Chanis by the hand and pulled her after him across the small clearing, kicking his way through the rubbish that had accumulated like fallen leaves on the floor. They made their way past the small conglomeration of huts and towards the shadowy ruins beyond.
As they passed the ramshackle huts and make-do accommodation, the few inhabitants retreated inside, like animals threatened by intruders.
'Hi!' shouted Kevving. 'Don't worry, we're not stopping. Just passing through.'
From within the cardboard-clad darkness, cold eyes watched them warily, ready to rush out and defend what little they had.

'See you later!' shouted Kevving giving a cheery wave.

It only took half a minute for them to pick their way through the debris and reach the front of the old, ruinous station.

Jave looked around him, through the dim, misty light. Way above them, the sun had made a brief appearance and, for a moment, the mist and gloom of the ground level was pierced with dancing shafts of light, shooting their way between the dark shadows of the walkways. For a moment, the ruin and squalor around them was illuminated by dancing, flickering strands, dappling the crumbling masonry and rotting plaster with yellow light.

A little to the right of where they stood was a set of railings which formed three sides of a rectangle. Above the railings was a sign, a red circle crossed through with a line. Jave strode up to it. Written on the sign were the words 'Victoria Underground'. Below this, enclosed by the railings, was a flight of steps, descending into darkness. Above the steps was another sign, hanging from a single, rusty bolt. 'Victoria Line', it read. 'Northbound for Green Park – Oxford Circus – Euston. Southbound for Vauxhall – Stockwell – Brixton.'

'There you are,' said Jave. '"Vic Stockwell" wasn't a person, but a place. Or between two places to be exact. The old tube line between Victoria and Stockwell.'

25

'He went down there?' said Chanis.

'Must have. That's how he seemed to disappear, you see.'

'So what do we do?'

'Well, er, I suppose we follow him.'

Jave looked at the entrance to the Underground with some trepidation. It was dark, dirty and full of refuse. Somehow it reminded Jave of his brother.

'Wow!' exclaimed Kevving. 'This place is bazzin' brilliant!' His four nostrils flared with excitement and suddenly Jave saw where the similarity lay. They too were dark, dirty and full of refuse.

'How can you say that?' Jave asked. 'It's filthy.'

'Yeah, but great atmosphere,' replied Kevving.

In the gloom, Jave could see a flight of stairs in the corner of the station entrance. The gerbil hummed.

'Scannin', baby,' said Frid. 'Them steps go way down.'

'Great,' said Jave, whose initial enthusiasm on finding 'Vic Stockwell' had now been somewhat tempered by the discovery of what 'Vic Stockwell' actually was.

'Hey, bruvv,' said Kevving, 'where's your spirit of adventure?'

'It's well hidden away,' said Jave. 'I keep it with other useless things, like my spirit of being totally killed.'

'We have to go,' croaked Chanis. Her voice echoed in the empty station entrance. 'The man who killed my father is down there somewhere.'

'Yeah,' said Jave. 'And what are we going to do if we catch him? Be nice to him? Overpower him with tea and biscuits?'

Chanis looked at him.

'You don't know, do you?' said Jave angrily. 'You haven't even thought about it.'

'I want to find the truth,' said Chanis.

'And what then?' said Jave. 'What are you going to do with the truth when you find it?'

Chanis turned away.

'Come on,' she said and started to descend the steps.

Chanis had brought a powerful torch with her. Jave had brought Frid, whose nose emitted a powerful beam that bounced off the walls and cast eerie shadows as they descended. Kevving, too, had come prepared. Or thought he had.

'I can't work out why this torch isn't working,' he said.

'Perhaps the batteries have gone,' suggested Jave.

'It doesn't use batteries. It's solar powered.'

Jave looked at his brother.

'A solar powered torch,' he said. 'Brilliant.'

A look of realisation came over Kevving's face. 'Of course!' he said. 'It's too dark. If only there was more light, the solar cells would work....'

'If there was more light you wouldn't need the torch in the first place, you stonking bazzer.'

'Oh yeah.'

There was a clatter as Kevving threw his torch away.

'Never wanted it anyway,' he said.

The stairs were old and rusty, but basically secure. They descended in a spiral ever lower, occasionally breaking into a straight passage before the spiralling descent continued. The walls, reflected in the flickering torchlight, were covered in old posters, their messages undimmed by time.

There were adverts for *Lord McCartney's Greatest Hits* (a forty CD set) and one that Jave realised must have capitalised on the first effects of global warming, that read: 'Holiday in Tropical Basingstoke.' There was even an old election poster: 'Vote for the PM,' it said. 'She's got a lot of bottle.'

By 2025 this was, of course, literally true.

When she returned to power in the dying embers of the twentieth century, a political myth had reached its fruition. She, whom they rejected, had returned from the dead. She was seen as the only one who could renew Britain, the only person who could halt the long slide into obscurity and ruin.

And there was no doubt that the PM did it. The death

of the empire was, if not reversed, then at least halted. The country had given her the call and she had not been found wanting.

But there was no doubt that a return to the seat of power for a lady of her age took its toll. Early in the new millennium, people noticed that she was beginning to show her age. She was not getting around as much as she used to. She no longer clutched the handbag with her accustomed strength. She was, in fact, getting old.

The answer came in a revolutionary new technique called Cryogenic Bottling, which allowed skilled medics to remove a person's brain and store it in a jar of nutrient jelly. There, it would continue to function and communicate by being hooked up to a small but immensely powerful computer.

The technique certainly sustained life in the strictly biological sense. But no one knew whether it would lead to a significant loss of such things as memory and personality when applied to humans . Experiments on various animals – rats, amoebas and Geoffrey Howe – proved inconclusive because none of them had any discernible personality before the operation. But, in the end, the Government's hand was forced when the PM took ill.

The operation, which could only be performed by a highly-trained neuro-surgeon and a milkman, took place amid maximum security, secrecy and other things beginning with an 's', and led to great anxiety.

Would the PM wake up? Would she be changed? Would the stress of a complete body-ectomy prove too great?

After a few minutes of tense waiting they had their answer. The computer terminal beeped; LEDs flashed agitatedly; the electronic voicebox cleared its throat and the voice of the PM ordered the bombing of France. It was clear she hadn't changed at all.

Instead, she had made political history. After being

the first woman Prime Minister, she became the first disembodied brain in a jar of nutrient jelly Prime Minister. There were those who were saying that spending the last forty-five years in a bottle was affecting her judgement. But since elections had been abolished as a foregone conclusion some twenty years before, there was little anyone could do about it.

Something stirred in Jave's mind on seeing the poster. Something about the Prime Minister and the Underground....

He put the thought out of his mind and continued on downwards. There were more important things to think about. What had Mikey meant about Marc Shoeban being a mixture? And what was Shoeban doing fixing people's teeth? It didn't square with the image Jave had built up of the man as a blackmailing murderer.

The steps led down and down and down. Each step had to be taken carefully; it was like the descent of a particularly difficult mountain climb. None of the party could be sure that the steps wouldn't give way at any moment, and no one relished the thought of falling into the pool of almost impenetrable darkness that lay below them.

'I hate this,' said Jave after they had negotiated another spiral of stairs and were standing on a short landing. Chanis nodded, her face looking pale and drawn. Her torch, which had been growing ever dimmer, finally gave out.

'Don't worry,' sang an echoing voice, 'be happy....'

'Look,' said Jave to the singing gerbil, 'we're relying on you for light, Frid. Maybe you ought to conserve your batteries by not singing.'

'No worries, baby-dude,' said the gerbil. 'All batteries OK. Good for another twenty-six hours. So I can keep singing.'

'Oh goody.'

They started to descend again, Frid still singing. After

a few more bars, Jave could stand it no longer and said, 'I wish you'd shut up.'

'Hey man,' said Frid, his noselight swaying around in the darkness, 'I is just trying to keep our spirits up. We should count our blessings.'

'Your singing wouldn't make anyone count their blessings,' replied Jave. 'Except, perhaps, deaf people.'

Suddenly something scuttled over his feet. Arms flailing, Jave stumbled forward and fell into the darkness.

He only fell for a few steps before coming to rest.

'You all right, bruvv?' asked Kevving behind him.

'Yeah,' said Jave, picking himself up. 'I reckon. The steps seem to have come to an end.'

There was another scuttling sound and, to his relief, Jave saw that Frid had joined him.

'Rats,' he said. 'I hate rats.'

'Hey, baby,' said Frid. 'That's my family you're talking about.'

'You're a gerbil.'

'We is an extended family,' said Frid.

As Chanis and Kevving joined them, Frid's nosebeam scanned around the area they were in. Ahead of them was a wall; to the right a tunnel stretched away into the darkness. On the wall was a sign with an arrow which said 'To the Trains'.

'This is great!' said Kevving. 'I bet no one's been down here for years!'

'Are you OK?' Chanis asked Jave, helping him up. In the torchlight, her face looked pale and vulnerable. Yet she was not the same. Jave knew that he had built an obsession around her without realising that, at the bottom of it all, they were separated by an unbridgeable gulf. Did she care for him? Maybe. But not as much as she disapproved of him. And the really worrying thing was that, deep down, Jave thought she might be right.

'I'm OK,' he said. 'Come on.'

The passage led them along for about 100 metres and then down another short flight of steps. Then there was a turn, and another, and then more steps. Surprisingly, down in the passages, the air was quite dry and comparatively warm. The passages were filled with heaps of dust and blocked by the occasional spider's web and, every now and then, they could hear scuttlings and rustlings in the darkness ahead of them.

Suddenly, the passage ended and Frid's nosebeam hit a wall straight ahead of them. The wall was slightly curved in at the top and the atmosphere was lighter, the air less thick. As Frid shone his nosebeam about, Jave realised they were in another, much larger, tunnel which ran at right angles to the one they had just emerged from.

There was even a slight breeze, the faintest of breezes, the kind of breeze that is produced when someone a few hundred metres away sneezes. Nevertheless, it was a breeze.

'Where are we?' said Jave.

Frid's nosebeam cast about them.

'Some kind of platform,' he said.

'I've read about this!' said Chanis. 'This was where people used to wait – you know, years ago. When they had trains.'

The entire Underground system finally stopped working in 2021. Not that it made much of an impact because most people had stopped using the Underground many years before. The invention of air cars, combined with the dirt and the crowds and the fact that a return to Shepherd's Bush cost £30,000.04, had finally driven all but the most die-hard commuters away. And the few who remained weren't enough to keep the trains running.

The end came on a Wednesday afternoon, when the chief executive announced to the entire staff that the Underground was closing down.

The entire staff were shocked and saddened but bowed to the inevitable. And in the end all three of them accompanied the chief executive down to the pub for a farewell drink.

'What do we do now?' asked Chanis.

'I don't know,' said Jave. 'I'm trying to think.' His hands and knees ached from the fall he had taken a few minutes back. And he was pursued by worrying thoughts. He didn't like being here in the dark, in an alien environment. If Shoeban was down here, and Jave was beginning to doubt it, then this was his home patch. He knew the place. He could pick them off one by one and they would never even see him.

He put such thoughts out of his head.

'Anyone ever see that old film *Aliens*?' Kevving asked.

All the thoughts rushed back into Jave's head. At the same time, slithering down the tunnel, there came a distant noise.

'What's that?' said Chanis, her bass growl moving, through nervousness, up to a sort of strangled gurgle.

'Frid,' Jave ordered, 'scan.'

Frid's whiskers revolved as usual.

'Something coming down the tunnel, man,' said Frid. 'Something big!'

'Get back!' said Jave.

'Where to?' yelled Kevving. 'Where's the entrance gone?'

They had moved down the platform and lost the entrance through which they had come. All they could do was back up against the wall as the noise grew louder and louder.

'Nobody move!' said Jave, having to shout above the

approaching din. 'Crouch down! Try and keep as low as possible!'

The next moment all hell broke loose. A rushing, pushing wind came down the tunnel towards where the group cowered in the darkness. Then the loud rattle became a thundering and then a deafening roar.

Into what had been darkness, there burst a monster of light – a huge, shaking, clattering, steel snake, rushing to-wards them and vomiting light and warmth and movement.

Jave, Chanis, Kevving and Frid pressed themselves back against the wall as the snake began to slither to a halt. After so long struggling through the dim light, the glare from this monster was painful and blinding. Shielding his eyes with his hand, Jave thought he could make out glass windows and doors and a dull steel coloured metal. It was some kind of vehicle. And it was carrying people.

The vehicle stopped. There was a hissing sound as doors opened.

A figure came out towards them. The light behind him, so startling to Jave's dark-accustomed eyes, seemed to blur the outlines of the man's body.

'Hello,' said the blur. After the rattling and roaring of the train, the man's voice sounded muted and small. Yet it had a kind of grandeur to it. A kind of unearthliness. Mindlessly, Jave pulled the weasel's knife from his pocket and held it in front of him.

The blur laughed.

'Don't be afraid,' it said, easily taking the knife from Jave's hand. 'I won't hurt you.'

Behind him, Jave heard Chanis draw in her breath.

The blur grabbed Jave's hand and started shaking it.

'My name is Abram Chones,' it said.

26

The hair was shorter, considerably shorter. And his beard had been trimmed back. Jave looked about him. Someone down here must have attacked the man with a hedge-cutter.

In fact, the haircut made Abram Chones look about twenty years younger. He looked remarkably like the photo of him and his young bride. The years had been trimmed away with his unruly, unkempt hair.

And yet there was still an odd aura about the man. The eyes still looked somehow old and careworn and it was only when you got close to him that you saw the wrinkles in his skin and the dark shadows of strain beneath his eyes.

Jave pulled his attention away from the man who had, so surprisingly, reappeared alive and well and living in a disused tube train. He shook his head, as if to rattle some reality back into it. But it was no use. Abram Chones had emerged from a subway train on the deserted platform of Victoria Station, and they were in some sort of dream-world.

As soon as Jave's eyes had recovered from the blinding light and his brain from the shock of finding a murder victim talking to him, Jave tried to question Abram. But the man refused to answer immediately.

'You've obviously had a long and tiring journey,' he said. 'Not to mention something of a surprise. Come with us first and have something to eat and drink.'

So they boarded the tube train and travelled north, to an old station called Green Park. Where Abram created the power to run the train, Jave did not know. But what did it matter? In a dreamworld anything was possible.

At Green Park, the train stopped and they clambered out. What was waiting for them there was scarcely credible.

On the old platform, Abram Chones had set up a little community. There were about a dozen people there, milling about the platform, busy with a variety of tasks. They were an odd collection – almost all of them seemed old and stooped. They looked up as the train arrived with an uncertainty in their eyes. Jave thought back. It was a similar look to the cowed, frightened, animal stare of the people who lived in the cardboard town in the shadow of Victoria Station.

The Underground train was used as living quarters and they had turned the platform into storage space and cooking facilities. The materials were the same mixture of cardboard and plastic and corrugated sheeting that had filled the muddy streets up above them. But here it was cleaner and more organised.

'There are only ten of us so far,' said Abram, 'but we will grow. Of course,' he added, 'we won't be able to let them all in, or that will spoil it for everyone. Isn't that so, Hagatha?'

'It's certainly that, sir,' said a collection of skin and bones at Abram's side. She was a little old lady with no teeth, grey hair and a face that looked like a landslide.

'How old do you think she is?' Abram asked Jave, as they moved on down the platform.

'Sixty? Seventy?'

Abram shook his head. 'She's forty,' he said. 'A lifetime of begging on the streets has all but wrecked her. Down here she organises cooking for the community. She's learned to care and be cared for. That's the kind of society we're building.

'Each member of the community has their own place, somewhere where they can keep their few personal belongings. Some choose to sleep on the train. Others prefer to sleep in the houses on the platform. It's the way of life they have been used to, you see...'

'How long have you been here?' asked Chanis.

'Not long,' replied Abram. 'Only a few days. But I've been planning it for a long time. You see,' the older man waved about him excitedly, 'there's so much we can do down here. We have our own power, our own defences. We get food from up above. It's safe and secure.'

'But Father,' rasped the beautiful girl, 'I don't know...it's not the real world, is it?'

The old man looked sad.

'Have you seen the real world?' he asked. 'Have you spent time there? The "real" world is evil. The "real" world is cold and miserable. Unless you have money. Then it's warm and miserable. This world is different.'

Jave interrupted him before he could restart.

'Yeah, great. Very laudable and all that, but if you don't mind, I've got about three million questions to ask you, beginning with: Why aren't you dead?'

'Please,' said Abram, holding up a lean hand. 'I will answer all your questions in due course. But first, let's eat.'

The meal they ate was well prepared and very, very tasty. A simple meat stew, with plenty of vegetables and a good thick, beery gravy, accompanied by hunks of home-baked bread torn from a large, communal loaf.

'Great stuff, Hagatha,' said Kevving. 'Where'd you get the food though?'

'If you go along the tunnel over there,' her hand indicated a small tunnel marked 'exit' at the far end of the platform, 'and you follow the red markings you come to the foundations of a big tower block. It's some kind of hotel, 'parently. Well, we just ups and sorts through what they throw down from way above. No problem finding good stuff to eat.'

Jave stared at his empty plate. He had just eaten garbage Cordon Bleu.

After the meal there were mugs of steaming hot coffee as the thirteen people and one gerbil sat round a fire that someone had made at one end of the platform.

'I haven't introduced everyone, have I?' said Abram Chones. He went round the group introducing the members of the community one by one. Each was called Brother, or Sister, and each had a similar story to tell. They had been destitute, they had been hungry, they had been dying. Brother Abram had befriended them and rescued them and brought them down to the Underground, where they were safe.

As each talked about their own story, Jave studied their faces. They were all shapes and sizes, yet not one of them looked like the man on the library card of Marc Shoeban. Not one. For a start they were all considerably older. They were probably, like Hagatha, relatively young, but battered by degradation and suffering. But none of the other members of Abram Chones' community could have been Marc Shoeban. And yet Jave knew that Shoeban was down here somewhere.

'Now,' said Abram, 'you have some questions?'

Jave looked at him.

'Couldn't we go somewhere more private?' he said.

'I am not afraid to answer before the brothers and sisters,' said Abram smiling. 'They have a right to hear my story.'

The brothers and sisters grinned and clapped each other on the back and murmured their assent. It was clear they were fans.

'Well,' said Jave, sipping his coffee, 'let's start at the beginning, shall we? How come you're not dead?'

Abram smiled and the group round the fire nodded appreciatively. Clearly the answer to this question was one they knew well.

'By the will of God,' said Abram Chones. 'That's all it could be.'

Jave sighed.

'You are not a believer, Mr Fleming?'

'No.'

'Yet your brother is, I am given to understand.'

'That's right.'

Kevving nodded, enthusiastically.

'You will not fully understand, then. I do not remember the night clearly. I had been sitting and worrying about a particular problem. I did not know what to do. The night was hot, so I went and opened the window, and stood breathing in the night air. Suddenly, there was a great pillar of fire in the middle of my van. I was like something out of the Bible – the pillar of fire that led the Israelites by night.'

The assembled community murmured happily at the comparison.

'It came from beneath the floor I think. Some kind of bomb. I found out afterwards. At the time, it hardly seemed that way. At the time, I thought it was a sign.'

He smiled. 'It was not such a mistake. In a way it was a sign. Anyhow, I think I told you I was standing by a window. The power of the blast was such that it threw me backwards, straight through the window and clear of the caravan. Not that I escaped completely unscathed. I put up my hands to protect me.'

He held up his hands. The palms were smooth; all the lines and wrinkles burnished flat by the intense heat. 'As soon as I was clear, I realised that someone had made an attempt to kill me. But, through a miracle, I had been thrown clear. I managed to escape. I realised then that I knew something dangerous. I realised it would be safer for me, and those who knew me, if I disappeared.'

'And what was it that you knew?'

In the empty platform, Jave's voice echoed like the

flickering shadow of the fire around which they were sitting.

'I had moved out of the M25 Housing Estate to help people there, to set up another church. I did not know the area. I didn't know the other churches around, so I went to have a look at one. What I saw saddened me. A huge, empty building, peddling a sham and empty religion by means of the TV screen. But what struck me particularly was the man on the TV screen, whom I recognised. It was peculiar...I was talking to the vicar in charge of the church when I saw the face of an old schoolfriend on this TV screen.'

'Charlie Harris,' said Jave.

Abram smiled.

'That doesn't matter now. The vicar looked very surprised and told me I must have been mistaken, but I knew who he was. One doesn't forget one's childhood friends that easily. I listened to him for a while. To my dismay, I realised that he was now a Bishop.'

'Why did that dismay you?'

'Because of what he was saying. What he was saying had nothing to do with poverty and hardship and helping those in need. It had a lot to do with money.

'A few days later the vicar came back and asked me to go with her to meet a man. I forget his name. We went to a tall tower in another part of the country. The man was a very big man. Very big and very greedy, I thought. He offered me money to keep quiet. A silly thing to do.'

'You didn't take the money?'

'Of course not. If Charlie no longer wanted to be called Charlie, that was up to him. What was wrong with him was the things he was saying, not the fact that he called himself something different.'

He gazed into the fire and poked at it with a long stick.

'It was not long after that that my lorry was firebombed. I realised then that the fat man was not only very greedy, but very dangerous. I had few friends in that area. I said to you that, although it was a bomb, I thought it was a sign, and in a way I still do. I had been thinking about moving to the ground level, but I thought I would take that one step further. So I came here.'

'How long have you known about this place?'

'Oh, a long time. Many years ago, I was a guard on these trains, you know. I realised a long time ago that the tube stations would make a perfect hiding place. It was only when I arrived on the ground level that I realised we could do more than just hide! We could build something here. Something for the future.'

'So how did you end up here?' asked Jave.

'Ah,' said Abram Chones, 'I have been thinking about this plan for a long time. I suppose the violence, the threat to me, spurred me into action. If I had to disappear, what better place to do it? So I came down and reopened the Underground. I used what engineering skill I had to get a small proportion of the network open again and use it as a base.'

Jave took a long draught of his coffee. It was good and hot and warming.

'Did you have any help in that?' he enquired.

'Help?'

'From other people. It's a big task for one man alone to get stations opened, to get a train running.'

'I had some help, yes, from my brothers and sisters.'

'What about MacWhirter?'

'MacWhirter?'

'You knew him. He ran a loan company and credit agency on the M25.'

'Yes, I remember. I remember him well. I took his confession.'

'Confession? What did he have to confess?'

'Jave, you surely don't wish me to reveal what one person has told me in confession. It's not about finding out people's secrets. It's about offering the forgiveness of God.'

Jave felt oddly humbled. The man had an atmosphere about him, almost a holiness, that Jave found difficult to come to terms with.

'All right, forget MacWhirter. What about Shoeban?'

'Shoeban?'

'Marc Shoeban.'

'I have never met this Marc Shoeban.'

Jave stared at the man.

'You must have,' he said. 'That's how we found you. We found a book in Shoeban's lorry that led us here. We found a gram of you in his wardrobe.'

'I tell you I have never met this Marc Shoeban. If he knows where we are, he has found out for himself.'

There was something wrong, thought Jave, suddenly. It should all link up at this point. For one thing, it should be Shoeban sitting there and not Abram Chones. And, as it was Abram Chones, Shoeban must have known about him, must have met him, talked to him. How else could he have found out about this underground retreat?

'I am telling you the truth, Jave.' Abram's eyes were pools of darkness. There was something frightening about him, something almost too pure.

'Yes,' answered Jave, 'I believe you are.'

He stared into the fire, watching the flickering flames create shapes and patterns in the dead darkness of the Underground platform. When he spoke again, it was almost by remote control.

'Do you know that they're dead?' he asked Abram. 'MacWhirter and the vicar you spoke to. They've been murdered. Whoever tried to murder you, has murdered them.'

Abram looked at him. Jave thought for a moment that he was going to cry.

'Poor people,' he said. 'Perhaps someone thought they

knew too much. In fact, like too many people, they never knew enough.' He shook himself ever so slightly. 'And now, my friends, if you would excuse me, I would like to spend some time with my daughter. I haven't seen her for a long time.' He rose from the floor and helped Chanis to her feet. Then he turned back to Jave. 'Jave,' he said, 'I am sure you have some questions. I will be happy to answer them in the future.'

Together the prophet and his daughter walked away into the shadows.

The party broke up. Members wandered away to do various jobs. Hagatha brought Jave another cup of coffee and he sat and stared into the fire.

'You OK?' Frid asked, sitting at his side.

'I can't make out the pattern,' said Jave. 'I can't pull it all together.'

He took another drink.

'Was the dude telling the truth?'

'Yes, he was telling the truth, so far as it goes.'

'Meaning?'

'Meaning that he was telling the truth, but he wasn't answering the questions.'

Opposite where Jave and the gerbil were sitting was an old poster, which had come to light some time in the distant past, as successive posters on top of it had peeled away. At the very top of the poster was a date, 'July 20–27, 2011', and a place, 'Wembley Mega Dome'. Below that was a picture of a man's back. The man was, perhaps, speaking at a meeting of some kind. Printed in large, white letters across the picture was the legend 'E.FIL' and below that, in smaller lettering, the phrase: 'He'll make sense of it again.'

'E.FIL?' said Jave. 'What the bazz is E.FIL?'

Frid buzzed.

'Life,' he said. 'It's an anagram. Mixture of letters.

According to my memory banks, they did it to advertise that old Billy Graham dude.'

'Never heard of him.'

'Dude was an evangelist. Came and did missions to Britain. Preacher.'

'I'm sick of preachers,' said Jave. 'You can't move in this case for preachers, evangelists, church leaders.' He looked at the gerbil. 'All this Christianity business,' he said. 'You think it's true?'

'You is talking to the wrong guy,' said Frid. 'I'm a computer, remember? I mean, I'm a great computer, but metaphysics is way beyond me.'

'Yeah. I forgot. You don't act like a computer.'

'Face the facts, baby. If I act on impulse it's because I've been programmed to do it.'

Jave smiled.

'Join the club,' he said.

THE SIXTH DAY

27

Jave woke early the next morning. Or at least he assumed it was early. His wrist unit told him it was early. Here, underground, however, all times seemed the same.

It had been a shock to him to look at his wrist unit late the previous night, as he sat at the fire, still thinking about the patterns and the problems before him.

'Hey,' he said to Frid, 'how long have I been sitting here?'

'About two hours.'

Jave looked around him.

'Where's Kevving gone?' he asked.

Frid nodded in the direction of the tunnel marked 'exit'.

'Up there, with the Hagatha chick,' he said. 'Exploring.' Jave yawned.

'We ought to get out of here, if we're going.' He looked at his unit again. 'It's late,' he said. 'Maybe we'd better try and stay here until tomorrow. Don't fancy finding the air car in the dark.'

So that was what they did. Abram had beds made up for them in various compartments in the carriages of the train.

'All right?' Jave asked Chanis, just before he turned in. Ever since her father had arrived, he had hardly talked to her.

'Um,' she nodded.

'You don't sound too sure.'

'Well, it's all this. I'm not sure about it. Oh, don't get me wrong, it's wonderful to see him again. I...I'd sort of given him up. But all this. He reckons it's the answer. I'm not sure.'

'Seems to be an answer for him, at any rate. They'll never find him here and he can wander about doing good to his heart's content.'

Chanis turned to him.

'You are so cynical,' she accused.

'I'm realistic.'

'Cynical,' she insisted. 'You don't believe anyone can have good motives, do you?'

'Of course I do. Don't be ridiculous.'

'I suppose,' she said angrily, 'it comes of spending your life prying into other people's secrets.'

Jave sighed. 'I don't want to argue with you. I do what I'm paid to do. And before you get too high and mighty, remember who it was who paid for me to do the prying on this job.'

Then he turned and stomped off to bed.

He didn't get to sleep for a long time. His brain was itching.

It was at breakfast the next morning that he saw Kevving again.

'Where have you been?' he asked. 'I've been worried about you.'

'Nowhere particular,' said Kevving. 'Just following my noses.'

'Long journey then. Have some breakfast?'

They sat down in a corner, each bearing a plate of pancakes that Hagatha had created. The pancakes were beautiful and light and smeared with a sweet and sticky syrup.

'So what do you make of all this?' Jave asked.

'Pretty neat set up,' replied Kevving. 'But you know me. I hate to be stifled.'

'Yeah. What puzzles me is how he got all this working

again. I mean there's a lot of engineering work involved. Must have cost a fair bit as well.'

Kevving nodded.

'Good point. But they all chipped in, you see. I mean they've got plans to extend it even further. I was talking to a zeke called Lezlee. Seems they've got to clear some blockages further down the line to extend the network. But he showed me all the gear they've got: diggers, drills, explosives. Lezlee is in charge of all that kind of thing. Apparently he was an engineer once, long ago.'

'I just can't fit Shoeban in. If I could just find him.'

'I'd give up, if I were you,' said Kevving. 'I mean, he probably doesn't exist any more.'

'What do you mean?'

Jave stared at his brother. For the briefest of instants, an idea had flickered to light in his brain.

'He's probably been rubbed out like the rest of them.'

The idea disappeared.

'Oh, yeah,' said Jave, 'probably. Well, I don't know about you, but I'm going to see if there's any more to eat.'

Jave took his plate and wandered up the platform past the cardboard shelters that housed this community's resources. Each shelter was clearly labelled and sorted – 'Bedding', 'Medication', 'Clothing'....

Jave stopped. He went back a few paces and into the 'clothing' store. There was a pile of old clothes on the floor reaching to about halfway up the wall. They were mostly old but serviceable garments. Jave began to sort through the garments.

'Can I help you?' asked a voice behind him.

Jave looked round. Hagatha was standing watching him.

'Where did all this stuff come from?' he asked.

'I'm not sure,' replied the little, hunched woman. 'I think Brother Abram brought them all. But these aren't the best clothes. The best clothes are kept somewhere else. Why don't you go and look there?'

'No, I'm all right,' replied Jave. 'I'm just browsing. I'm just looking for something. Or rather, I'm not looking for something. Or is it both?'

Hagatha left him to it, shaking her head at the idiocy of this strange man. After a while, Jave came out of the store with something bundled underneath his arm and quietly made his way to the far end of the platform.

He found Abram Chones with his daughter in the end car of the Underground train. They were talking excitedly.

'Of course it's right!' Abram was saying. 'Look at what it's done for these people!'

'I'm not arguing about that, Dad,' said Chanis. 'It's just that it...it feels like a retreat, that's all. It feels too much like hiding. When we came here, I saw the most horrible things – people living in rubbish dumps, people begging to survive. I can't believe all of that has been going on up there, while we've been living the good life in the tower blocks. How could we have been so blind?'

'No one wanted to see.'

'But the point is that we should be up there changing it, not running away from it and creating our own little world! How can you alter anything from down here?'

Abram smiled.

'Stay with us a while,' he said. 'You'll understand.'

'You've changed,' said Chanis. 'I don't know what's happened to you, Dad, but you've changed.'

'Nonsense.'

'It's true,' insisted the girl. 'I can tell. Something's happened.'

'Excuse me,' said Jave. 'I wonder if I can have a word?'

Chanis looked startled by his appearance.

'In private,' said Jave. 'With Abram.'

Chanis rose from her seat.

'More detecting?' she said.

'No. I...I want to make my confession,' said Jave. He felt a tinge of shame at the lie and even more at the way Chanis smiled at him as she passed. 'It's not what you think,' he said to her as she walked back up the platform. She didn't look back. 'Nothing is what you think,' he muttered.

Abram Chones looked up at Jave as he stepped into the carriage. It was an ascetic, sparsely furnished carriage. All the old seats had been removed. In their place, at the far end of the carriage, was a simple mattress for a bed. Halfway down, there was a table and a book. And, apart from three large, old chairs at the other end of the carriage, that was more or less it. Abram Chones was sitting in one of the three chairs, his hands resting lightly on his knees, sitting up straight and tall, like a king on some badly upholstered throne.

He smiled at Jave. Once again, Jave felt the sense of purity about the man. Or was it purity? No, it was something darker. There was an infection festering beneath the surface.

'What can I do for you, Jave?' asked Abram.

'That's a fine daughter you have there, Mr Chones,' Jave said, walking further into the carriage and putting his bundle on the floor. 'She really believes in you.'

'I fear she has reservations about my scheme here. She thinks I should be up above, getting involved, rather than creating something new down here.'

'She's got a point.'

'What do you think?'

Jave looked about him, and replied, 'I'd say you've already been more involved than you ought up above.'

'Yes,' agreed Abram, 'but that wasn't my fault. I didn't wish to become involved in the business of Charlie Harris. It was an accident.'

'I didn't mean that,' said Jave. 'Or maybe I did.'

'Perhaps you had better sit down,' suggested Abram. 'You sound a little confused.'

'Confused? No, I'm not confused. For the first time this week, I can definitely assure you I am not confused.'

Jave sank back into the soft cushions of the old armchair. Here and there the covering had burst, revealing clumps of coarse horse-hair bursting from inside.

'Why did you cut your hair, Mr Chones?'

Abram looked surprised at the question. Unconsciously, he dragged a thin hand across the grey hair of his head.

'I am not quite sure. I think it was something about starting again. The medieval monks shaved their heads, you know, to show their devotion, to symbolise the decision they had made. It set them apart.'

'You feel like that?'

'I certainly did after my narrow escape from the bomb. I felt...special. Somehow set aside. Chosen for a purpose. That is why I made my way here, Jave. I believe this community, these people, is the thing for which I had been saved.'

'It's not a tonsure, though, is it?'

'I didn't say it was. I was merely using the tonsure as an illustration.'

Jave stared at the ceiling of the carriage.

'Last night I asked you a question,' he said. 'I asked you if you had heard of Marc Shoeban.'

'And I told you that I had never met the man.'

'So you did. Which is a bit of a problem really, because Shoeban's been the problem in this case all along. We could never find him. We found out about him all right – that just led us here – but of him, of the man himself, we never saw a trace. Apart from a photo on a residential permit, we had no information at all about the man.'

'Surely someone had met him?' suggested Abram.

'Oh yes. Two people have certainly met him. Mikey and his tooth, for one.'

'Mikey?'

'A part-time human being we met on our way here. The details were very sketchy, but it appears that Shoeban met Mikey one night and healed his tooth. But he said something very weird to Mikey; he said that he was a "mixture". What do you think that meant?'

Abram Chones shook his head. 'I have no idea,' he said quietly. 'Perhaps he meant that he was mixed up. After all, he does sound a little mad.'

'And then there was the vicar. Marc Shoeban received a large amount of money from Anson, which was delivered by the vicar. The money was part of a blackmail payment.'

At the mention of the word 'blackmail', Abram Chones frowned.

'Didn't I tell you?' asked Jave. 'Shoeban was blackmailing Anson Enterprises using the same information you had. The fact that Charlie Harris equals Lou Blynell. Apparently, Shoeban managed to extract quite a bit of money out of Anson before disappearing. But anyway, the vicar must have met Shoeban as well,' continued Jave, 'because she delivered the money. She knew where he lived.'

He paused.

'Go on,' prompted Abram.

'Well, I got to thinking. Supposing this Shoeban doesn't actually exist? Supposing he's never existed?'

'But he met people. And you have a picture.'

'They met someone called Marc Shoeban, certainly, but that doesn't mean there actually ever was someone called Marc Shoeban. It only means they thought there was. He's like that poster.'

'I don't follow.'

Jave looked at the man, still sitting calmly in his chair and smiling his inscrutable smile.

'Don't you? There's a poster out there on the station wall – an anagram.' Chones looked baffled. 'It's quite simple, really,' said Jave. 'Shoeban isn't a person. He's what he said he was to Mikey that night up above. He's a mixture. An anagram.'

'An anagram of what?'

Jave smiled.

'Abram Chones,' he replied. 'Marc Shoeban is an anagram of Abram Chones.'

Abram Chones looked at Jave and laughed.

'Do you mean Marc Shoeban is pretending to be me?' he asked. His eyes weren't laughing or smiling. His eyes were as cold and hard as nails.

'No.' Jave looked the old man straight into those cool, clear eyes. 'I mean, you pretended to be Marc Shoeban.'

28

There was a moment's silence.

'You have proof?' said Abram Chones, staring unwaveringly at Jave.

'Not really. But a lot of it makes sense if you look at it this way. You've already admitted that it's too dangerous for you to go up top under the name of Chones. As Shoeban, however, you wouldn't have any problems. Abram Chones has long grey hair and a full beard. Marc Shoeban has short black hair and no beard.'

'I do not have black hair.'

'Not now, you don't. But when Shoeban met Mikey, he didn't have black hair. When I showed Mikey the photo of Shoeban, he noticed at once that the guy's hair was a different colour, although at first I thought Mikey was talking about something else. I thought all along that Shoeban's face looked pasty and pale. Now I realise it's the kind of pale skin you find when people shave their beards off.'

'You are suggesting that I cut and dyed my hair, shaved my beard and put on sunglasses as some kind of disguise?'

'Now, how did you know that Marc Shoeban wore sunglasses?' asked Jave.

There was a long pause.

'I...' began Abram, then he was silent.

'But what puzzled me,' said Jave, 'was why you would want to do this. I mean, I could understand that if people bomb you you would want to disappear, to come down here. I could even go for all that stuff about a sign that you came out with last night. But that doesn't explain why you would go back, disguised as someone else.'

'And why do you think I did?'

'Revenge.'

Jave took a deep breath. Abram's head had dropped. His hands were clutching and not resting on his knees.

'Well, maybe "revenge" is the wrong word. Maybe you were looking for some kind of justice or fairness. As Shoeban, you can go back to the vicar and get all the money you want for being quiet. And you could use it as well, building a new community down here; a community where people are safe from bombs and fake Bishops. A bit of the Robin Hood syndrome. But that doesn't explain it all, does it? I mean, there's such a big change. It seemed to me that it would take much more than a firebomb to make Abram Chones suddenly turn to blackmail, even if it is for a good cause.'

Abram Chones raised his head and looked at Jave, almost sadly.

'Do you really think I would blackmail someone?' he asked. 'Even for something as worthwhile as this community?'

Jave sighed.

'It was Marc Shoeban who blackmailed,' he said. 'But, no, I don't think that you could resort to blackmail, pure and simple. I think it was a lot more complex than that.

'When you first went into the church you had no idea about Charlie Harris, about what he'd said, or done,' Jave continued. 'You just came right out with it; Bishop Lou Blynell was your old schoolfriend. So that tells us that, at that time, you didn't know anything about Charlie Harris, nor why it should be such a big secret. And, when you were taken to meet the business bosses, you readily agreed to requests from Anson that the secret should be kept. After all, you had no reason to tell anyone. At that time, all that worried you was what Lou Blynell was saying. So, according to my theory, at some time you had to find out what Charlie Harris had done. Last night, you told me that you heard MacWhirter's confession.'

An almost imperceptible shudder shook Chones.

'A man's confession is secret,' he said.

Jave continued, 'MacWhirter saw you as a holy man, a man of faith. Someone he could trust. He saw in you a chance of some kind of redemption. You were his only friend, the only one who cared about people like him. So he confessed his sins to you. I'm sure it took some time. He confessed how he had once worked for a black marketeer called Charlie Harris. He told you all the details. He told you all about Charlie Harris' worst crime – and, incidentally, the crime which resulted in MacWhirter going to prison – the withholding of much needed antibiotic drugs from hospitals who wouldn't pay.'

Jave looked at Abram Chones. There was a great sadness on the man now, a heaviness. Jave felt like a torturer, and yet he knew he had no choice. He was the one outside, the one who saw the whole picture.

'Of course,' he continued relentlessly, 'MacWhirter didn't realise that it was in one of these hospitals that your wife gave birth to Chanis. Chanis told me that your wife died because they couldn't get her the right drugs. We know why they couldn't get the right drug. Charlie Harris refused to sell it to them. I think that was what really turned you. It wasn't the money for this place. It wasn't what Charlie Harris was saying. It was the fact that the man was directly responsible for the death of your wife.'

The man in front of him slumped further into his chair. Jave carried on, a knife twisting in a wound.

'So, anyway, what do you do when you find this out? What can you, as Abram Chones, do? Nothing really. These are dangerous people. They know about Abram Chones. They may even know about Abram Chones' daughter. But Marc Shoeban, that's another matter. Marc Shoeban would be safe.

'Now we come to the really clever, but simple, idea. It's so simple I should have seen it a long time ago. All the time I was acting, not only on the assumption that Abram Chones was dead, but that someone had tried to kill him, because of what he knew about Charlie Harris. Well, in a sense that was true. But all the time something bothered me about the bombing. If you're going to firebomb someone, I mean professionally, you make sure it works. The pros don't allow people to escape; they have the exits blocked. You certainly wouldn't have got out of there alive if it had been a professional job. So that means that an amateur did it. And one particular amateur.'

He pointed at Abram Chones.

'You firebombed your lorry that night. You destroyed the old life of Abram Chones. It wasn't hard for you to arrange. You'd bought explosives to clear out some of the tunnels down here, according to Kevving. And weren't you once employed on the North Sea Tunnel, years ago? Anyway, you planted the bomb.

'But, before that, Marc Shoeban was born. A simple job – you cut off your hair and shaved off your beard, which explains the hair they found in the wreckage. Then the bomb went off and that was that. Everyone fell for it – Social Security, Anson's mob, me – because you'd chosen a bomb that tended not to leave any trace. As a way of stopping people hunting for you, death is pretty effective.

'Of course, I'm not saying that you came up with the

name "Shoeban" there and then. I think that only occurred when you had to get a residential permit for your base of operations. You had to have somewhere for them to bring the money, somewhere to meet. So you came up with Shoeban – the avenging angel. Someone who would make people pay – both in cash and in other ways – for what they had done. All you had to do was to get in touch with the vicar and arrange it. Then you sit back and wait and plan your new community deep below the streets of London.

'A terrific irony, isn't it? Getting Lou Blynell himself to pay for the setting up of a community totally opposed to his point of view. Anyway, you got the dosh.

'But it was never about money, was it, Abram? The money seems almost incidental. No, it was what I said – it was about some kind of justice. That's why you could never stop at just the money.

'MacWhirter was first, strangled with the belt from a coat.' Jave scratched his head. 'You know, I knew that belt as soon as I saw it. It was the belt from the coat you were wearing in the gram that Chanis had shown me first of all.'

He unwrapped the paper parcel he had brought with him and spread it out on the floor. It was a brown coat, old and stained and creased where it had been stuffed at the bottom of the pile. Abram didn't look at it. The belt was missing.

'That's the one, isn't it?' asked Jave. 'I found it in the clothing store on the platform there. No belt, of course.

'Anyhow,' he continued, 'the next day, you murdered Shamworth. A bomb in the C27. Easy for someone with your engineering experience and with the explosives that you'd bought to unblock these tunnels down here. I'm not totally clear on why you killed Shamworth, though. Was it because she'd met Shoeban and guessed who you really were? Was it because she was such a strong supporter of Charlie Harris? Why?'

He waited. There was no answer from Abram.

'Well, anyway, she was killed. After that, there was no need for you to hang around, so you disappeared, quickly. In the rush, however, you left the A–Z and the photo. They were enough to lead us back here. And here we are.'

Jave stopped.

There was a long, heavy silence, then Abram raised his head.

He was crying.

29

'I loved her very much,' he said.

'I know,' replied Jave, taken aback.

'You don't. You can't.' Abram almost spat out the words. 'You don't realise. After all these years, finding out who did it...finding out who was responsible. I had to do something. They were judged. All of them.'

'Was that up to you?' asked Jave. 'Who appointed you the judge and the jury?'

'Who?' cried Abram. 'Who else but God? Look about you, Jave Fleming! Look at the filth and degradation and suffering. Look at the poverty and humiliation and hunger that we have inflicted on people. And then ask yourself who is responsible. The people who live in the tall towers, that's who. The people who make all the money and keep it to themselves. The businesses, the Government, even the church. If you were God, wouldn't you want justice done?'

'Sure, I'd want it,' said Jave, 'but I'm not God.'

'I loved her,' said Abram again. He wiped away the tears on the sleeve of his coat.

'I loved her and I loved the people up there. And were betrayed by others. On that night, after MacWhirter's confession, for the first time in my life I saw things as they are. I saw how the rich get richer and the poor get poorer. I saw how murderers get away with it and how innocent people are punished. I saw the whole spread of injustice before me and I decided to do something about it.'

Jave stared at the man. There was a fierce and frightening anger about him.

'Marc Shoeban was merely a name. You have turned him into another side of me, a Mr Hyde figure. That's not the case, Jave. Marc Shoeban was merely a badge, or a piece of protective clothing. Inside the armour, I was still Abram Chones.'

He broke off and closed his eyes for a moment. When he opened them and started speaking again, he voice was very quiet.

'Do you know what the worst pain in the world is?' he asked Jave. 'It is not physical pain, but the pain of injustice. The pain of impotence in the face of evil. The pain of watching others, richer, stronger, more powerful than you, getting away with the most terrible evil, while you can do nothing about it.

'For too many years I have lived with such pain. Not only in my life, but in the lives of other people. I have lived with and tried to help those without work, those without families, the lonely, the poor.'

Suddenly, he raised a thin hand and slowly folded it into a frail fist.

'This country is a degradation!' he whispered. 'What happened to it, Jave? What happened to the Britain that we knew? Who sold it and turned it into the place that we live in now, where the rich live so cleanly and the poor live in the stinking mess on the ground? Who made it a place where only the rich can afford good health and clean water and food and education?'

His whole body seemed to sag under the weight of his speech.

'Oh,' he sighed,'I can't expect you to understand. You never knew it before all of this, did you? Even I hardly remember it. But this is a plastic country now, Jave. A plastic country filled with plastic people with plastic souls. It was time someone did something about it.'

There was a pause.

'Didn't do very well, though, did you?' asked Jave. 'I mean, who have you punished? Not the big boys. Just the minnows.'

Abram Chones shook his head. There was a hardness in his eyes that frightened Jave.

'MacWhirter died in my arms,' he said. 'He knew why he was dying and he accepted it. He even welcomed it. I loved him, but I could not let him get away with what he had done. Because I loved him, I punished him.

'The vicar was different. She came in after I had killed MacWhirter.'

'She saw you?'

'No, but she knew the truth. Why else would she visit the man? She must have known his part in the story and, therefore, the truth about Lou Blynell. So, all along she knew. Can you believe that?'

'It doesn't necessarily mean she knew. She might have been told that MacWhirter was a suspect for the blackmailing. She might have been told anything.'

'She knew!' spat out Abram. 'Like the rest of them she was nothing but a fraud!'

'So, she was a fraud. Did that mean she had to die?'

'She was a woman of God, collaborating with evil and wrongdoing. She, and the church she represented, had become a servant of money. So she had to die. It was the best way.'

Jave shook his head.

'How was it the best way?' he demanded angrily. 'The

woman was blown to pieces! How is that the best way?' There was silence. 'And anyway,' he continued, more calmly, 'they were just pawns. They were hardly at the heart of the conspiracy. They're not responsible for what happened to this country.'

Abram stared at him.

'Did you really think that I would not continue the task the Lord had given me?' he said quietly. 'Did you really think that such injustice, such deceit would be allowed to flourish within his church?'

Jave's heart missed a beat.

'You mean....'

'He died this morning. Very early. While you were all asleep. He was to open a new centre for the groundlings in the heart of London today. Can you imagine it?' He began to laugh. 'Him! A man who has done nothing but exploit people all his life. A man who has no faith, but professes to lead others. The blind leading the blind, Jave.'

'You blew him up?'

'No, nothing like that. Charlie Harris knew why he died.'

'How?'

'I told him. He was in a tower, a tall tower near this station, but many metres above us. Its base has a service shaft that comes out not far from here, in an upper tunnel. Not the usual school reunion, is it, Jave? No, at the last Charlie Harris knew me and he knew why he had to die and he knew that God had appointed me to bring justice.'

'This isn't justice. This is revenge. This is murder.'

'Murder?' shouted Abram angrily. 'How dare you talk to me of murder? Do you think it was easy to do all this? Do you think it was easy for me to kill these people? You think I enjoyed doing it? I did it because I had to, because it was the only way to bring any kind of justice. Why should we go on living with such injustice? Wasn't it time that we did something about it, instead of always helplessly giving in?'

'What about God? Doesn't he figure in this? Shouldn't

you have left him to mete out the justice in his own way?'

'What do you know of God?'

'Not a lot,' replied Jave, 'but didn't he give in? Didn't Christ suffer, helplessly? And don't you think he was God?'

Abram slumped in his seat, his head hanging before him.

'You don't understand,' he said. 'This was God's way.'

'I don't think so,' said Jave sadly. 'I don't think he had anything to do with it.'

Abram began to cry again.

'Don't say that,' he said. 'Of course he was to do with it! Why else would I have done it?'

Jave got up from his seat and went to the door. The air blowing in from the platform was cool, like water. Somewhere down the platform he could hear echoing noises. People building their new lives, safe from the terrors above. People believing. Suddenly Jave felt very old and very tired.

'He laughed,' said Abram, behind him.

'What?'

Jave turned back to see the old man, his head resting in his hands.

'Charlie Harris. When I told him. He laughed at me! He wasn't sorry, or ashamed, or anything. He killed my wife and he just laughed.' He stared at Jave, his mind rewinding the years to find the pain waiting, the same as ever. 'Her name was Lisa,' he said.

Jave looked away.

After a while, Abram spoke again.

'What will you do now?' he asked.

'I don't know.'

'If you choose to arrest me, I will not fight. My fight has never been with you, Jave.'

'I said I don't know.'

The air was cool, like water....There was still something scratching at the back door of Jave's mind. His memory raced back to their journey down here, to the political poster, to the Underground.

'But if you do take me,' said Abram, 'don't tell my people. They...they trust me. Look at them. I've rescued these people from the sewers.'

A door swung open in Jave's mind and the thought that had been waiting since they had first entered the Underground rushed in.

'The sewers!' he cried. 'The skagging sewers!'

30

Jave careered out of the train and raced up the platform, his shoes slipping drily on the dust. Chanis was standing halfway up the platform.

'What's the matter?' she called as he raced towards her.

'Everyone!' shouted Jave. 'Get out of here! They're going to flood the place. We've got to get out of here!'

'What?'

'The Government!' shouted Jave. 'They're going to use the Underground as a water mains. I heard it on the radio days ago. I've been trying to remember....'

The inhabitants gathered round him.

'What is it?' said one.

'Look,' said Jave, trying to remain calm, 'they're going to flood this place. I heard it on the radio some days ago.'

'Flood?' said someone.

'Yes, flood! With water!'

'Flood?'

'What are you, a skagging parrot? Flood! As in death by drowning and all that!'

The ten people gathered went silent. From the other end of the platform, Abram Chones joined them. His face was back to what it had always been – placid, gentle.

'Abram,' said one of the brothers, 'is it true?'

'Is what true?'

'That this place – our home – is going to be flooded?'

'Is that what you heard, Jave?' said Abram.

'I heard it on the radio a few days ago. It's to do with the water supply in London or something. I can't remember....'

'Well, Brothers and Sisters,' said Abram to the assembled crowd, 'it may be true. Perhaps you ought to go, just to be safe.'

'But this is our home!'

'That's right,' said Abram. 'But don't worry, I shall stay and look after it for you.'

'But if they flood it, you'll be killed, Father,' said Chanis.

'As the brother said, this is home. I created this place. I made it. I don't think I have the strength to leave it.'

Jave stared at Abram, open mouthed.

'But you can't....'

He was interrupted by Hagatha.

'Then we will stay with you as well,' she said to Abram.

'Are you mad?' said Jave angrily. 'Look, pretty soon this place is going to be the world's largest underground swimming pool. If you stay here, you'll die!'

Hagatha smiled at Jave, as she might to a confused child.

'Young man,' she answered, 'maybe you don't understand. This is our home. This is the only place we've ever called home. And Brother Abram is the only person who ever cared for us. Maybe it's madness to stay, but it is a good madness.'

Jave looked about him. They were all agreed. He stared at Abram.

'Can't you do something?' he said.

Abram looked at him.

'I can only let them do what they think best,' he replied. 'I have had enough of forcing people to change.'

He turned away. 'Brothers and sisters,' he continued, 'will you forgive me?'

'Forgive you? For what?' said Hagatha.

'I have sinned. I have sinned very badly. I want you to pray for me. I love you all and...' his voice faltered slightly, 'I...I just love you.'

There was a distant rumble. A slow trickle of despair slid down Jave's back.

'Come on!' he yelled. The rumble was growing, there could be no doubt about it. Hardly thinking now, Jave grabbed Chanis by the hand and dragged her after him along the platform.

'Frid!' he called. 'Way out?'

'Thanks, man,' said the gerbil. 'You ain't so bad yourself.'

'I mean the exit, you stupid rodent.'

'Oh, right!'

Frid scampered ahead of them, a beam of light flickering from his nose.

'What are you doing?' yelled Chanis.

'Saving your life – again!'

But his words were drowned out by a deafening, shattering roar. As they reached a flight of steps, Jave turned to see the group of people standing at the other end of the platform. They were standing in a circle, heads down. Jave guessed they were praying.

Then, from the tunnel behind them there burst a seething, muscular blackness. For a moment the whole community was framed by the wall of water before it crashed down onto the platform in a great, sinuous, oily wave.

'Father!' screamed Chanis.

'Run!' yelled Jave, his voice all but lost in the noise.

They turned and ran up a flight of stairs. Behind them they could hear the water roaring through the tunnel and smashing against the steps.

They scrambled along a short corridor, stumbling in the

darkness. Dragging Chanis behind him, Jave followed Frid's light to a high, disused escalator. Behind them, the water was gaining as billions of litres of water were forced through the old system. Frid started running up, his whiskers whirring and his noselight playing on the walls. There was an old poster on the wall. 'Become an H_2Owner' it said.

There were too many steps. There were just too many steps. Heart pounding and muscles aching, Jave pushed Chanis ahead of him, urging her forward. They stumbled in the darkness and, momentarily, Jave felt an ice-cold splash against the back of his legs.

'One last effort!' he yelled. At the top of the escalator, they raced towards a last set of steps. The water chased them into the deserted hallway, bubbling and frothing as if it boiled. Leaping up, two at a time, with lungs that felt like they were being beaten with a meat tenderiser, Jave pushed Chanis before him.

They were almost at the top when Chanis tripped and they both fell back. Desperately, Jave grabbed a handhold and tried to heave himself up, but, before he could move, the water had pounced. In a split second it swarmed over his feet, raced up his legs, up to his waist. The steps were slimy underfoot now, and the swirling pressure made it impossible for him to hold on to the handrail. Above him, Jave could hear Chanis scream. 'Run!' he cried, as his hand slipped and he was dragged back into the swirling flood.

The water was up to his neck as he scrabbled for a foothold. His foot found a step, but he slipped again and suddenly his mouth and nose were full of water. This is it, he thought, as the water pressure started to spin him round like a top. This must be what it's like being flushed down the toilet.

His right arm flailed wildly and then was caught. Someone grabbed his hand and pulled him up, out of the blackness.

As Chanis dragged him out of the water, he realised that the level had now stabilised, the roaring and buffeting was gone. The surface of the water was now smooth, sleek and impenetrable.

Someone above them threw open an old door. They were near the old entrance to the station. The light flooded in, making them blink. Jave looked at Chanis, sweating and shaking. He looked down at his clothes, sodden and pouring water from every inch. Then he looked back down at the pool below him which lapped against the old stairs.

'Father?' There was a tremble in the gravelly bass of Chanis' voice.

Jave looked down.

'Kevving...' he whispered.

'Yes?' said Kevving.

Jave turned to see a figure framed above him in the doorway. It was Kevving who had opened the door.

'Kevving!' he yelled. 'Where have you been?'

'Well,' said Kevving, 'I dunno. I came up to talk to a few people. Tell them about all that down there. Invite them down, maybe.' He stopped as he caught sight of the water that filled the tunnel. 'Wow!' he said. 'That's a heck of a plumbing problem they've got there.'

They stood outside the station in silence. It was just before dawn and the slum streets were quiet.

Jave looked at his wrist unit. It was broken.

As they stood there, the sun began to rise over London. Around him, the poor began to come to life, coughing like badly starting engines. Lights flickered on in the shanty houses. Flickering clouds of rubbish began to descend as, many metres above them, the robots began the daily task of cleaning the walkways.

In the dim light, Jave turned to Chanis.

'Let's go home,' he said.

31

They dropped Chanis off at her flat. Inside, a matronly woman was waiting. Kevving told Jave that she was a member of the church that Chanis led.

'She'll be all right,' Kevving assured Jave as they flew away. 'She'll be well looked after.'

They arrived back at the flat and Jave showered and changed, while Kevving punched up some hot food. While he was dressing, an announcer on the radio reported that the Bishop of Swindonopolis had been found strangled in his hotel suite.

Jave turned the radio off.

The stew that had arrived through the tube was warming and strong, but it was not like the one they had eaten on the station platform, and the whisky tasted of plastic.

'So did you ask him, then?' said Kevving as they sat on the loungers afterwards, drinking syntho-coffee from plastic mugs.

'Ask who what?'

'Abram,' said Kevving. 'Did you ask him why he killed all those people.'

Jave spilled his coffee.

'How did you know?' he asked, wiping it off his bathrobe.

'Oh, I guessed. Well, I mean, you said that the zeke in the Underground was the zeke we were looking for. Had to be Abram, really.'

'Yes, I asked him,' replied Jave.

'So why did he do it?'

'I don't know,' replied Jave. 'Because he felt he had to. Because he loved his wife. Because he got it all terribly wrong. Why do any of us do anything?'

'Because we want to make things better,' replied Kevving.

'Yes,' said Jave, 'that was it.'

His wrist unit was going again. It was six days since he had begun his search; six days in which his life had changed. In six days, his old world had disappeared as completely as Abram Chones' alternative society, to be replaced by the same kind of black oblivion. He punched himself up another cup of coffee and slowly explained the story to Kevving.

'Should I tell Chanis?' he asked.

'She already knows, I reckon,' replied Kevving. 'Well, maybe not the whole thing. But she knew something wasn't right with her father the moment she saw him.' He scratched his left nose. 'Funny,' he continued, 'it was seventeen years ago, but he still loved the woman.'

'It wasn't only that,' said Jave. 'It was the whole show. He'd spent his whole life trying to help the poor. One day he looked around him, and found that the poor were still poor and the rich were getting richer. He wanted to see things fair and right. He wanted justice. I think finding the truth about Charlie Harris was just the final straw.'

He turned to Kevving. 'So what will you do now?' he asked. A thought struck him. 'You don't fancy joining me in the investigating business?'

Kevving laughed.

'Thanks for the offer, bruvv,' he said, 'but I've already got something set up.'

'You have?'

'Yeah. Going to go and live with the zekes in that village down there.'

'What...on the ground?'

'That's the one. I went to see them this morning, have a look round, like, while you were being put through the sheep dip.'

He shrugged.

'They've got some serious stuff going on there. There's little kids running around in the garbage. There's all kinds of diseases in the place. So, I reckoned I had to do something.'

'Why?' said Jave.

'I dunno. Because they need it, I guess. I mean, they need to know that God cares about them, that he loves them. We just need to find the best ways of showing it.'

'Kevving,' said Jave quietly, 'if God loves them, why doesn't he do something about it?'

Kevving looked at Jave.

'He is. He's sending me.'

Jave shook his head.

'Boy, are they in for a disappointment,' he muttered.

Kevving laughed.

'Yeah, well, that's God for you,' he said. 'Always chooses the weirdest people to work for him.'

'I just wish it all made more sense,' said Jave.

'Always your trouble,' replied his brother, cheerfully. 'You want everything to fit together neatly, all easily explained and methodically organised. But it's not like that, bruvv. Life is full of contradictions. Good people do bad things. Bad people are better than you know. Only God sees it all.'

He picked up his bag from the corner of the room.

'You off already?' Jave asked.

'No time like the present,' replied Kevving. 'See you around, bruvv.'

He waved, slung his bag over his shoulder and headed for the lift.

'Kevving,' said Jave.

Kevving turned.

'Take care.'

The door to the lift hissed shut and the flat fell silent.

Jave climbed up from the lounger. Tomorrow, this would all be a jumbled memory and a better credit rating at the bank. Tomorrow, he would rest.

He walked across to the window.

London lay in front of him framed by grey, acrid clouds. The tower blocks glowered black in the rapidly fading afternoon light, walkways spun between them like webs. Somewhere, the sun was shining. Somewhere, there were green fields and mountains and streams and burnished bracken, glowing red in the autumn twilight. Here, it was raining.

He thought about his job. He thought about the gerbil that lay curled up by the heating duct in the kitchen. He thought about an old man, sitting and remembering in a room made of old files. He thought about a boy with two noses and a beautiful girl with a voice like a tree-frog with laryngitis. He thought about a Bishop who lied and who was dead. He thought about a man who lost his wife and who never lost the pain.

'Only God sees it all,' Kevving had told him.

Jave turned away from the window.

'Rather him than me,' he said. 'Rather him than me.'

The Wounds Of God

by Penelope Wilcock

'Clarity, simplicity and depth . . . Penelope Wilcock is a genuine storyteller. I loved this book and so will many, many others.' **ADRIAN PLASS**

Abbot Peregrine was an aristocrat, scholar, priest and authoritative leader of men. He could be fierce and intimidating, but there was also a tenderness about him that he had learned in the bitter school of suffering. A man with a broken body, he was familiar with fear and pain.

The monks of his community, sharing Peregrine's path of poverty, chastity and obedience, wrestled with pride, faced disillusionment, tasted grief and struggled with despair.

Yet they, and Peregrine, persevere. Each glimpses the love that stands firm in disappointment and grief: the steady love of the wounded God.

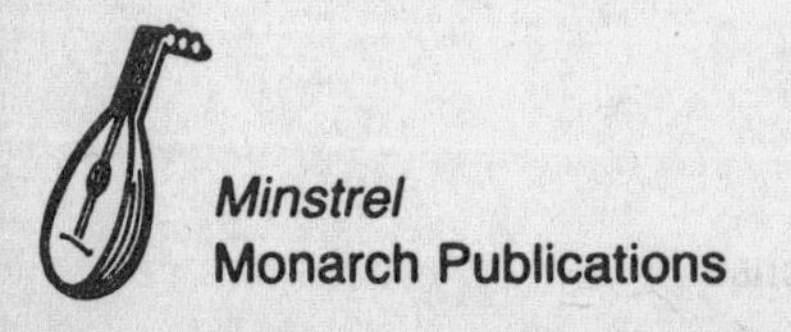

The Hawk And The Dove

by Penelope Wilcock

'Lifts and transports us into another world...I was hungry to read more.'

- JANE GRAYSHON

THE HAWK. An aristocrat of the thirteenth century and a renegade from his own passions, Peregrine entered monastic life still fierce and proud. When thugs from his past beat and crippled him, they left him helpless as a child. Bereft of his independence, he could finally teach true strength to his brothers.

THE DOVE. Melissa is a modern teenager, direct descendent of the hawkish abbot, who encounters the same struggles he did. As she listens to her mother's stories of her distant ancestor, Mellissa discovers that times do not change: that people, pride, resentment and love stay much the same, and that it is the grace of God on the inside that changes things.

'I enjoyed reading this book and saw once again more of Jesus - for me always the final test of a good book.'

- ROGER FORSTER

'Not only a joy to read, but also the kind of experience from which you come away feeling cleansed, whole and determined to live life more generously.'

- JOYCE HUGGETT

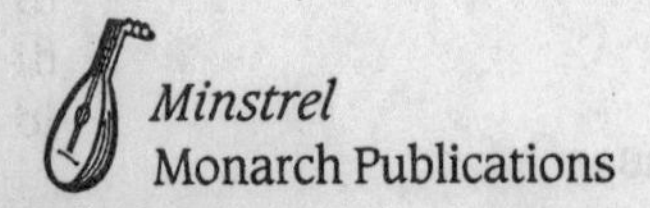